Heat of the Moment

Jason vanished through a door that linked with the kitchen, returning almost at once with a silver salver on which stood white china ramekins filled with dark chocolate pudding. He served these with warm mocha sauce and extra-thick pouring cream, finished with a generous helping of vanilla ice cream.

'This is melt-in-the-mouth stuff!' exclaimed Amber, her taste buds pleasantly titillated. 'Where did you learn to cook like that?'

He reached across and wiped a smear of chocolate from her lips with his little finger, then licked it, and the sight of his tongue, and the way he used it, transformed this simple action into something lascivious. Amber eased her bottom down against the brocaded upholstery of the Chippendale chair.

'I took a course,' he said. 'The experts like to shroud it in mystery, but it's all a matter of common sense really. I like to do everything I undertake to the best of my ability. And this applies to sex. I always make sure that my lover is satisfied. You won't have to fake it with me.'

Author's other Black Lace titles:

Earthy Delights
All the Trimmings

Heat of the Moment
Tesni Morgan

BLACK LACE

Black Lace books contain sexual fantasies.
In real life, always practise safe sex.

First published in 2002 by
Black Lace
Thames Wharf Studios
Rainville Road
London W6 9HA

Copyright © Tesni Morgan 2002

The right of Tesni Morgan to be identified as the Author of
the Work has been asserted in accordance with the Copyright,
Designs and Patents Act 1988.

Design by Smith & Gilmour, London
Printed and bound by Mackays of Chatham PLC

ISBN 0 352 33742 7

1

'Good God, what a night! It's lagging it down,' Sue exclaimed, squinting through the rain lashing the windscreen, the wipers squeaking like agitated bats as they thrashed backwards and forwards.

'Are we nearly there?' Diane asked anxiously, seated in the rear, her face appearing in the driving mirror.

'We're not sure, are we, Sue?' Amber replied, trying to read the road map in the greenish glow of the dashboard. 'I don't think I've ever been to Elberry.'

'I have,' said Sue. 'Had a fussy old bag of a made-to-measure customer once who lived there. Wouldn't it be weird if she turned up tonight? A right bossy cow.'

'I hope we don't get stuck anywhere,' Diane ventured.

'Don't worry,' Amber said, with a reassurance she was far from feeling. 'We've got our mobiles.' She was beginning to question the wisdom of their expedition. There had been flooding in the area, roads swamped and cars getting into real difficulties. She made light of it, joking, 'Don't tell me you'd mind a night away from Ray? We might have to be rescued by the police and the fire service. Think of that.'

'I *am* thinking of it,' Diane murmured. 'I wish I'd brought my wellies.'

'Nothing's going to happen,' Sue said firmly. She had elected to drive so that the others could have a drink or two. Now she halted at a barely legible signpost, and added triumphantly, 'There you are, oh ye of little faith. "Elberry Two Miles". Forward troops!'

On occasions like these, Sue always reminded Amber of

a Scout mistress. All she needed was a tan linen uniform, a woggle and a whistle, and she'd be fully equipped to deal with any emergency. She always took charge, slipping easily into the role of leader of the pack. Amber imagined that if, by a fluke, they *did* end up stranded, Sue wouldn't let it get her down. Oh, no. She'd have a fire alight in a jiffy, produce something nourishing and have them singing jolly Girl Guide songs to keep their bodies warm and their spirits up till help arrived.

The dark road and storm-wracked branches gave way to the yellowish uncertainty of street lights and a scattering of houses. Then, right beside the high steepled church, there was an open gate, a notice that said 'The Village Hall' and an unexpected congestion of traffic and a shortage of parking space.

'I told you so,' Sue declared, and angled her car into a gap between a muddy green Land Rover and a red Massey Ferguson tractor.

'*A tractor*? They didn't drive here in that, did they?' Amber was sure her worst fears were about to be realised. The evening was going to be a total disaster and a colossal waste of time and effort. She got out, straight rods of rain belting down, ruining her hair as she made a quick dash to the promise of shelter offered by the village hall.

There was a table set up in the vestibule, and a balding, youngish man in a dog collar (clerical not bondage) seated behind it. Two of his acolytes, who looked as if they were in charge of flower arranging for the church services, hovered around dutifully, wearing tweed skirts and cardigans, and with no-nonsense old ladies' perms. Among the flyers drawing-pinned to the notice-board detailing a jumble sale, bingo and the playgroup for under fives, Amber clocked a torrid poster depicting dancers in frilled skirts and mantillas. *El Fuego* was announced in vivid letters that twisted like flames, along with the blurb, 'A warm, intimate show of live flamenco dance, song and guitar.'

Anybody can make that kind of claim, she sneered inwardly, and resolved to wait and see before she bought one, or spent a tenner on a CD. She could always get one in the interval if the group proved to be worth remembering, which she very much doubted.

Sue and Diane arrived, dripping, just as Amber was buying the tickets. 'My treat,' she insisted. 'Whose birthday is it, anyway? It's a good deal ... six quid a shot and that includes a Spanish supper, no less.'

But she still regretted listening to Sue who had suggested this expedition into the wilds of Somerset. Sue had picked up a brochure in the library, and had enthused about the flamenco event, describing it in her caustic way 'as bringing culture to the peasants'.

'Sounds awful,' Amber had said dubiously. 'It's probably a bunch of amateurs who've never travelled further than Bournemouth.' She thrilled to Spanish music, had been there, done that and had the T-shirt to prove it. She'd seen and heard the best of dancers, singers and guitarists.

'Why don't we give it a whirl?' Sue had insisted.

'Spend the evening watching a bunch of sad wannabes stamping about thinking they're Carmen? Give me a break!' Amber had groaned.

'Oh, come on. I'm sure Di will be into it. It's either that or we get rat-arsed.'

'Or I stay in and put my feet up in front of the telly.'

'Saturday night is crap on the box and you know it. Nothing but game shows and pathetic *Blind Date* fools seeking their fifteen minutes of fame. Let's do it. It'll be a crack.'

It had been the wettest winter on record and Amber smiled wryly now that she was actually there. Sunny Spain? Hot-blooded gypsy passion? It took a long stretch of imagination. It was only the English who could have dreamed up such a show, organised by local council members under the auspices of the Mendip Arts and Leisure Foundation.

Damp people were flocking in behind them and when Amber led the way through the double doors into the hall proper, she was surprised to see that it was already crowded. Some bright spark had transformed it, setting up little round tables covered by check cloths and adding candles stuck in wine bottles and dishes of olives, sun-dried tomatoes and sliced onions in virgin oil, like a regular tapas bar. It was obvious that he or she had once been on vacation to the Costa Brava.

Not only the body of the hall was buzzing with anticipation; members of the audience were also seated on the stage. A space had been kept clear near an exit on one side, and chairs were positioned there and paraphernalia that suggested that this was where the action would take place. Mouth-wateringly delicious smells tinged with exotic spices wafted from mysterious, out-of-bounds quarters at the rear where W.I. stalwarts held sway over the cooking pots.

Amber and Diane found a vacant table edging the dance floor, and Sue queued up at the bar to buy a bottle of red wine. 'It's not exactly Chateauneuf du Pape,' she said, after returning with it and filling three glasses, 'but here's to you, Amber. Happy birthday tomorrow, and many of them.'

'Thank you,' she replied, smiling and raising her glass. 'I should have asked Alastair to come along but he's in lust. He's absolutely useless as an assistant at the moment.'

'What's he like!' Sue exclaimed, eyes lifted to the ceiling.

'At least he's getting some,' Amber answered, popping a green olive into her mouth, the succulent flesh crunching beneath her teeth. It was stuffed with garlic. I shan't be able to kiss anyone tonight, unless they have been eating vampire deterrent, too, she thought. Fat chance, any way. Looks like all the men are spoken for.

'Too right, but then, so could I be if I'd gone along with Gareth, instead of giving him the elbow.'

'Oh? I thought you were planning to do the deed last night.'

'I was and I did,' Sue replied, her tone of voice indicating that it hadn't been love's young dream.

'And?' both Amber and Diane chorused.

Amber was curious. Unlike herself and Diane, Sue had never married or had children, being career-oriented and well known in the rag trade as Sue Tucker, designer. What she didn't know about haute couture wasn't worth knowing. She loved fabrics and used them to satisfy her own artistic flair, but earned a living by making exquisite garments for women with more money than sense.

'I played it cool,' Sue said, pushing her fingers through her deliberately tousled burgundy bob, and grimacing at the No-Smoking notices on the walls. 'Gareth and me got on well, or so it seemed. He didn't try to rush me into the sack like men usually do, their brains in their crotch. We'd been meeting for a month, dinner dates, a few tongue kisses, and a feel or two outside the clothes, but he'd made no attempt to get off with me. I began to wonder about him. Was he gay? Or was it me? Was I losing the old pizazz? Then I thought, what the hell, let's go for it, and seduced him when we got back to my place.'

'Was he any good?'

'He knows where the girly spot is, but treated it as if he was trying to rub verdigris off brass. I got stuck and couldn't come. I told him to get lost.'

So, dismissing the inept Gareth, Sue threw back her mock-leopard jacket and displayed a mulberry satin boned bodice laced down the front over her pert breasts, her long legs encased in skin-tight velvet jeans. She was as chic as a catwalk model. 'What about you, Di?' she said. 'How does Ray rate these days in the Y-front stakes?'

Diane shrugged, and her cheeks went pink. 'Not Mr Sexy,' she said. 'But we did do it in the shower when I was getting ready to meet you guys.'

'Oooh, get you! And did you reach your moment of ultimate pleasure?' teased Sue, but Amber shuddered inwardly. As far as she could see, Ray had absolutely nothing going for him, whereas Diane was a natural blonde, blue-eyed and buxom, with a warm, bubbly personality.

'Yes, I did,' Diane confessed. 'Can't explain why. He really doesn't turn me on, but this adds to the excitement when I'm in the mood. Debasing myself and doing something I really shouldn't makes me randy as hell. It's so impersonal, and this makes me feel even dirtier and more excited.'

Diane had that half-ashamed, half-defiant look on her face. Amber had gathered that she was in constant conflict with herself about her husband. She fidgeted, crossed one solid leg over the other and tugged her skirt down, covering her knees. She never could achieve Sue's sleek sophistication or Amber's individualistic, ethnic styling. Diane tried, enlisting their aid, but lacked that certain knack for making the most of herself. Some people are blessed with an eye for blending colours or putting this with that to make a harmonious whole. Not so Diane.

'Forget Ray. Let's view the talent and see what's on offer,' Sue suggested, assessing the throng without being too obvious.

The hall was rapidly reaching the state of standing room only, and still people were coming in. Amber noticed that there was a plethora of attractive men, though they all seemed to be attached. Certainly, this show had not attracted the lower orders. If these gentlemen and their ladies had anything to do with the land, then they didn't work it themselves; they were owners who employed labourers. The men were thirty plus, wearing check shirts, no ties, possibly canary-coloured waistcoats, corduroy or drill trousers and brogues. They were handsome in a well-bred way, and their hair in the main was short and styled. They talked a lot and laughed loudly, and liked to think themselves patrons of such cultural events as this.

They would have looked ravishing dressed in hunting pink and hard hats, flourishing riding crops. The thought made Amber feel horny. She had never been whipped or caned, but had sometimes wondered about it, especially when playing with herself.

The women were of that fine-boned, straight-haired, peaches-and-cream complexion found only among the county set. They were casually dressed. Some wore tiny babies hanging in slings round their necks as if they were ornaments; others coped with wilful toddlers who should have been in bed long since. They had disobedient little boys called Freddy or Charlie and precocious little girls who answered to Emma or Vicky and looked as if they should be grooming their ponies.

Amber stared and ruminated and wondered why on earth they had turned out on such a night. Supporting village functions, she dared say. Liking to think they were a part of rural life, which they were, without a doubt. She felt a twinge of envy, wanting to be married to one of these well-heeled, well-connected gents, with several equally blue-blooded children and a beautiful old manor house and a paddock and horses.

You'd be bored out of your tiny mind, she told herself. No flat over your shop, no auction sales and bargains and deals. No phone calls from my sons enjoying a sabbatical in America. I've very nearly forgiven them for wanting to stay with their father, the selfish little ratbags! I'm a fraud when I try to present myself as a hard-bitten trader.

Underneath I'm a big splodge of marshmallow – no, even worse – a pink blancmange. I go all gooey over romantic music and babies' starfish fingers and wriggly little toes. If one of the boys were to call me up this minute, I'd probably cry – to myself, of course. I wouldn't let on.

Now the atmosphere was becoming tense. The hour was approaching when, if the posters were to be believed, the fire of Spain was due to burst forth upon the phlegmatic British scene. A ruddy-faced man who might have had 'I'm a Young Farmer' written large across his perspiring brow, grabbed a microphone and boomed into it as loudly as if he was addressing horse trials.

'Ladies and gentlemen. Give a big hand and a warm welcome to *El Fuego*.'

The door behind him opened and every misgiving Amber had harboured melted away as they came in, led by a man with a mane of flowing gypsy ringlets, a white shirt and black form-hugging trousers.

'Gosh, look at that. He's small but beautifully marked,' hissed Sue in Amber's ear. 'Talk about "give that boy a wash and send him to my tent".'

He walked with lithe grace, followed by a taller, blond man carrying a guitar, a statuesque woman in the traditional red and white polka-dot flounced dress, a rose tucked among her sepia curls, and a shapely girl with fair hair pulled back into a bun and kept in place with a comb and mantilla. She, too, wore a flamenco dress, tight to the hips, then flaring out in a series of frills. They took their places on the chairs, poised and still as ballerinas, and the dark man spoke through the mike.

'Good evening. My name is Camilo, and before we start, I'm going to explain a little about flamenco. Let me introduce Juan on guitar, Angelita who performs *Canto Jondo*, the "Deep Song" of the gypsies, and Carmencita who dances,' he said, in the slightly lisping accent of Southern Spain.

Amber could not keep her eyes off him, listening enraptured as he talked about the meaning and history of the dance, then when the guitarist strummed and the rhythm set feet tapping. Angelita clapped her hands and started to sing in that odd, grating, spine-tingling manner of *canto*, pouring out songs of unrequited love, of death and sorrow and being imprisoned. It was all very dramatic.

Carmencita rose, took up a pose, bending as gracefully as a sapling in the breeze, yet with her feet planted firmly in the earth and her tits raised to Jesus. Camilo joined her. Castanets clicked and they stamped and gyrated, passed and repassed, bodies held in a haughty stance. Arms alternatively raised and descending in spirals, they wove intricate patterns in the air, seductive and fiercely passionate.

When they had finished, Amber said to Sue, under the cover of applause, 'He's fit. I'd give him breakfast in the morning.'

'He's OK, but I think he's in love with the guitarist. I've been watching the way he looks at him.'

Amber was not convinced and continued to lech over Camilo. She loved this expression of emotion through dance, song and music. It was unique. Nowhere else in the world was human desire portrayed in such a pure form. Of course, it was all about sex, jealousy and unappeasable longing. She sat there and watched and drank the raw red wine and wanted Camilo with a hunger beyond all reason.

She imagined the smell of him – his hair scented with the verbena oil so much favoured by Mediterranean men; his wiry, muscular body, olive-skinned and smooth as velvet; his tapering hands and soulful black eyes under those incredibly curly lashes; his small feet in the heeled flamenco boots. Then there was his hawk nose and arrogant mouth, and that interesting package that she glimpsed under the restraint of his form-hugging trousers.

In love with the guitarist? No way.

She went hot all over when he looked across at her, caught her eye and smiled faintly. All she could do was clap her hands to the beat – *palma claro* or *palma sombra* – and shout *olé* and send out signals to him through the ether. Why am I bothering? she thought. He's probably a devout Catholic with a wife back home and half a dozen kids. What chance do I stand? Or do I really want one? But a quick shag with him, no ties or commitment, would be ace.

By the time they reached the interval the audience had been won over completely. The troupe made for the exit, still singing, still strumming and swaying and hand-clapping. The door closed behind them and Amber lined up for the supper that was now being served. Diane stayed to help her, but Sue went outside to have a cigarette, falling by the wayside in her attempt to kick the habit. After buying a poster and a CD, Amber returned to their table where she examined her purchases. Sue was now on the coffee, while Amber and Diane polished off the wine. The meal consisted of tortilla and paella.

'Someone has been boning up on their Spanish recipes,' Amber observed. 'This isn't half bad.'

'Know about Spanish food, do you?' Sue asked, with a lift of one finely arched eyebrow.

'Well, no ... not much,' Amber admitted. 'I've only visited once, and that was years ago when Mum had the boys for a fortnight and I booked a package holiday. The plane landed at Malaga and it was all pretty grim really, a crappy hotel and dreadful yobs and slappers all getting drunk and singing "Viva Espania". I felt ashamed to be English and took a train to Granada ... a very smelly train, I might add, but infinitely preferable. I had a wonderful time, went native and drifted up to Cordoba and then down to Seville.'

'I'll bet there was a man involved,' commented Diane, digging into the slice of omelette that Sue couldn't finish.

'There was. Matthew had decamped by then, and divorce was in the offing. I hadn't had sex for months. I met this Canadian called Bob. He knew the area like the back of his hand, studying guitar with a professional in Granada. I didn't keep in touch and haven't thought of him for ages, though I am eternally grateful. He taught me a smattering of the language and took me to the gypsy quarters in Triana, and bought seats on the *sombra* side of that magnificent cathedral of bullfighting ... La Maestranza, in Seville.'

'How could you? It's a horrible sport!' Diane said with a shudder.

'It's not a sport. It's a ritual. Taken very seriously by the aficionados,' Amber tried to explain. 'Just wait till you've seen matadors with rock-star status wearing ball-crushingly tight satin pants, flaunting their fighting capes and providing afternoons of great emotion.'

'It's cruel. The poor bulls!' Diane continued, stubbornly refusing to relent.

'The world would be a dull place if we all liked the same things,' put in Sue the peace-maker.

Amber brooded into her wineglass, quite accustomed to meeting this reaction if she so much as mentioned the ancient art of tauromarchy. Football, which she found deadly boring, was praised, even venerated, so was wrestling and boxing, all so-called sports in which men were injured and huge amounts of money exchanged at the betting shops. Yet, if she tried to explain the art of the bullfight to her friends, she was condemned as barbaric.

'I wonder if I could go backstage and meet Camilo when the show's over. I'd like him to sign the CD,' she murmured.

Sue shot her a glance. 'You can't be serious, can you?

You *can*! You mucky tart! And what are we supposed to do while you're tripping the light fandango with lover-boy?'

'Have another coffee and, when the tidying-up brigade finally turn you out, then you can wait in the car. Please, Sue. It shouldn't take long. He'll probably be so overloaded with adrenaline that he'll go off like a rocket,' Amber said and, as she moved her legs under her softly flowing jersey skirt, she could feel the seam of her lace panties digging between her pussy lips, and was aware that the crotch was damp. She examined the cover of the CD, admiring the photographs of *El Fuego* in general and Camilo in particular.

'You can't really be going to do it,' Diane said nervously. She was the least adventurous of the three and, after a quick glance at Amber's face, added, 'You are, *aren't* you?'

No more time for speculation. People were taking back their empty plates. The intermission was over and the second set about to begin. Several couples had left with their grizzling, overtired young. Those that remained were the hard core, and others who'd never seen flamenco until that night, but had found their epiphany and were likely to be fans for life. Maybe it really spoke to their souls, or maybe it was simply Carmencita's cleavage or Camilo's wide shoulders and tight-muscled arse. Whatever the reason, the posters and CDs were selling out fast.

El Fuego returned, all smiles and confidence, warmed by the wave of applause that met them. Carmencita had changed into a low-necked black dress that fitted her curves closely to her knees where it exploded into Valenciennes lace, not by the metre but by the mile. A storm of frills swept into a train at the back and had to be held away from her patent leather court shoes. At one point, she caught hold of the hem and stretched a fan-shaped length high above her head.

The crowd roared their appreciation of this proud,

sullen-mouthed beauty, but Amber gave her hardly a glance. All she was interested in was Camilo. His hair was brushed back and tied in a ponytail. This threw his features into prominence, the typical high cheekbones and aquiline nose of a Romany. Amber swallowed hard and clenched her hands in her lap. It was hard to sit there when every instinct was urging her to leap on to the dance floor and seduce him, then and there, with everyone looking on, including the ever-so-hip vicar and Mrs vicar and two or three little vicars, spawn of their loins.

Camilo now wore a dove-grey suit, with a short jacket, a white shirt and a thin red tie. His trousers shouldn't have been allowed, Amber decided. They were just too provocative. Extremely tight and high waisted, they were kept in place by braces worn under his closely buttoned waistcoat. Yanked up, one might say, drawing attention to his lean hips, tight buttocks and the deep hollows in his flanks.

'Gosh,' muttered Sue, goggling at his crotch. 'Talk about lift and separate! He's obviously not wearing a jockstrap, and I can't see a knicker line, can you?'

'No,' Amber managed to reply, his bulge drawing her eye like steel to a magnet. It was all there: the twin hillocks of his balls, the long baton of his cock pressed against the inside of his left thigh. No underwear, not even his shirt tucked down decently to conceal this flagrant display of masculinity.

'My word,' breathed Diane. 'It's a wonder his trousers don't cut him in two.'

Amber couldn't answer. It was worse when he danced, his brilliant, flashing footwork making his equipment jiggle. He was good, oh so good, and so was Carmencita, and the hour was soon gone, with that bucolic audience completely losing their reserve and joining in, clapping and shouting *olé* and demanding encores.

When at last they let them retire, Camilo deliberately

looked towards Amber and flashed her a smile. She could feel herself going bright red, touched a hand to her hair, clutched her CD and stood up. She was about to walk up to him boldly, when she saw that he was surrounded by several women who had been seated at the side of the floor near the door. They were expensively dressed and from the upper echelon, and jealousy stabbed through her as she saw how he was smiling and nodding and gesturing with his expressive hands. A wicked waste when he should have been using them on her.

'Of course, I helped to organise this,' a horse-faced woman was drawling. 'So wonderful ... and your dancing was sublime.'

'Thank you. That is so kind,' he responded politely.

'Would you care to come back to my house for supper?' Horseface continued, and she could hardly control herself. Amber wondered if she too shared her own desire to palm his crotch.

'Thank you, but no. We have to leave almost at once,' he said. 'Our next performance is in Taunton tomorrow.'

Damn and blast! Amber fumed. But it seemed that he had escaped Horseface, bowing and then disappearing through the door leading to the dressing rooms. Amber moved like greased lightning, elbowing Horseface aside and diving after him. She caught up with him in the deserted corridor. He turned, his dark eyes sparkling and his smile embracing her.

'I thought I'd never get away from that lady,' he said, and his husky voice turned her legs to jelly. 'I've been watching you, and you have great sympathy for the dance. *Si*?'

'Oh, yes. I mean *si*,' Amber mumbled, clutching the CD like a shield and feeling extremely foolish. 'Will you sign this?' She opened the plastic case and thrust it forwards, along with a ballpoint.

'My pleasure,' he said, taking it with courtly, old-world

grace and scrawling his signature across the bottom. He handed it back, then hooked a finger into the band restraining his hair, shaking it free.

She knew she should go, but . . .

He stood, still as a snake, staring at her, and then he reached out and clasped her breasts in his hands, one on each, those hands that had clapped their way through the evening's entertainment, and now wanted to go on performing, it seemed. She gasped but didn't draw back. It was he who moved, stepping closer and bringing his mouth down to hers, then leaving her breasts and pulling her body close to his. He smelled as she had imagined, of perfumed oil and body spray and male sweat, his hair falling over her like a dusky cloud.

His kiss shocked through her, womb clenching, clit thrumming, nipples peaking. He was very thorough, delving and exploring, licking her tongue, her teeth, the inside of her cheeks, leaving a tiny trace of the garlic and wine that spiced his breath. After this he withdrew, and used his lips on hers, first the outer corners, then the cushiony centre, bringing her to limp, lubricious surrender. She would have gone mad if he had stopped.

Stopping was far from his mind.

He was holding her, this fantastic man, holding and caressing, touching her breasts and running a hand down to lift the hem of her skirt. His fingers encountered the tops of her mink stockings and traced round one suspender, the back of his hand brushing against the silky triangle covering her mound.

His face darkened; his mouth hardened, then he exclaimed harshly, 'Guapa! Guapa!'

And she knew what this meant. It was the expression murmured by men as a pretty woman passed down the streets in Andalusia. A term of praise, endearment and admiration. It thrilled her. To have this compliment handed to her on the eve of her birthday made her feel

15

ten feet tall. She wasn't over the hill, not by a long chalk. Had masses of living yet to do. She almost fell in love with Camilo then and there, but put the brakes on just in time, sensible enough to realise that this was it – this quick meeting in a dingy passage, the memory of which would warm her during any barren times ahead. It appealed to every romantic bone in her body.

She gasped as his fingers found the edge of her panties, very gently stroking over the taut fabric, then dipping in, parting her swollen sex-lips and cruising along the wet cleft. She tried to pull back, but his other hand clamped across her lower back, pressing her against his iron-hard cock. Her blood pounded and she came out in goose pimples and couldn't help bearing down on those artful fingers that rotated on her clit, then dipped into her centre, going deeper, her inner muscles clenching round them.

'Where can we go?' she moaned. 'Your dressing room?'

'The others will be there. They want to get away. If we leave soon we shall reach our hotel by two in the morning.'

'Are you married to either of the girls?' How much she hoped it wasn't so, an irrational hope for this was going nowhere.

He chuckled and his busy fingers were almost her undoing. She didn't want to come – not quite yet. She needed to feel a hard, hot, fully primed cock attached to a man, pumping in and out of her vigorously – not any man – it had to be Camilo.

'Angelita is married to Juan, and Carmencita is married to our manager. I'm not married. I am free ... free to dance and to make love to gorgeous women, like you,' he replied, so disarmingly that she couldn't condemn him. He was not being unbearably conceited. He was simply stating a fact.

Sue might rate him as cheesy, but Amber didn't think

there was anything false or insincere about him. What you saw was what you got. Nonetheless, she laughed and said, 'Bullshit!' though she was willing to suspend disbelief. Nothing must spoil this interlude. It seemed that nothing would.

She was suddenly aware of a doorknob boring a hole in her back. 'It must be a storeroom,' she said.

'That's good? A storeroom, *si*?'

'Very good. Very private,' she answered, trying not to fall into the habit of speaking pidgin English. 'You have a good command of our language,' she added, trying the knob.

'I was a waiter in Malta,' he explained and, as the door opened, he steered her inside.

She found the switch and a bare, forty-watt bulb lit the crowded interior. It was as she had suspected, filled with plastic stacking chairs and gear associated with the playgroup: easels and slates, Lego, a rocking horse, a doll's house, a bin filled with stuffed toys, a farm and small animals, a Noah's Ark.

'This OK,' Camilo said, and seized Amber under the haunches and sat her on a narrow, Formica-covered table, sending a box of bricks flying. They fell to the floor, scattering like shrapnel.

He pushed her back and pressed against her between her wide-opened thighs. She heaved her pelvis up and he found her panties, pulling them down and off. She could feel her juices, wet and sticky, anointing her crack. He played with her slick folds, tickling her clit until she could no longer hang on, her climax building and building, ripping through her belly and soaring to her brain until she exploded, coming in a welter of bliss that made her head spin.

Camilo growled his satisfaction in making her surrender, then felt for his fly, unbuttoned it and pulled his penis from the gap. Sue had been right. He wasn't wearing boxer shorts or even a thong. His was an impressive organ, long and thick and swarthy, with a flushed, shiny helm. She reached between their bodies and touched it, fondled it, ran her fingers up and down its length. She wormed her hand beneath it, encountering his tense balls and tugged gently at his wiry thatch.

'No, wait,' she commanded as he lunged at her. She felt suddenly very much in charge. In common with most men, Camilo was putty in her hands while he was obsessed with shooting his load.

She reached for her shoulder bag and fumbled in one of the compartments. Though she had not had a sexual encounter with a man for over a year, she had got into the habit of carrying a pack of three, just in case she should get lucky. She fished one out and broke the packet open, then took the condom and rolled it over his bulging cock and up the heavily veined shaft. Then she lay back, hooked her ankles on his shoulders and he paused with his dick at her moist niche.

'I'm going to fuck you, hard,' he grated, and pushed himself into her all the way in one rapid stroke.

He withdrew, then slammed in again, his hips meeting her raised inner thighs with a sharp slap. My God, I must look lewd! she thought, with my suspenders stretched and my white flesh showing above those mink stocking tops, my bare bottom lifted to heaven, and his mighty, foreign, sexy prick plunging in and out with a squishy sound. She groaned with pleasure and he snarled and pounded into her again and again, as hard as possible, using all his strength, subduing her when she wanted to be subdued, showing her who was boss when she wasn't even arguing the case. So macho, her Camilo – her dark comet, her star dancer.

As he continued to shaft her, she knotted her fingers in his hair and clamped her mouth against his, revelling in every stab of his tongue and every ravaging thrust of his cock. This was not love or affection; just sex, pure and simple. He hadn't even asked her name. He built up speed, pumping into her savagely, bruising her tender skin and hurting her inside. She thought he had reached his limit and couldn't possibly go any faster, but he was like something possessed, chasing his climax with the ferocity of a madman. He worked his solid penis brutally with such fierce thrusts that pleasure and pain merged into one and it was impossible for her to orgasm again.

Like an animal driven by a primitive urge, he threw back his head and bared his teeth as his body shook with the intensity of his crisis. His cock throbbed once, twice, thrice, and she felt the heat of his spunk shooting into the rubber, wanting to remember this amoral, relentless, bestial lust. She lowered her legs and Camilo pulled away from her, the condom teat filled with milky white semen. He unrolled it, knotted it and wrapped it in a tissue, presumably ready to be disposed of down the nearest loo.

He had recovered remarkably quickly. Due to long practice? she wondered, smoothing down her skirt and retrieving her knickers from where they were draped over the ears of a one-eyed, push-along dog.

'I must go,' he said, and handed her a business card. 'My mobile number. You can reach me anywhere.'

'Why should I want to do that?' she asked, and wondered at herself for being so blunt.

He looked hurt and pulled his mouth into a wry grimace, shoulders lifted, hands outspread. 'You might. Look me up if you're in Andeluz. I'll teach you to dance. I'd like to see you again. What's your name?'

'Amber Challonor,' she said, relenting a little, knowing she was only trying to protect herself from hurt, and she handed him her card in exchange.

They slipped out of the storeroom undetected, and he bent to kiss her full on the lips. 'Please ring me. You're very beautiful,' he whispered.

'So are you,' she answered, and watched him disappear along the passage, his tumbling hair covering his shoulder blades.

Amber headed towards the near-deserted hall, and looked in vain for Sue and Diane. She stepped out into the night and the carpark. It had stopped raining. Her thighs and sex ached and she felt very thoroughly used, her entire body quivering with echoes of the pleasure Camilo had given her. She felt inspired and excited and thrilled by what she had done, and not in the least ashamed.

Sue lit up a cigarette and sighed impatiently as she gazed out of the car window and said, 'How much longer is she going to be?' Then she spotted her walking quickly from the hall. She flung open the passenger door and shouted, 'Come on, Amber, for God's sake!'

'Sorry,' Amber said breathlessly, as she climbed in. 'Didn't mean to keep you waiting.'

'It's over and above the call of duty, but we'll let you off this time,' Sue replied. 'I only hope it was worth it.'

'It certainly was,' Amber said, her eyes sparkling in the interior light.

'Well, get on with it. Tell all,' demanded Diane, bouncing on the back seat. 'Is he big? Did he satisfy you? When are you seeing him again?'

'Give me a chance!' Amber exclaimed indignantly. 'I can say yes to the first two questions, but as for the other . . . I don't know if we'll ever meet up.'

'Oh, that's tight,' Diane complained. 'All this fuss for one screw?'

'It's quality not quantity that counts,' Sue put in. Knowing Amber, she didn't question her motives, but was curious. She had never found her to be promiscuous, and wondered why she was acting out of character.

Amber's not like me, she thought, not hurrying to drive off now that they were all present and correct. I've always been one for experimentation, right from the time I entered my teens. Boarding school did it for me – a college for genteel young ladies that was a breeding ground for heated amorous adventures. I lost my virginity to the head gardener's son, and that was only the beginning. Some of the other girls had brothers; there were end of term dances and visits to best friends' homes and ample opportunity for fornication. I sailed through it emotionally unscathed and physically alert to most aspects of human sexuality. It was there that I bonded with my first love, a girl called Trudy who introduced me to the passion and ecstasy that could exist between persons of the same gender. It was a lesson I never forgot and one that has stood me in good stead ever since.

University and a degree in design and clothing technology had kept her so occupied that she had never seriously considered marriage. Finishing a three-year course and then branching out on her own had been exhilarating, taxing and expensive. An older man had backed her financially, asking no more in return but that she become his dominatrix. This role had come easily to her. She never sentimentalised about men and had no illusions.

'Shall we go?' Amber asked, obviously reluctant to supply details about Camilo.

'Spoilsport,' Diane accused. 'You might have let us enjoy it by proxy. All I've got waiting for me at home is Ray.'

'Camilo's a nice guy. He was sweet to me. I can phone him any time I like. Does that answer your questions?'

'You know damn fine it doesn't,' Diane grumbled. 'I want to know how long it is . . . eight inches? Nine? More?'

'Shut up, Di,' Sue said, and pressed the starter button. 'Let's go. I could do with a strong cup of coffee. What they served there was weak as gnats' piss.'

'It's been a great evening. I can't believe *El Fuego*. So

genuine, and to find them in a dump like this,' Amber said, and Sue could see that she was still high from the music, and Camilo.

'The Mendip Arts seem to be an enterprising lot,' Sue said as she drove out on to the road. 'I've been thumbing through their leaflet and there's all sorts going on, all year round,' and she thrust the brochure under Amber's nose although it was too dark to read. 'They're holding drumming workshops, and having visiting theatre companies and folk concerts ... even encouraging badminton and t'ai chi at the sports centre. We should go. Try something different. I feel the need for vigorous exercise and a bit of mind stretching. We're getting to be real old stick-in-the-muds. What d'you say, Amber? Shall we go for it? Or are you sold on Spain?'

Amber, sitting there with soggy knickers, a tingle in her groin and a silly grin on her face, rather thought that she was.

2

No hangover; just that deliciously warm, slightly aching feeling inside that follows being well and truly fucked.

Amber snuggled down under the duvet, promising herself five more minutes. The church bells pealing out, summoning the tardy inhabitants of Lyncroft to attend morning service, reminded her that it was Sunday. She squinted at her wristwatch lying on the nightstand. Eight-thirty, which meant that she need not hurry. She opened the showroom on Sundays, but not till ten. Trade would be slow today, she guessed, looking forward to the spring when the historic market town would once more be bursting with tourists, both British and foreign, trawling through her bric-a-brac like fishermen in search of sprats. Shopkeepers like herself and Sue could reduce their overdrafts, and Diane's café would be in demand.

Inspired by this thought, and filled with a sudden surge of get up and go, she swung her legs over the edge of the bed. She had saved her cards, more controlled than Sue who would have torn them open as soon as they arrived, and now dragged on her robe and wandered into the kitchen, carrying them. While the kettle boiled, she ran a knife carefully under the flaps.

The one with an American stamp came first. It was from Christopher, her youngest son. It was like him to remember, but there was nothing from Andrew. He was too much like his father, a chip off the old block, she thought ruefully, getting a quick flash of her ex-husband's face – Matthew Challonor, that suave, handsome, obsessed-by-ambition businessman with his big cock and even bigger ego, his womanising and lying and generally infantile behaviour.

The cordless phone trilled and it was Sue. 'Hi, there, birthday girl,' she carolled.

'I'm just looking at my cards. Chris sent one.'

'Good.'

'I was pissed off when they elected to live in the States with Matthew,' Amber said, voicing a resentment months old. 'All those years of nurturing, changing nappies, emptying potties, coping with toddler tantrums and teenage angst, and where does it get you? No bloody where.'

'Forget it,' Sue advised. 'How d'you feel this morning after being shagged stupid by Don Juan?'

Amber was aware of a smile tugging at the corners of her mouth. 'Great!'

'How about a spot of lunch?'

'OK, but I'll be opening the shop.'

'That's all right. I've Mrs Hartley coming in for a fitting. It's her daughter's wedding soon and, as the mother of the bride, she's demanding a show-stopper.'

'I'll call in for you.'

As Amber clicked the off button, she poured boiling water over the tea bag in her mug, added milk and sweeteners and went back to the bedroom, cards tucked under one arm. She usually started the day with the power shower, but felt perverse. She wanted to hang on to Camilo's scent for as long as she could.

Dwelling on him, and glancing at his mobile number, she wondered whether to ring. Then decided against it. A glance in the mirror told her that he had done her a power of good, even though there were smudges under her green eyes. Didn't the Italians rate these as sexy indications of nights of fucking instead of sleeping? She followed her hairdresser's advice and, bending forwards, gave her hair a big 'whoosh'.

'Now it looks like a haystack,' she said aloud. 'Thanks a bunch, Armand.'

It was naturally curly and had a reddish tinge that Armand kept alive with frequent applications of henna. 'Haystacks are in, darling,' she could hear him reply jauntily.

Sunday, and she'd better make the effort, she supposed. You never knew what might happen in the antiques game. It could be quiet as the grave or, just when you were about to give up, a rich American might bowl in and buy half your stock. Best to look casual and on the ball. Jogging pants, maybe, and a sweater. She wore sandals and trainers mostly, rarely cramming her feet into high-heels, though often admiring them and wishing she could drum up an excuse to justify the expense. Once, long ago, she had tottered around on stilettos, in those halcyon days when she was a student, before meeting and marrying Matthew.

Wish I was taller, she thought, instead of five-four. Sue's tall, and leggy with it, but Diane is a tiddler, a mere five-one. She dragged open a drawer and took out some lingerie. In an extravagant moment, egged on by Sue, she had treated herself to a coffee lace underwired bra and matching tanga. She slipped into them, adjusting the briefs that came no higher than the sharp delineation of her pubes, and easing her breasts into cups that held them in an upthrusting, aggressive way. She wished she had been wearing them last night

'Umm,' she murmured, taking up a stance, legs spread, one hand at the back of her neck, pushing her hair high, the other akimbo. 'Slut,' she commented, pouting and gazing at herself through hooded eyes. She dropped the pose, muttering, 'Tart, more like it,' and grabbed her sensible clothes, though with a passing regret at covering the delicious underwear.

She pulled on a black T-shirt, then a sloppy jumper and blue jeans. It was essential to be comfortable when working. This sometimes necessitated leaping on boxes to reach pictures and rummaging among the second-hand furniture on sale. Warm socks and moccasins completed her outfit and she went sparingly with the make-up.

A lovely old oak staircase led down to the ground floor. Amber let herself into the shop from an inner door at the back. At once its familiar smell filled her nostrils with its conglomeration of dust, must, polish and woodworm preservative, though it wasn't the worms it preserved, but the furniture in which the creatures took up residence and reared their young.

She was proud of her achievement. Having inherited on the death of her mother, she'd used the money to buy this property and open Collectibles. Matthew had decamped with a younger version, and the shop had provided a steady income for herself and the boys. Some of her family possessions had been used as stock, the rest acquired through auction sales and house clearances. Her close neighbours were Sue in her boutique and Diane, doyen of the Honey Pot.

Amber drew in a breath, bracing herself to meet the day, and switched on the lights, stepping from the storeroom to the show area.

There was a scuffling sound from behind the curtains of an oak four-poster bed that took pride of place, a ticket for £5,000 dangling from the tester. Cheap at half the price, she thought, having at least two customers 'thinking about it'. But who or what was inside it, snug in intimate darkness? She twitched one of the curtains back with the clash of wooden rings on a pole.

'Oh, dear,' exclaimed her assistant, on his hands and knees as he looked up at her. He made no attempt to move from under the young black man who had his cock buried to the hilt in his arse.

'Well really, Alastair!' she said, exasperated. 'You know damn fine that the Jacksons are interested in buying this. I hope you haven't messed up the mattress or pillows or valance. These are included.'

'Not a bit. I swear it,' Alastair declaimed, all wide-eyed innocence. If Sue and Diane were her mates, then he was the friend of her bosom, definitely one of the girls.

Now, totally shameless, he withdrew from his compromising position, wrapped a pristine white towel round his slim hips, slapped his partner on the firm brown rump and said, 'You'd better meet the boss-lady, Yusuf.'

The young man grinned good-naturedly, and Amber hazarded a guess that it was he who had been making Alastair act like a lovesick girl. He stepped unselfconsciously from the bed, yawning and stretching like an adolescent lion, his shiny wet prick standing to attention. The shaft was chocolate brown, the helm circumcised and showing purple, and Amber was sharply aware of the desire that had been worrying at her gut since she woke. She wanted Camilo for a repeat performance, but he wasn't there and she was eyeing up Alastair's gay lover.

He smiled at her disarmingly, his features delicate and finely chiselled, his body lean, his dreadlocks cascading down his back. 'I'm so pleased to meet you,' he said. 'Alastair has told me so much about you.'

As if pre-empting her questions, Alastair said, 'Yusuf's a musician. He plays the *kora*. That's a sort of African harp.'

Not another musician, she thought bitterly, remembering the photo she'd seen of the father she had never known. He'd died of booze and drugs before she was born, back in the era of Love and Peace.

'Oh, I thought he was just one of your pick-ups,' she said unkindly, then went on, 'How come you brought him here, instead of taking him home?'

'Ooh, get those claws!' Alastair said, sidling up to her. 'Wasn't the flamenco thingy any good? Didn't you pull?'

'As a matter of fact it was, and yes, I did.' Amber couldn't keep back a smile.

'And aren't you going to recite the rude bits?' he said persuasively. 'If you're wondering about Yusuf, he's not a pick-up, as you so crudely put it. I met him several weeks ago at an Aid for Africa concert. And anyway, he's been home with me lots.'

Home was the cottage next door that was also Amber's property. He had it as part of his wages and it was an excellent arrangement. He was fussy and immaculately tidy and kept up the decorating and took pride in the garden.

'Then why spend the night in a very valuable four-poster?' she asked.

His good-looking face broke into a smile. 'Because, my dear, it's your birthday and I wanted to be here to make a fuss of you,' he declared, then dived under the lace-edged pillow and produced a parcel wrapped in coloured paper featuring teddy bears and balloons. 'I thought we'd sleep here so I didn't miss you. The bed's solid as a rock. It doesn't shake, I promise. The Jacksons will be able to fuck like rabbits. This is for you, and a card, too. Happy birthday,' and he leaned forwards and kissed her cheek, his tawny curls breathing out the fragrance of Obsession.

'You old trollop!' she said affectionately, touched by his kindness.

The parcel contained an elongated box. Inside, wrapped in tissue, was the biggest vibrator she had ever seen, complete with spare batteries.

Amber leaned forwards with her elbows on her knees, holding a catalogue with a page open and ticks against the items she intended to bid for.

The auction sale was being held by Beale and Co., but

it was not the one organised on the first Saturday of every month when top gear was on offer: Chippendale, Victoriana, bronzes, paintings in large gilded frames, nothing contemporary, all eighteenth or nineteenth century. These encouraged foreign buyers and telephone bids. Midweek events took place between, where more humble articles went under the hammer: interesting objets d'art, boxes of china and ornaments and lace-trimmed linen, an old doll's pram or two and garden relics, most of which might be bought for a song and passed on for a profit.

These were Amber's stamping grounds. One of the lots she had earmarked that day was a biscuit tin full of junk jewellery, necklaces, bracelets, rings and brooches possibly around forty years old. Unless there were several other dealers after it, she would probably get it for ten pounds and, once the contents were displayed in her shop, she might sell each piece for a handsome sum. It could take a while to start recouping her outlay, but this was all part of the buzz of wheeling and dealing.

The large room was full, a section of the Beale empire that incorporated valuation and furniture removals and storage. Their auctions always attracted interest. Everyone loves a bargain, and there were members of the public in evidence, besides those like herself who were in the trade. She had a nodding acquaintance with some of these shrewd operators. Rivals they might be, but there was a camaraderie among them, too. If your van broke down or you were struggling to load an unwieldy settee, a stone statue or a tallboy, then they'd be sure to lend a hand, particularly if you were a halfway presentable female. Amber was never backwards in coming forwards if she decided she needed assistance.

She had arrived early, viewed the lots and noted anything interesting that would be within her budget. A bunch of picture frames seemed promising, a cabin trunk of pre-war vintage, and a wicker pilgrim basket of silk

shawls, feather boas and T-bar ladies' shoes with sparkling rhinestone buckles from the 1930s. They would all
add to the medley of antiquities draped over bentwood
chairs or looped across painted screens or gracing the bow
windows of her bottle-green shop front, beneath the sign
in gold lettering that read Collectibles.

She had left Alastair in charge. He was almost as good
a sales person as herself, though he was a little off form,
thrown when Yusuf left him to go on tour with his *kora*.
She could sympathise, missing Camilo, though it was
weeks since she had met him. She had resisted the temp-
tation to phone him, being very sensible and grown-up.
He could always ring her if he was that bothered. His
silence told her that he was not. But she thought about
him often, playing his CD and giving her imagination full
rein when she consoled herself with her birthday vibrator.

His memory made her restless. It was a warm day, one
that a chill March had dropped into the lap of April as if
begging forgiveness for the diabolically wet and windy
start to the year. She wished she had worn a cotton skirt
instead of trousers, a T-shirt in place of her jumper. She
always worked up a sweat when waiting to bid. It was
almost as exciting as having sex.

The punters settled down as the auctioneer took his
place on the rostrum. 'This morning, ladies and gentlemen, we'll start with Lot 1. A collection of kitchen equipment ... saucepans, dishes, frying pans, a canteen of
cutlery, not silver, of course, but what do you expect?' he
quipped – William Beale in person, who owned the whole
shebang. He was corpulent and thinning on top, and had
a falsely jocular manner, hard as nails beneath. 'Who'll
start it off at fifty pence?'

'You're not after this?' said Sam Ridley, bending over to
speak to Amber from the seat behind.

'Not my sort of thing. I'll leave it for the car-booters,'
she replied with a smile.

'Very wise,' he agreed.

He was a rugged fifty-something who she often came across in their mutual line of business. A pleasant man, very knowledgeable and with that nose for a bargain essential if one was to become a successful trader. She had picked up many a tip from him and, though it was apparent that he fancied her, he wasn't pushy. Sometimes she wondered how it would be with him. He was single, attractive in a positive, solid, no-nonsense way, and she felt instinctively that he wouldn't mess her about, but couldn't make up her mind whether she wanted to be bothered.

'You're interested in Lot 34, I'll bet,' said another voice, close to her this time. 'The tin of baubles?'

'Perhaps,' she answered cautiously. She could feel herself blushing, avoiding glancing at him.

He was another dealer who turned up most times: Jason Ansley, a lanky, personable man with a quirky smile who owned a shop several streets over from Collectibles. He often pipped her to the post, having an annoying habit of bidding just that bit more than she intended to pay, throwing down the gauntlet and daring her to pick it up. But with a wilfulness she couldn't control, her body responded to this unrepentant rogue in a wanton manner. Already her nipples were peaking, whereas the presence of reliable Sam left her unmoved.

She fought her base urges while Beale craftily upped the bidding. Cold fingers inched down her spine as Jason's breath tickled her cheek. He leaned his shoulder against hers in the confined space, making her acutely aware of his desirable body under the demin jacket and battered jeans. They were baggy and faded to light blue round the fly, yet even this looseness seemed to emphasise that which lay behind. He moved easily, was loose-limbed and rangy, with unruly brown hair. He had an air about him and an accent that reminded her of the crowd at Elberry

Hall on that never-to-be-forgotten night of rain and passion. He might deal in antiques through necessity, but he managed to make it appear that he did it as a hobby and was really the recipient of a private income. In actual fact he was, as she put it to Sue when describing him, 'rough as fuck'.

'When are you coming out for a drink with me?' he persisted, while Beale brought his gavel down smartly after the final bid for the kitchen miscellany.

'I don't know. Never, perhaps,' she faltered, wishing he would leave.

She needed to concentrate, though Lot 34 was ages away. There were a mass of items to get through first, including the picture frames. And after the jewellery came the other things she wanted, along with items she didn't. It was all set to be a long morning and afternoon, with only a short break for lunch.

She sat there, resolutely trying to ignore the not very subtle message in Jason's predatory grey eyes, and the way he touched her whenever he could. The out and out physicality of this man played havoc with her senses. She crossed and recrossed her legs, and this brought pressure to bear on her pussy where it contacted the firm seat of the upright wooden chair. Her nipples were hard as cherry stones, teased by the lacy underwired baskets of her bra. She swivelled round, deliberately turned her shoulder on Jason and talked to Sam, discussing the merits of the sale.

When Beale's assistant, wearing the compulsory brown cotton coat and flat cap of his breed, carried in the next lot, her interest sharpened and she forgot Jason momentarily.

'That's it, Fred,' Beale said encouragingly, as his henchman lifted the object on to a side table. 'Here's a novelty, ladies and gentleman. You won't see another like it for miles around, if at all.'

Amber's mouth went dry, completely at variance with

her damp crotch. She had already made a note of this article and wondered if it would be worth an outlay of say, fifty pounds. It was about eight inches tall, a cast-iron Edwardian money-box depicting a jolly minstrel with a straw boater, white gloves and a wide grin. When coins were laid on his tongue, he swallowed them. The piece was in good condition considering its age, and highly desirable. She had seen several dealers examining it. No hallmark or provenance, but it looked as if it had been made in America at the beginning of the twentieth century. A child's toy once, probably costing a few cents, but now, in a consumer age where people harked back to an earlier era when quality workmanship counted, it might well go through the roof.

The bidding commenced at fifteen pounds. She raised her catalogue and caught Beale's eye. 'Ah,' he said. 'I have a bid from that lovely lady on my right. Mrs Challonor, isn't it? Do I have any advances on fifteen? Shall we say twenty?'

He leered at her and his patronising attitude put her hackles up, but she was trembling with eagerness to win this prize. It was not to her taste, but immensely saleable. There was a movement beside her. Beale nodded at Jason and continued. Amber was furious. The bugger was at it again, bidding against her. She was convinced he was doing it for devilment, not because he really wanted the thing.

The bidding continued and now several others were entering the fray, but it was Jason who annoyed her most, not the lady in the floppy hat who was winking at Beale, nor the obliging Sam who had just retired from the lists. Jason was doing it to prove something – to her or to himself? Probably trying to display his superiority as a dealer, and she couldn't let him get away with it. She did rapid calculations in her head and decided that if she stuck with the jewellery, the basket of clothing and left the rest, then she could afford to go higher than she had intended for the money-box.

It reached her fifty-pound limit and sailed over it. She went to seventy-five and Jason topped it by another five pounds. A hush held the saleroom in thrall, as it always did when the competition was keen.

'Eighty I'm bid. Is there any advance on eighty?' asked Beale, eyes twinkling at her behind his steel-rimmed glasses.

'I'll drop out now, if you promise to come for a drink with me tonight,' whispered Jason.

'Get knotted!' she hissed.

She shook her head at Beale and sank back in her chair. 'Eighty, it is,' he said, and brought his hammer down three times. 'Sold to Mr Ansley.'

'That was silly,' Jason murmured, trying to gain possession of her hand. 'You know it's worth a lot more.'

She avoided his grasp, and replied scornfully, 'You'd have just gone on pushing it up,' then regretted this phraseology, hoping he wouldn't see it as an innuendo.

'Not if you'd done as I ask,' he pointed out blandly.

'Listen, Mr Ansley. I don't do married men,' she snapped, glad when the person next to her got up and left, giving her the chance to move away from him.

'I'm not married,' he said, with a chuckle. 'What gave you that idea?'

'Isn't that your wife who has just come in?' she asked, nodding to the nondescript, mousy-haired woman who was waving to him. Amber had seen her with him before.

'Not my wife. My partner.'

'Same difference. I wouldn't touch you with a barge pole. I have too much respect for women,' Amber said and sat there in stony silence, except to bid, not always successfully, for small lots that took her fancy, until the break at twelve-thirty.

When she returned after lunch, she moved to a different part of the room, well away from Jason, and cheered up a little when the jewels, the basket and the trunk became hers. But her depression refused to lift entirely as she paid for them and humped them out to her Bedford van, with the assistance of Sam. Even he, she concluded, was driven by ulterior motives; to put not too fine a point on it, he wanted to get into her knickers, too.

She headed for home in a gloomy mood, lonely and frustrated and, in a way, kicking herself for her principles that had stopped her taking up Jason's offer. By now, she could have been looking forward to an evening of flirtation ending in bed. As it was, she'd now dump the stuff off at the shop, leave Alastair to sort and fuss over it, and go round to Sue's for a cup of tea and a moan.

She took a side road instead of the main drag, needing the peaceful rural scene to calm her. It was a beautiful day and, as she drove, she concluded that there were few places on earth as glorious as the English countryside in early spring. The narrow road was winding and she kept the pace down, though handling the van came as second nature. The trees grew thicker and, as she rounded a corner, a mounted man suddenly rode out in front, forcing her to brake sharply.

'Bloody idiot! What the hell are you playing at?' she spluttered, winding down the window, shaking with shock and rage.

He rode round, and she stared up at him, unable to believe her eyes. He was flashily dressed in a velvet, gold embroidered doublet, with a white, lace-edged collar open over a brown, hairy chest. A black cloak flowed from his shoulders to the horse's withers. His breeches fitted his muscular thighs tightly, and he wore brown leather riding boots pulled up above the knee. They had floppy tops and red welts and heels. A swept-hilt rapier swung at his left hip, supported by a finely worked baldrick. He reminded her of Frans Hals's painting *The Laughing Cavalier*. He had that same look on his face, jaunty, confident and with just a hint of provocation.

Several other men, all on foot, now appeared from the hedgerow and surrounded the van. They also wore old-fashioned costumes, but these were more muddied and down-at-heel. It was surreal. The modern world as she knew it had faded away, and she remembered tales told by travellers about suddenly finding themselves surrounded by a Roman legion or even a gang of barbarian Vikings. Was this what was happening to her? Had there been a time warp? Or was it simply that she'd stumbled into the middle of a film shoot?

'Don't be alarmed.' The horseman's voice was humorous, and he was handsome and audacious, his thickly curling, chestnut hair making his tanned face seem darker, his full lips curving under the thin line of moustache, a goatee beard forming a narrow wedge on his firm chin. He bent almost to his saddle bow in ironic courtesy, sweeping off his feather-loaded, wide-brimmed hat and adding, 'We mean you no harm, lady.'

'Is this some sort of sick joke?' Amber demanded in a tone that could have smashed rocks, but her eyes were going over him. He was big built and powerful and he sat on his horse like a conquering hero. Her pulse was racing and the lust aroused by Jason was threatening to get out of control.

'No joke,' he said, grinning at her as he openly admired her breasts outlined by the fine woollen sweater. 'We're collecting for charity. Show her, lads.'

The 'lads' duly stepped forwards and a couple of younger ones rattled tins that bore labels advertising famous charitable organisations.

'What is all this?' Amber was losing her fear, wanting to know more about this dashing man.

'We give our services free,' he replied, one large hand gentling his gelding who was fidgeting and tossing his mane. 'I request a contribution in aid of the poor and needy and homeless.'

Amber reached under the seat for her bag and extracted a five-pound note, then hesitated. 'How do I know this isn't a load of bullshit?' she asked crisply. 'I could call the police.'

He threw back his head and laughed – laughter came easily to him it seemed. He pulled out a very modern-looking wallet from an inner pocket, flipped it open and handed it to her. Inside was an identity card with his photograph (wearing conventional attire but no less sexy) and his name – Ian Barrett, Captain of Horse. 'Call away,' he said. 'They know all about it. We have their blessing, just as long as we don't cause traffic jams.'

Amber felt immediately extremely foolish, imaginative and dotty. She hastily stuffed the fiver into the slit of the nearest box. He bowed again and wheeled his horse so that she might pass. 'Safe journey,' he said, and the look in his eyes made her sex leap as he added, 'May I hope that you'll come and watch our display?'

'I might,' she said, slipping the car into gear and moving off.

She could see him in the side mirror, a gallant, romantic figure, and she suddenly yearned to be the horse between his hard, velvet-covered thighs, or the reins under his sun-browned hands. She had always revelled in historical novels and swashbuckling period movies and this episode had fired her. It made her think back to her teens when she had gone to the cinema and often sat through the entire programme twice, if she could get away with it, just to experience those strange, exciting, dimly understood feelings stirring in her belly as she watched the sword-play and love-making of the hero. These sensations were much in evidence now but, unlike then, she knew all too well what they portended. She wanted to shag Captain Ian Barrett.

Spain and Camilo seemed very far away at that moment.

The Honey Pot was usually quiet on Wednesdays. It was early closing in Lyncroft, though the supermarkets ignored this tradition, but today the town was busier than customary. It was Easter Bank Holiday the coming weekend.

Diane was preparing teas backstage in the café. It was hectic: women taking the weight off their feet after doing extra shopping, and enjoying a gossip with friends before the storm broke. The children would be home for a week, starting on Good Friday and, encouraged by the fine weather, their husbands were bound to want to play chef, showing off at barbecues. Rolls had been purchased, and sausages, chicken drumsticks and chops, tomato sauce and bottles of wine and cans of beer. It was small wonder that the women were looking harassed, and cynically observing to one another that it was a pity these exponents of open-air cuisine didn't help in the kitchen sometimes. Who'd be doing the clearing up when hubby was comatose after too much slaving over beds of glowing charcoal and too free an indulgence in tinnies? The women, as usual.

Diane liked being busy. It stopped her thinking about Ray and what she was going to do to repair their crumbling marriage, or even if she wanted to. The lively atmosphere of her café never failed to lift her spirit. At least she had that, and it was in her name. If the crunch came, Ray would have difficulty in getting his hands on any of her assets. Poor Ray, she couldn't help feeling sorry for him. He was so blinkered, stubbornly refusing to take advice from anyone. He was always right, or so he imagined. His mother has encouraged this, she thought resentfully. That woman has a lot to answer for. Her boys can do no wrong, in her eyes, never mind that she had brought them up to be spineless twats.

She washed her hands for the umpteenth time and prepared another salad. She didn't only do cream teas; snacks and toasted sandwiches were also on the menu, all freshly made and with wholesome ingredients. The prices were moderate, and customers came back again and again.

She daydreamed as she went through the routine; she was working out how she could manage a break, the first for years. She wanted to go away alone, or with maybe Sue or Amber. Ray didn't come into the picture. She wasn't sure where this might be, but had been intrigued by holiday programmes on the television about Ibiza. It looked so glamorous and racy. All those confident, busty lasses in their bikinis or less, their strident, in-your-face attitude, their determination to get as drunk as the lads and go on the pull. She wished she was that young again.

All right, not Ibiza, but how about somewhere in England? She sighed and sought an answer in the heart of an iceberg lettuce, staring down as if it was an oracle before slicing it with her sharpest knife. She had the feeling this wouldn't be exciting enough for her two friends: they'd want fresh fields and pastures new – maybe New York or Florida, the Seychelles or Bermuda. This was a daunting prospect and she was reluctant to commit herself to these far-flung reaches of the globe.

'Two pots of tea and buttered toast. Wholemeal,' trilled Toyah as she swept through the swing doors, a skinny, sharp-featured girl who wore the Honey Pot's colours with an air. 'I don't know what's got into 'em today. Ever so busy for midweek,' she opined, pushing an escaping curl back under her red cap. 'I want to get off early tonight, Mrs Wexford. I'm meeting my Derek.'

'It's the Easter rush,' Diane reminded, while Lisa, plain and stodgy, a behind-the-scenes worker, got the order together.

'You going to the fête?' Toyah asked, sweeping up a tray and retreating out of the door, pushing it open with her hip.

'I didn't realise there was one,' Diane called after her. 'Where's it being held?'

'Lyncroft Castle,' Toyah's voice came back faintly, then was lost among the general mêlée.

Now Diane remembered vaguely. Her attention had been taken up with her daughter, Karen, home from university on vacation and already bored, missing her mates, missing the student life, lounging about, getting up late, doing sweet FA, and constantly demanding money. She resembled a baby cuckoo, but nothing like as cute. Though Diane had been looking forward to her stay, it was already proving irksome. Now she had two overgrown children to look after instead of one.

'I don't want to be a mother,' she muttered under her breath.

'Did you say something, Mrs Wexford?' asked Lisa, her eyes on the neat rear of Toby, the general help who was supposed to be receiving an education in the rudiments of cookery. Diane thought he needed to be taught the basic rules of being alive. Lisa was smitten, looking at him with the glazed expression of a rabbit mesmerised by a stoat.

If they had two brain cells between them they might be dangerous, Diane concluded.

She straightened up, rested her knuckles on her hips and said loudly, 'Yes, I did. I'm tired of being a mum. Sick of being at everybody's beck and call. I need a holiday. I feel like marching through the town centre with a placard saying, "Don't ask me to do anything. Fuck right off!"'

'Oh, right-ho, Mrs Wexford. Well, I'm sure Toby and me and Toyah could manage for a few days,' Lisa offered and Diane was immediately ashamed of her irritability. It wasn't even as if she had PMT.

It was pointless taking it out on the staff, especially these two simple souls. She should be addressing her grievances where they belonged: with Karen, and – even more – with Ray. She patted Lisa on the shoulder.

'Thanks for the offer. I'll think about it.'

'I don't mind how many hours I do, just so long as I can go to fête,' Lisa vouchsafed eagerly, never stopping in her task of sandwich making. 'It's going to be ever so good. There's a funfair and a cheese-making competition and a tent where they sell booze and, I dunno, everything. I'm going along with me mates. You coming, Toby?' she added, greatly daring.

He shrugged and then shuffled his feet, unable to cope with his hormones and her panting, though inexperienced, eagerness to fulfil his fantasies. 'I might,' he grunted.

'Of course I know about it. There's been a poster hanging in the window for over a fortnight,' Diane said heavily. An earnest member of the Lyncroft Country and Garden Show had been round distributing them.

Black lettering on a day-glo yellow background. As Lisa said, there was much to entertain the populace. 'Featuring The Silver Banner', it stated, and what the hell was that, Diane had wondered, scanning it before she applied four knobs of Blu Tack to the corners. 'Famous Greyhound & Pigeon race, Falcon displays, Owl display. Duck racing.' (That sounded bizarre, Diane had thought.) 'Civil War battles.' (What!) 'Living history displays.' (What! What?) Rural craft demonstrations.' (Something for everyone, or maybe not.) 'Aura Photography.' (Eh?) And all the other things Lisa had mentioned. None of them appealed to Diane particularly.

Then Toyah burst through the swing doors, flushed and bright-eyed, a sure sign of males somewhere in the vicinity. 'Mrs Wexford,' she cried, voice up several octaves. 'Come and see!'

'What is it?' Diane asked wearily, longing for closing time, but it was some way to go yet.

'People in fancy dress ... men ... that is!'

I knew it, Diane thought with a kind of grim satisfaction. Toyah always perked up in the presence of men. 'Fancy dress? What are you on about?'

'They're sort of like soldiers, armour and that, and some of them have gone into the White Swan over the road, and left horses tied up outside.'

'Hey, wait a minute, you two,' Diane said crisply, using her boss-lady tone that stopped Lisa and Toby who were poised to desert their posts and go take a look. 'You stay here and I'll see what this is all about.'

When she stepped out into the main body of the café, it was to find that Toyah hadn't been exaggerating. Her regulars, particularly the bored and family-weary housewives, were goggling at the colourful collection of a dozen men who stood around, a bit sheepishly, looking like escapee extras from *The Three Musketeers*.

They clanked when they moved, or rather their weapons did. Diane wondered briefly if it was legal to wear a sword or heft a long-barrelled gun or carry a pike. Apart from these macho accessories that distinguished them from her usual clientele, they wore scruffy jackets and breeches, grubby shirts, thick socks and scuffed shoes. Their hair either straggled from under battered felt hats, or was close cropped. Their stubble had nothing to do with fashion; it was caused by several days of razor avoidance. They acted tough; a gang of mercenaries perhaps, fighting for whoever paid the most. They swaggered and eyed the women, emitting clouds of masculine hormones, a ruthless brigade of devil-may-care troopers, but it didn't quite come off. Diane thought them a bunch of self-conscious plonkers.

Toyah, all of a twitter, had found tables for them and was taking their orders. Not scones and cream, apparently, but something substantial like black pudding and eggs and baked beans. 'And don't forget the fried bread, love,' added a sandy-haired man in green, rather better dressed than the rest, who appeared to be their leader. 'We've marched all through the town, and need a good nosh-up.'

The penny dropped. The Civil War battle promised as part of the fête. Diane walked up to the leader's table and said, 'You must be appearing at the Easter shindig?'

He stood up and removed his hat, then bowed, smiling at her engagingly. 'That's right. The Silver Banner, at your service, ma'am. We're camping near the showground. Been mustering for a couple of days now. It's part of our policy to give the town a sample of what we look like and how we march. You missed it. Pity. My name's Colin Fielding, sergeant if you like, and we're foot soldiers. The officers are over the way, in the pub, but we're gasping for a cup of tea, to make way for the ale, you understand.'

He had astonishingly bright eyes of a colour that matched his hair and sandy lashes. He was attractive in a lean, wiry way. Diane's nipples peaked under her thin nylon overall, and a shiver ran right down her spine into her belly. This was something new – something to break up the monotony – I must phone Sue and Amber, she thought, while thought was at all possible.

'I'm Diane Wexford,' she said. 'I own the Honey Pot. So, what's this you do?' she asked, while an agitated Toyah, knocked completely off kilter, took their orders. 'Dress up and gad around the countryside having battles?'

Colin grinned and his rather ordinary face took on a sparkle and personality that almost robbed her of breath. She rested a hand on the back of the settle and, standing just above him, caught the personal smell of his hair, the tang of fresh sweat, the fascinating odour of leather that rose from his protective buff coat.

'It's for people who want to be either Cavaliers or Roundheads. They fought each other all over England from sixteen forty-two, and onwards for five years or so, but we do it for the crack,' he explained, then added, 'Can we smoke?'

'Sure. This is a smoking zone,' she said, pulled out a free chair and sat down. Colin wasn't alone. A hulking red-headed, ugly-handsome man with the face of a prize-fighter added his bit, 'It's a laugh, Mrs Wexford. It really is. We go all over the show in the summer, sieges, skirmishes and battles. No shortage of crumpet. They like soldiers. And I'm a pikeman. We form a square and are bloody well near unbeatable when it comes to push-of-pike. This really gets the girls fired up. I'm Josh, by the way.'

He was built like the proverbial shit-house, and was nursing a plumed steel morion on his knee. This heavy helmet had left a red mark round his low forehead. The chair creaked under his weight as he sat with his broad knees apart, feet planted firmly on the floor. The sheer animal magnetism oozing from his every pore was enough to convince Diane that most women would be up for it. Not herself, perhaps. She preferred Colin.

'What do you do when you're not on the march and battling it out?' she asked, aware that he was staring at her breasts, then up to her face, and back again.

'I'm a history teacher,' Colin replied.

'And your wife doesn't mind you going off like this?'

'I have no wife,' he said, and it was as if he brought this out to let her know he was free, even if she wasn't. 'But a lot of women go with their husbands, kiddies too, all wearing seventeenth-century costume. Some of the girls want to be she-soldiers and fight with the men. No one is barred, but they must adhere to one side or the other ... support King Charles the First, or the Parliamentarians who are his enemies.'

'Cor, yes,' put in Josh, smacking his full lips. 'There's some goings-on going on, I can tell you.'

A glance down at the prominent parcel resting on the seat between his bulky thighs told her that the thought of snatch recently enjoyed and plenty more to come was turning him on. Diane began to see the advantages of belonging to such a group. Camping, caravanning, dressing up, surrounded by fit men for weekends at a time – away from Ray, away from Karen and responsibility, yet able to return to her café at the end of it.

'And which side do you support?' she asked Colin.

'We're the King's men,' he said proudly.

'We don't have nothing to do with those damned rebels, the bloody, canting Puritans,' snorted Josh truculently.

'But you lost, didn't you? Wasn't the King executed?' Diane said, ferreting back to school days, but even then she hadn't been much good at history.

'We don't talk about that. Least ways, not while we're marching and battling and trying to beat the Roundheads,' Colin answered, and she could see that whereas Josh and some of the rest might simply use the Silver Banner as an excuse for boozing and fornicating, Colin took it very seriously indeed. But then, after all, he was a teacher.

'I see. Well, you'll have to fill me in on the subject. Now, if you'll excuse me,' Diane said, rising, and disappeared round the back of the pay desk. She picked up the phone and dialled Sue's number.

'Hello,' said Sue, almost immediately.

'It's Di. Listen. Take a look out of the window. You're bang opposite the White Swan. Can you see horses and hunks in costume? I've got a gaggle of 'em in here ... the guys not the horses. They're part of something called the Silver Banner, and they're camping at Lyncroft Castle.'

'Hang on. I'm in the workroom at the back,' Sue answered. There was a pause as she moved, and then she said, 'Yes, I can see them all right, and heaps of steaming horseshit. There's quite a crowd gathering to watch, and a reporter from the *Western Courier* has just arrived, and a photographer. This needs looking into. I'll ring you later.'

'A nice place you've got here,' said Colin, materialising beside Diane. By rights, he should have been at the other side of the desk, but she was glad he wasn't. Though not a tall man, her shortness made him seem much bigger than he actually was. She had to look up at him, but found this hard. She kept blushing.

'Is Toyah seeing to your orders?' she asked, for want of something to say. He was just too close in that confined space. She could smell the outdoors, the sunshine, the lush grass and greenery, and the acrid odour of wood smoke from campfires that clung to him after two days and nights of sleeping out. Back to the earth earthy, she thought, and melted inside.

'Toyah's treating us just fine,' he answered.

'It's not every day we have something as exciting as this happen,' she said, knowing that she was prattling but unable to stop.

'This is our first meet this season. We only campaign from March to October. Like the real Civil War armies. It was impossible in bad weather. Tarmac hadn't been invented and the roads were dirt tracks. Imagine trying to march in the mud, and think of the train of artillery, massive cannons, pulled by teams of Shire horses. Impossible.'

'You love this subject, don't you?' she said, admiring his enthusiasm, wanting to get closer to this interesting person.

'Always have,' he confessed. 'Ever since I read a book called *The King's War*, and realised just how fascinating and exciting and significant the Great Rebellion was.'

Diane wanted to keep him talking, there in that secluded nook. It wasn't only the man, though this was tempting enough, it was what he was doing – something different and adventurous, beyond the day-by-day, hum-drum activities of ordinary life. He went back in time; they all did. They recreated an age when there was no electricity, or television or cars or planes or phones (mobile or landline), no medicine as she knew it, only crude surgery, and cruel punishments for wrongdoers. Yet Shakespeare had not long been dead and, while Diane found his plays difficult to follow unless in cinematic form (thank God for Kenneth Branagh), she was aware that he was England's pride and joy.

How can I join? she wondered. Join what? questioned her inner self. The Silver Banner, or Colin? Both, she decided.

3

The White Swan was crowded, more than usually so on a weekday, space taken up by men and women in costume who blended with the blackened oak beams, horse brasses and open fireplaces of the ancient inn. The regulars took it all in good part and the taproom and bar parlour reverberated with talk and laughter and folk tunes scraped out by a fiddler, the beat accentuated with sticks hitting a tambour.

'Bit like an Irish band,' Sue commented as she weaved through the colourful crowd.

'Old English, I guess,' said Amber. 'Very hey-nonny-no. It must have been top of the charts in the sixteen hundreds.'

Not only the men were dressed up to the nines, but the women, too. Some were simply 'wenches'. This seemed very popular, the most respectable women leaping at the chance to wear off-shoulder white blouses and extremely tightly laced black velvet corsets that pushed their breasts so high they bulged over the tops. Bum rolls exaggerated the fullness of their hips and made their waists shrink in comparison. Their skirts were full and they flaunted lace-edged petticoats, and flashed woollen stockings upheld by fancy garters and shoes with low heels and cut-steel buckles and boasted that they were naked of knickers.

'No drawers?' Amber asked, grinning at Sue. 'How draughty.'

'It's accurate, though,' Sue said, nodding her approval. 'Drawers were considered to be very immodest in those days, too much like a man's garment. You were a right slag if you wore them.'

Sue and Amber had reached the pub before Diane. She couldn't close the café till six-thirty and, in any case, according to her last telephone call, was more than happy to stay where she was for the moment, surrounded by a plethora of soldiers.

'All this must be to do with the guys you told me about, who waylaid you when you were coming back from the auction,' Sue said. 'Members of the Silver Banner, so Di informs me.'

'I know. I've seen the posters, too,' Amber replied – a tad huffily, Sue thought – and they carried their drinks over to a corner table where two young women dressed as cavalry officers shifted up on the settle to make room for them.

They wore crimson. Not exactly uniforms, too individualistic, but similar in style. Slashed sleeves, epaulettes, much gold frogging. Wide sashes spanned their waists, and they had basket-hilt swords at their left hips, supported by baldricks that crossed their chests. Gauntlets lay on the table, serviceable though heavily embroidered, and they were drinking beer from pewter tankards.

'Hello,' Sue said, admiring their panache. 'I love your outfits.'

She had studied the history of costume at college and could see that their clothes were authentic. Only the finest cotton lace adorned their wide collars and cuffs, with no trace of nylon. There were no zip fasteners or Velcro on their doublets and breeches. These were fastened with horn or silver buttons, or tied with cords tipped with metal points.

'We're dead fussy about getting it right, and so is our commander,' replied a striking, dark-haired girl who appeared to be the spokesperson. 'This isn't a game, you know. We're serious about it, but that doesn't mean we don't have fun.'

Her sherry-coloured eyes were warm as she looked at Sue through lashes that were naturally thick and long, owing nothing to mascara. They held a message that wasn't hard to interpret. Sue wondered, and not for the first time, if she had 'I'm a dyke' tattooed across her forehead. This handsome creature was flirting with her, and it wasn't simply because she was dressed as a man and playing a part. Sue instinctively recognised that she would have done so anyway were she wearing a little sequinned halter, a minute scrap of skirt and high-heeled, strappy shoes. The signals were there, plain as one of the pikestaffs leaning against the wall. It was an I-fancy-you-rotten sort of look.

The officer rose, swept off her plumed hat, held it to her heart, placed the heel of her left riding boot to the instep of the right, and bowed low. 'I'm Lieutenant Prudy Hemming,' she said, straightening up, nearly as tall as Sue. 'Part of Captain Barrett's troop. Your servant, ma'am.'

A sharp poke in the ribs and there was Amber, hissing, 'That's the bloke who stopped me. I remember his name. Not likely to forget it. He was sexy as hell.'

'My name's Sue Tucker, and this is Amber Challonor,' was all Sue could manage, lost for words as she looked into Prudy's smiling eyes. She was flattered, impressed by this gorgeous person with the abundant lovelocks who had taken on the mannerisms of a soldier and was being laddish, yet all female underneath.

'Is your captain here?' Amber broke in, leaning across Sue and fixing Prudy with a sharp stare.

Prudy's companion, small and compact, with fair curls poking out from under her broad-brimmed felt hat, gave her a smile, dimples flashing like those of a wayward cherub, as she said, 'Sure. Ian's not far away. He doesn't trust us not to get plastered. He rounds us up at last orders and we ride back to camp under escort ... that's him and his bullies ... no cars allowed, not for us anyway. We're supposed to be living like three hundred and forty years ago. It's not unusual for someone to fall off his or her horse. This really bugs Ian and we're put on fatigue-duty ... cleaning out the Portaloos, if there are any, or digging latrines if there aren't. It's a drag. I'm Corporal Stapleton ... Jess to my mates.'

'Are there many women in the Silver Banner?' Sue asked, wondering if Jess was as gay as her friend.

'Dozens,' Jess returned, sipping her ale. 'And in the other skirmish societies ... the Romans, the Vikings, the medieval lot ... the American Civil War. They're all at it and the gals can't wait to don armour and make like Zena, Warrior Princess, though not in that dull old Confederate bunch. The costumes aren't so fetching, unless you want to be Scarlett O'Hara.'

Prudy resumed her seat, and stretched out her legs under the table, her thigh brushing against Sue's. 'Yes,' she agreed with Jess. 'A lot want to fight, especially those who can ride. There's nothing quite so exciting as a cavalry charge. It's almost better than sex.'

'With men, that is,' Jess added, clearing the air about which bus she was on.

Sue wondered if they were partners. She hoped not, for Prudy was very attractive, though not exactly beautiful. Her nose was too strong and her mouth too big, but her wide-spaced, intelligent eyes and winged brows made up for this. So did her confidence and ease of manner. Here was a woman comfortable with her body and her sexuality, and proud of it. Sue could feel herself responding in a way she never had with Gareth. Sometimes she tried it with men, just to see what her reactions would be and toying with the idea of producing a child before her biological clock ran out, but this wasn't high on her agenda. Prudy might well be.

'Tell me more,' she said, and her foot in its elegant

calfskin pump, idled across Prudy's ankle, lingered for a second, then slid higher.

'Well, there are not only fighters,' Prudy went on calmly, and Sue admired her cool, 'but camp-followers, too, just like there were in the real armies ... women who go along to look after their men ... cooking, washing, tending the wounded, and those who supply other comforts ... the whores.'

'Wherever there have been armies, you'll find hookers keeping the troops happy. It makes it easier for the commanders to control the pillage and rape,' put in Jess, grinning at Sue's expression of disbelief. 'OK. I'm only kidding, but ravishing the enemy's women was part and parcel of warfare once.'

'Might you be interested in signing up?' Prudy asked, resting her shoulder against Sue's, and making no attempt to avoid her naughty foot.

'I was only saying to Amber the other day that we ought to try something different.'

'Do you live together?' Prudy voiced this question, then the tip of her tongue emerged to lick off a morsel of froth from her full lower lip. Sue knew that her answer would be vital to the furtherance of contact between them.

'No, but have places just across the street from here, practically next door to each other. I've a dress shop where I sell my designs. It has a workroom at the back. I live above it, and Amber owns an antique emporium and has a flat, too. Our other friend, Diane Wexford, runs the Honey Pot café. She's coming in later, and I think she'd be into this.'

As Sue talked she was speculating about what went on under Prudy's doublet. With her eye for measurements and fittings, she guessed that she would have boyish hips and a supple waist, while her breasts would be small and firm with brown areolae and nipples hard as stones. Her own tingled at the thought.

'You and Jess ... are you partners?' she asked. She liked to get things straight from the onset. It was not her policy to come between couples, unless of course it happened to be a threesome, in which case they all came.

Jess giggled and shook her head, hat off now and those springy curls making her look even more like Bubbles from the old-fashioned Pears Soap advert. 'No, we're friends, but that isn't to say that we haven't tumbled in the sack together at times ... or should I say the sleeping bag, when nights turned chilly and we were out under the stars.'

'She likes to exaggerate,' Prudy said dismissively. 'As far as I can remember, I've never slept in the open, even at the most grotty muster.'

'So what do you do? Live under canvas?' This didn't appeal to Sue much. She liked her creature comforts and doubted that even the possession of the desirable Prudy would make up for their loss.

'We have tents ... individual or big, shared ones. Some bring along caravans, and this is allowed, providing they park away from the area that is supposed to be like a real army camp, with open fires and benders and tents that don't look like something from Holiday Med. Families usually put up six-manned ones, where they can do their own thing and control their children.'

'Fat chance,' Jess interjected. 'They're awful mostly, little horrors who can't keep their hands off anything and haven't a clue about the "no" word.'

'So this is a strictly Royalist muster, is it?' Amber enquired, though Sue thought she seemed somehow distracted and wondered briefly if she was missing Camilo and would have shown more interest had they been discussing a Romany encampment.

'Oh, no. It's Roundhead, too, but we keep to our own parts of the field,' Prudy answered seriously. 'They support the Parliamentarians. We've got to have someone to fight.

They're all right till we get to the battlefield, then it gets serious and we go for one another, hammer and tongs. Some take it personally, and carry on vendettas from other skirmishes. It makes it more exciting, having a foe to hate, so that you're not just hacking around with your sword and chasing Roundheads without a real purpose.'

'Does anyone get hurt?' The more Prudy told her, the more intrigued Sue became, and she could see that Amber was now sitting up and taking notice. Yes, Amber would find this stimulating, with her love of spectacle and fencing and movies based on armed conflict and 'battles long ago'.

'Not seriously, but the St John's Ambulance people are kept busy during the action. It's organised properly, with rules and regulations and, if you want to take part, then you'd better come along tomorrow and go to the administration tent where they'll take your details and fill you in. Will you come? There's nothing quite like it, I promise you.'

'I'm going to find the loo,' Amber said, squeezing past Jess and narrowly missing tripping over her sword.

She needed fresh air, finding the interplay between Sue and Prudy too arousing for comfort, her inner core moistening as she watched them. The bar was reduced to standing room only and she could not see Ian Barrett anywhere. He had drifted in and out of her thoughts all through the conversation with Jess and Prudy, and now, thoroughly restless, she elbowed her way towards a door with the men's and women's and disabled symbols above it and found herself outside in a draughty corridor.

It was deserted, stone-flagged and echoing. The smell of cooking wafted from the kitchens, for this was also a restaurant. She realised she was hungry, having come straight from the shop to meet Sue. And was it worth it? She wasn't as struck with the idea of the Silver Banner as Sue and Diane seemed to be. Camilo still floated in her dreams and had become her prime masturbation aid: Crowe, Brosnan and Cruise would have to look to their laurels.

She found the ladies' room and used the lavatory, then washed her hands and held them under the drier. For some reason she felt suddenly dispirited and wanted to go home. Why hadn't Camilo phoned her or at least sent a card postmarked Spain? She was manless, though this was nothing new. If she got really desperate there was always that reprobate, Jason Ansley. He'd not be backwards in coming forwards.

She left the toilets and moved in the direction of the bar. By the noise, it seemed that the party was in full cry, wenches shrieking and men laughing raucously. Lost in thought, she wasn't looking where she was going. A man stepped in front of her. They collided. He was colourfully costumed, all lace and furbelows, feathers and leather, but no dandy this – a tough-looking soldier. It was the chestnut-haired, bearded and mustachioed Captain of Horse, Ian Barrett.

'Sorry,' he said, steadying her with one hand.

'That's all right,' she replied automatically, though her heart was jumping all over the place.

'No, really. It was clumsy of me,' he insisted, treating her to a blast from amazingly blue eyes. He smiled and clapped himself on the brow. 'I know you, don't I? Aren't you the road-rage lady?'

'I'm bloody not! I never get road rage,' she fired back at him, her vehemence sending him into paroxysms of laughter that revealed white, slightly irregular teeth and a dimple in his cheek. This made her hopping mad. How dare he poke fun at her?

But the truth was that she was finding him overwhelming. He was a good six foot two now that he stood beside her, not on horseback. Broad shoulders under that ridiculously fancy doublet, a broad chest and strong arms, long legs, too, straight breeches with buttons running all the way down the outer seams, thigh boots with the tops turned down around his knees, lined with linen, trimmed with lace.

She could not resist glancing down at the engine room, checking his equipment. It could have been difficult to detect for the breeches were not tight, but there, sure enough, she glimpsed the outline of his cock. It looked long and thick. Could it be getting bigger because he was standing close to her?

Oh, dear, she thought, her anger melting as it sank into a sea of lubricity.

'I owe you an apology, really ... I'm laughing with you, not at you,' he averred, and did not take his hand away, cupping her elbow. 'Let me buy you a drink?'

'I've friends w ... waiting,' she stammered.

'I know. I saw you with Prudy and Jess, and a good-looking woman with odd-coloured hair.'

'You mean Sue, I suppose, and she's a fashion expert,' Amber said, flying to her defence.

He shrugged and stood with legs apart, opening his arms wide in an expansive gesture, a virile, genial, handsome man. 'You're so prickly,' he chuckled. 'Chill out, girl. I'm not getting at you or your friend. You find the exploits of the Silver Banner interesting? Let's talk some more. Better still, will you come to see us rehearsing tomorrow? I don't want to lose sight of you again. Are you married, committed, in a relationship?'

'No. Not that it's any of your business,' she began, but the breath left her with a rush as he lifted her effortlessly, literally sweeping her off her feet and raising her to his mouth.

His kiss was extraordinary, wet, tongue-filled and divine. His little chin beard felt soft, his moustache tickled and she had never felt so small and insignificant, or so completely kissed. He smelled of horses, of leather and mist and the night, and something else, too. A whiff of danger, of reckless bravery and derring-do.

He led her into the bar and heads turned. An almost primordial rush seized Amber. Civilisation as she knew it fled away. She felt in her blood the maddest, purest and most magnificent triumph, staring down the other women who had the hots for him. He had chosen her, or maybe she had made the choice ... whatever. She intended to fuck him to the point of exhaustion.

'I'm going out tonight, Ray,' Diane said as she loaded the industrial dishwasher.

'Oh? Where's that then?' he asked, seated in the gleaming kitchen, tucking into a generous portion of home-made scones, strawberry jam and cream, one of the Honey Pot's specialities.

'Over to the White Swan. I'm meeting Sue and Amber. Nothing you'd be interested in,' she said casually, hoping that Colin would be there, though he had said his troop might be visiting the Dog and Whistle on the way back to the castle. It was closer to camp and the march from town was long.

'I thought we could have a bit of a chat,' Ray began, in that sheepish, crafty way which usually meant he wanted to borrow money.

'What about?' she said, switching on the machine and listening to its hum with a satisfaction that never left her. She could remember the days when she had to do the washing up in the sink. Not funny when you were catering for a steady stream of customers.

Now she had Toyah and Toby and Lisa, and a cleaner who came in every day. It was no longer a one-man band. Ray had never been much help, barely able to cope with his garage business and taxi service, let alone anything else. He seemed incapable of taking on board more than one idea at a time.

'Well, you know I've been looking for a genuine London cab?' he began, and she stared at him pitilessly, pent-up antagonism and dislike churning within her.

Why did he have to go to Razor Ted, the high-street barber, and have a Number Two haircut? All right, so he was going bald, but did this shaven, convict look do other than draw attention to it? And too many scones and too much booze was robbing him of his waistline and giving him a beer belly.

'You've talked about it, yes,' she said slowly, freeing her hair from the white cap worn at the insistence of the health inspectors. 'So what's new?'

She leaned against the worktop, subjecting Ray to the kind of scrutiny she applied to the produce she used. Had he been a carrot, he would have been rejected. Too ugly, too grubby and long beyond its sell-by date. Yet old habits die hard and she momentarily regretted the loss of whatever it was that had drawn them together in the first place – neediness, pheromones or simply Dame Nature urging a young couple to get it together and carry on the species.

'I've found one,' he exclaimed through a shower of crumbs. 'My mate Trevor on the Whitchurch Trading Estate got it at a car auction in Battersea. The real thing, honest. I'll make a bomb with it. Everyone wants to hire a genuine London taxi. We could do weddings and all.'

'How much?' She stabbed a glance at the digital wall clock. It gave a quarter to seven and she wanted to get away, but knew the crunch was coming and braced herself.

'Three grand,' he said, bringing this out casually, as if he was talking in pence, not pounds.

'And you're going to buy it?'

'I'd like to ... but ...'

'You haven't the cash?' Surprise, surprise, she thought wearily. He was hopeless with money. It burned a hole in his pocket.

'That's where you come in,' he replied with a brashness that was shocking. 'I'm willing to let you in on the deal. You lend me the dosh and I'll make sure you get it back with interest.'

How many times have I heard that? she wondered bleakly. Ray was as inept in business as he was in bed. Tired of being constantly hard up, with Ray's money going on pie-in-the-sky, get-rich-quick schemes that always failed, she had struck out on her own once Karen was at junior school. With a loan from the bank, she had rented the café that had been allowed to run down by the two old ladies who owned it. It was very convenient, situated as it was beneath the flat that she and Ray had taken not long after they were married.

By dint of hard slog and long hours, the Honey Pot became a profitable venture. Diane was able to purchase the entire property when one of its former owners died and the other went into an old people's home. Karen wafted off to university, leaving Diane and Ray very much on their own. An uncomfortable state of affairs as far as she was concerned, for they had grown apart, or rather the holes were showing. Maybe they had never been that close.

'What makes you think I've three thousand pounds to spare?' she countered, though knowing that she had. If it had been anyone else but him, she might have seriously considered the proposition.

'You can't lose,' he said, getting up and coming towards her. 'It's a snip. An automatic with a diesel engine. It's been sprayed maroon and is in very good nick. I'll take you out in it. You'll feel like a princess.'

'I'd rather drive myself. I've my own car,' she reminded, wondering for the umpteenth time why she had married him. This had been brought home with a bang that afternoon with the arrival of Colin and his merry men.

I expect it was because I was a country girl who'd never

been further than a day trip to Burnham, plus a couple of school outings to London's Natural History Museum, she thought. Or was it because Ray was the first boy who'd paid me any attention, fumbling and awkward though it was? I must have been mad to walk down the aisle with him, nineteen and gormless. Of course, both sets of parents were relieved that it wasn't a shotgun wedding.

'We get on OK, don't we?' he said, changing tack and employing that wheedling tone that may have got him his own way with his mother, but didn't work on Diane. He sidled up to her and slipped an arm round her waist. 'We're a team, you and me. Say yes, and I'll ring Trevor right away.'

'I'll think about it,' she said cagily.

'Can I tell him that?' Ray murmured, rubbing up against her, a glint in his eye and a bulge in his trousers. She knew he had the muddled notion that if he screwed her it softened her up, made her pliable and ready to do what he wanted. This might have worked once, but that was long ago and far away.

'Tell him what you like, but I'm not making any promises. I'll need paperwork to prove that you, or should I say *we* haven't been sold a pup ... *again*,' she couldn't resist adding, angry with him and more so with herself.

She wanted to move away, but part of her, that unfulfilled potential for sensuality that had never been realised, made her linger. She knew she was attractive. The soldiers' eyes had told her that earlier – Colin and Josh and their mates. She was always getting glances and come-ons from men. It seemed that your average bloke was more interested in a curvaceous figure than the fashion magazines would have one believe, although the corny old adage that gentlemen preferred blondes appeared to be based on fact. But it was a long time since she had met any man who remotely ruffled her hormones.

As she had complained to Sue, 'I think I've thrown out

my libido with the garbage. Either that or it's gone on holiday.'

Colin, however, had performed a miracle – finding it for her in that all too brief encounter over tea and bacon butties.

Ray, convinced that his caveman tactics had won her over, trapped her against the unit, coming up behind her and pressing his erection into the crack of her bottom. 'You'll say yes about the taxi, won't you, poppet?' he crooned, using that patronising pet name that put her back up. 'I'll treat you really nice if you do. Give you a right good seeing-to.'

'Promises, promises,' she countered, her irony lost on him. Playing for time, she was half hoping that the phone would ring, or someone try the door – anything to interrupt this amateurish foreplay.

She was wearing a short-sleeved, button-through overall with nothing beneath except panties and a bra. It was always warm in the kitchen. She didn't much like the feel of Ray's hands coming round and clasping her breasts, didn't care for the combination of cheap aftershave (a Christmas present from his mother), and sweat and thermal underwear that hung around him like a miasma, and it was a long time since love had been blind to his bad breath. But her nipples peaked despite this, and her clit – disloyal little beast – quivered in anticipation.

He slipped a hand down and felt between her legs, then lifted the overall's hem, worked a finger into the side of her knickers, tangled with the soft bush, and began to tease her into wetness. She couldn't stop herself from undulating round his artful digit, pressing back against the rigid stem of his cock trapped between her buttocks.

'It's a bit public,' she reminded, though she had locked the outer doors.

'Don't you worry about that, my lovely,' he muttered and pushed her overall higher, then hitched his fingers in the elastic and pulled down her panties. 'What we needs is a nice dollop of butter,' he added, and reached round to open the refrigerator.

Oh, damn! she thought He's in one of those moods, is he? He wants a *Last Tango in Paris* scenario. I'd rather mop the floor.

There was no stopping him, however. He quickly found one of those little individual pats wrapped in foil. It was the work of seconds for him to free it and spread her legs with his knee. She gave a whimper of protest as his butter-coated finger pressed into the tightly clenched mouth of her anus.

'Jesus Christ! That's cold,' she cried, saddened because the protest in her voice would have told a less insensitive person that she wasn't into being buggered – not just then – but was prepared to go along with it to keep the peace.

Ray was launched and, 'I'll soon warm it up,' he muttered. 'Bend over. God, but you've got a lovely arse.' He pressed the small of her back, making her lie across the granite work surface.

Her breasts were flattened by the cold hardness, and he took her wrists and stretched her arms above her head. Then his hand slid beneath her, massaging her clit too roughly and, at some point in the proceedings, she wasn't sure quite sure when, he released his cock from his trousers and fixed its snout at her entrance. He pushed, opening her sex and, lubricated by the melting butter, it slid in further, filling her full of him. At the same time, he inserted a finger into her greasy fundament and wriggled it around. He continued to rub her clit with his other hand – too harsh, too much. She knew what he wanted to do and it wasn't her favourite way of fucking, though she enjoyed it sometimes. When Ray had first suggested that they try it, she had found it excruciatingly painful, but had got used to it, stretching to accommodate him, even finding a dark, salacious pleasure in so doing.

But not today. Today she wanted to get it over with so she faked an orgasm.

'That's my girl,' Ray said, triumphant. 'I can always make you come.'

Feigning ecstasy, Diane flopped over the unit and Ray withdrew. He took a finger away from her clit and drew the other out of her anus and replaced it with his slippery cock-head. Not lubricated by me, she thought wryly. More thanks to the latest in spreads, Dairy Filled. And a sucker for telly ads, she visualised that wholesome young actor in his farmer's smock and heard him saying: 'Try Dairy Filled. Packed with the golden goodness of pure butter-milk. It may help to keep your heart healthy.'

What a load of toss, she thought. I'm only stocking it because of a promotional deal. As for Ray, he wouldn't care it if was machine oil as long as it greased his way to rectum heaven.

Ray heaved and she felt herself expanding to take him. She gripped the edge of the unit and tried to relax. Talk about close your eyes and think of England, she reflected, wincing.

She moaned as his hot prick penetrated her; anything to get him going. It wasn't particularly uncomfortable, or even humiliating – just incredibly boring.

'Oh, yes! Yes!' she cried encouragingly, spurring him on in the hope that it would be over soon. She heaved her bottom high, feeling the slap, slap of his balls against her crack every time he thrust his cock into her.

'Oh, baby, you're so tight!' he gasped, and his fingers dug into her hips, holding her to his frenzied jabs.

He hadn't an inkling that she was pretending, absorbed in his own sensations, panting hard as he chased his crisis. With a final, desperate thrust he forced his throb-bing cock deep into her and, as he started to spurt, fell forward with a groan, crushing her beneath him.

Diane moved, heaving him off. She had done her duty

and wanted no more of him. She stood up, feeling melted butter and spunk trickling down her inner thighs. She tore off a section of kitchen roll and dried herself, then found her panties somewhere under her feet and dragged them on, padding the gusset with a wad of tissue. She couldn't bear to look at Ray, that selfish, greedy, what's-in-it-for-me bumpkin, with his slow wits that only fired up if he thought there was money in the offing.

She was filled with disgust and self-loathing because, once again, she had allowed him to slake his lust in her. That's all it had been: sheer, unadulterated lust. He had copulated like an animal. No love. No tenderness. Not even liking or affection.

Ray wiped his tackle and tucked it away in his trousers. Then he washed his hands under the hot tap and said, 'If you're meeting the girls, then I might as well go down to the Snooty Fox ... find Trevor, have a pint, tell him what you've said, and try to knock him down a few quid.'

'OK. See you later. I don't suppose I'll be late,' Diane said, stiff as a board as he planted a kiss on her cheek, picked up his anorak and let himself out.

She made sure that the security system was on and the lights off, then went upstairs to the flat. Far from feeling relaxed and at peace with the world as one should after intercourse, she was edgy, disgruntled and upset. It was a horrible situation to be in when the only man she could have sex with didn't really turn her on. She never creamed her panties just by thinking about him. Masturbation gave her more satisfaction than putting up with the unpleasantness that was the greater part of Ray. Yet in many ways he was considered to be a good husband: he never strayed; was only occasionally paralytic – a binge drinker who went over the top when celebrating football matches or birthdays or the New Year; a moderately devoted father – no more or less than any other average man; and he let Diane do pretty much as she liked, as long as she paid the bills and came up with the cash to finance his schemes.

But surely to God there's more to life than this? she thought despairingly as she showered and dressed and did a quick make-up job on her face. Do I really want him plugging my arse? Or getting anywhere near me, for that matter? The answer came back as a definite no. She felt trapped, like so many other women she knew, apart from Sue and Amber.

And what about the lovely Colin? Would he be at the White Swan? Her heart lifted and her generous red lips curled up in a grin. Karen was sleeping over with a friend, so there was no need to worry about her. It had cost Diane twenty pounds to get rid of her for the night, but it was worth it.

She shrugged on her fleece, picked up her bag and left the building, heading up the street towards the pub. Before she got there, she could hear the cheerful uproar from inside, and saw several men in clothes like those of the soldiers who'd come to her café that afternoon.

She stopped one of them, a beefy fellow in a leather waistcoat laced across the front. 'Is Sergeant Fielding inside?' she asked, while he grinned at her, waving his mug and hefting a musket.

'Aye, he is,' he said, staring at her blearily. 'He's a good mate, is Colin, and a first-class sergeant. He looks after us. Doesn't he, lads?'

'Yes. That's right,' they chorused, staggering from the effects of the home-brewed cider.

'Go easy on that,' she warned. 'It's been known to work as paint stripper. Too much of it and you'll end up pole-axed.' Then she threw them a dazzling smile, and sauntered into the bar to find Colin.

4

'Once it used to be hot-cross buns and those yellow, deckle-edged biscuits with squashed flies in, and chocolate Easter eggs and fluffy toy chickens,' Amber declared, settling herself in the rear of Sue's car. 'That's when I got the boys guinea pigs one year. Kids always bang on till you buy them pets. We kept them in the garden, lawn chomping, chirruping, shitting everywhere. They were sweet really.'

'I know where you're coming from,' Diane agreed, swivelling round in the passenger seat to smile at her. 'Karen had a lop-eared buck rabbit. In spite of a visit to the vet to have his pockets picked, he still humped anything that breathed. And there were boringly placid goldfish that had to be cleaned out regularly or they went belly up.'

'And now you're both child and pet free and off along the Yellow Brick Road to find your fairy-tale princes,' Sue commented ironically, her eye on the traffic. 'It's kept fine for it, anyhow.'

It had, and a holiday spirit prevailed. Knowing how crowded such events could be, they had left Lyncroft early, but even so had to endure a tailback when they reached the junction that forked to the castle ruins. The car boot sale would be a big draw, and the other entertainments promised on the posters. Amber's dealer nose was twitching and she couldn't wait to rummage through the stalls, bargain hunting. But there was something else now, hovering large on her horizon – watching the Silver Banner doing their stuff. Not the actual battle: this would not take place till tomorrow with a repeat on Sunday, but they would be drilling and exercising and generally flexing their muscles and being put through their paces. Ian had told her what to expect. Ian, who had astonished her by leaving at closing time last night, refusing her invitation to come back for a coffee (i.e. a screw).

'Sorry, no can do,' he had said, taking her hand and lifting it to his lips. The hairs on her arms and back had stiffened in response to the brush of his moustache on her skin. 'Must get my troopers safely to camp. I'll see you tomorrow and we'll take it from there.'

'OK,' she had said, while inside her she was shouting, I want you to suck me between the legs, like lemon before tequila. Supper's ready. Come and get it.

'He didn't come home with me and fuck me!' she said aloud now, quite offended. 'It was like being wooed or something. I'm not used to it.'

'Colin was the same,' Diane complained. 'I hoped we might have a bit of a full-on snog but he marched off at the head of his platoon, or whatever they're called. They take their duties very seriously.'

'We'll simply have to enlist. There's nothing else for it,' put in Sue, edging the car through a gate into a field where a man in a weatherproof jacket and green wellingtons took their money, handed them tickets and pointed in the direction of the improvised carpark. 'That's the farmer who owns the land,' Sue went on. 'He must be making a packet, even though a percentage goes to charity.'

'I don't mind enlisting, but I don't particularly want to fight,' Amber said, yet the glamour of the whole thing appealed and it seemed to be the only way to get to know Ian.

'I've thought about it all night,' Sue declared, in pursuit of a spotty youth who was making a pig's ear of stacking the cars. Several irate drivers were leaping out, fists waving, fingers pointing. 'What about I start making costumes? I've history books and patterns and all. I can get out flyers and add this service to my website. I fancy having a go with a sword from horseback.'

'Having a go at Prudy, you mean,' Diane said pointedly.

'That, too. We've talked about clothes and she's willing to advise me and spread my name among her friends and get orders.'

'Hey, wait a minute!' Diane wore the expression of someone who has just had a road to Damascus revelation. 'Who caters for them? I'll bet they work up huge appetites. Supposing I buy a hot-dog and chip van and have it converted so that I could supply other things, too ... coffee and tea and soft drinks ... shish kebabs ... pizzas? We could run it round the clock, a twenty-four-hour service.'

'Laying on victuals. In costume all the time?'

'Of course. Though it's such a brilliant idea, someone else must have taken it on by now.'

'You can but ask the powers that be.'

'Let's go see 'em.'

'I'm into it.'

Sue parked up, finding her own spot where she wouldn't be bumper to bumper and unable to get out. They found the main entrance and passed beneath the bunting and a huge banner declaiming: THE LYNCROFT COUNTRY AND GARDEN SHOW.

'Somewhat misleading,' Amber said. 'It's too early for flowers and whopping big vegetables.'

'Don't be so picky. There's a marquee up,' Diane pointed out, 'and a flag. I expect there will be bonsai trees and floral arrangements, and shrubs contributed by the Brookside Horticultural Centre.'

'And prizes given for the best cakes.'

'And more prizes for guessing the weight of them.'

'And jam and marmalade and conserves getting awards.'

A Boy Scout took their tickets, tore them across and handed back half. His mates lazed against the fence, gazing aimlessly at the crowd and making brain-dead remarks that were supposed to be the acme of wit, though miraculously galvanised into what they hoped to be impressive action if any teenage girls appeared. Amber felt sore inside. Her boys used to be, somewhat reluctantly, members of B.P.'s famous band. Cubs, then Scouts. Camping, winning badges for proficiency in cooking and fire-lighting and those other skills supposed to set a young man up for life when all that really interested him was showing off and wanking.

'Andy and Chris were Scouts,' she muttered.

'I know,' Sue replied and hooked her arm in Amber's. 'I miss them, too. I watched them growing up, remember? What were they? Around ten and twelve when you moved here?'

'That's right. After Mum died, and I sold the family house and bought the shop. Last Christmas was the first one without them, and this will be the first spring and summer.'

'Matthew's a plonker. I only met him a few times and on each occasion he tried to bed me. As if I would. They'll soon see what a dickhead he is when they've been with him long enough. Come on. Concentrate on the advantages of being footloose and fancy-free.'

They struck out across the first field. People were milling about all over the place, though a steady stream were making for the car boot section: newly-weds supplementing their household furnishings; children looking for Beanie Babies and Pokémon card swaps; greedy pensioners who had studied *Miller's Antiques Price Guide* and were determined to make a profit on jumble sale buys.

Then there were dealers like Amber and Jason. She spotted him as soon as she entered the first lane between the kosher, canvas-covered stalls and the battered family saloons spewing forth dingy objects, mostly clothes that she wouldn't have had the bottle to offer the ragman.

He treated her to a wide grin, astonishingly tidy in a pin-stripe suit and pale lilac shirt. He even wore a tie and his brown hair coiled into tight rings at the nape of his neck. In spite of her resolutions about keeping him at arm's length, he was looking remarkably dapper, like one of those charming, Lovejoy-type characters gaining popularity in Attic Treasure programmes on daytime telly.

'Cor, you're smart. Where're your jeans?' she asked, getting in the first thrust.

'The whistle and flute impresses you? I'm a man of many parts,' he said, in that wicked way of his that made her pussy twitch. 'Rumour has it that the press will be here today. I'm told that I'm photogenic, and don't intend to let those poncy Royalists steal all the thunder.'

Her nipples crimped as she looked at him, adding to the mayhem in her pants. This wasn't right. She shouldn't be responding to his sex appeal. She was here to lure Ian, wasn't she? He was the reason why she had put on tight, black, kickflare trousers, a figure-hugging black camisole with a low neck and a pane velvet jacket in tobacco brown, livened by self-coloured Indian embroidery. She wasn't quite sure what she was aiming at, but wanted to appear arty, independent, ready to embrace new concepts, like becoming a Cavalier's doxy. She hoped her signals would not be misread if she bumped into any acquaintances on the fête committee, for she was not in the least inclined to offer her services as a raffle-ticket seller or a steward or anything tediously helpful like that.

Seeing Jason had spiked her guns somewhat, though she cursed herself for being surprised. When had he ever passed up the chance to make a few shekels?

'This your pitch?' she asked as casually as she could, avoiding staring at his kissable mouth by running a critical eye over the contents spread out beguilingly on a crimson chenille tablecloth with bobbing fringes. Not for him the modern-style throw.

'For today,' he replied, leaning against the edge of the trestle nonchalantly, long legs crossed at the ankle, his fly area thrown into prominence, impossible to ignore. She wanted to kiss that, too. 'I'm surprised you didn't turn up with your gear. You're a booter, aren't you?'

'I have been known, but not this time. I'm thinking of joining the Silver Banner.' She dropped this into the conversation casually, thinking, let's see what you make of that, Jack the Lad.

A lop-sided, slightly mocking smile lifted his chiselled lips, although he never took his eyes from several would-be customers who hovered, picking up this article or that, staring at the price tag, before replacing it, or hanging on, subjecting it to closer scrutiny.

'Want to play Cavaliers and Roundheads, do you? Several of them have bought things from me this morning. They're giving a demo later on,' he said, then glanced to where her breasts rounded out her skimpy top.

She blushed, disconcerted because her nipples were still hard as cherry stones, a part of her body over which she had no control, in league with the tyrannical jewel that crowned her cleft.

'I know all that,' she said icily. 'This is why I'm here.'

Jason, however, now fastened his eagle eye on a punter, flirting blatantly. 'Yes, my love. Genuine Goss china. It's yours for a tenner, though I'm cutting my own throat to let it go so cheaply. A nice piece and you've got good taste. Collect Goss, do you?' He was off on his spiel and the woman, blinded by his looks and patter and forgetting to haggle, parted with her ten pounds while he wrapped the china ornament in tissue and tucked it into a plastic carrier. It was like taking candy from a baby.

'Don't rush off,' he said to Amber, sotto voce. 'I want to talk to you.'

Such a peremptory tone was more likely to send her scuttling away in the opposite direction, but her feet seemed glued to the turf. His customer departed in a welter of delighted embarrassment at his innuendoes, and he turned back to Amber.

'I've got to go,' she said defensively. 'People to see. Things to do.'

'Why are you always trying to avoid me?' He had dropped his tone an octave, his voice a spine-tingling caress.

Amber darted a glance round. Where were Sue and Diane? She didn't want to be alone with this man whose aura was pure sensuality, although she could hardly describe their present situation as solitary. 'Avoid you, Jason? We've hardly met. A couple of times at auctions. That's all.'

'And you insist on pretending that you're not interested?' He rearranged the stall, closing the space vacated by the Goss china, his weather eye on an old gentleman in a tweed cap who was examining a marble chiming clock. 'Forty pounds to you, gov'ner,' Jason offered. 'Genuine Victorian.' The man grunted, shook his head and hobbled away

'I've told you before. I don't break up partnerships,' Amber said flatly.

'Oh, you mean Ellen? We've split anyway. She was getting too demanding,' Jason said with a callousness that put her right off him, mentally but not physically. She gave up trying to deny that he was terribly, fatally, wantonly attractive, but then bad boys always were.

'I really must go,' she repeated.

He reached out and detained her, pushing something into her hand. 'My card,' he said. 'Mobile and home numbers. Give me a buzz sometime . . . sooner rather than later.'

'And who is that smarmy operator?' Sue wanted to

know, pouncing on Amber from the shadow of a junk jewellery tent. It also stocked hash-pipes, incense, packets of extra long Rizlas, meditation tapes and other things cosmic.

'You dark horse. You've got men everywhere,' Diane chipped in, flaxen hair tied back in a scrunchie, and dressed in a pink linen trouser suit with the jacket secured, if it could be called that, by a tie belt. Her opulent breasts strained at the opening as she gestured unselfconsciously, and Amber envied her deep cleavage.

'Men? That's not true. And Jason is just another dealer I run across sometimes. I've told you about him, haven't I?'

'You described him as a bit of rough,' Sue said.

'He usually is. "Fine feathers don't necessarily make fine birds." He can be a pain. So bloody arrogant and patronising.'

'He does it for the same reason that a dog licks its balls. Because he can,' Sue returned pithily. 'Come on. Let's find the Silver Banner headquarters.'

The sea of canvas seemed to stretch for miles. Not only were there avenues of stalls piled with second-hand furniture and knick-knacks, but others selling cheap-jack goods that could be found at street markets any day of the week. DIY jostled shoes and trainers; health foods were on sale next to a butcher's van; vegetables, organic or chemically assisted and mass-produced, elbowed bras and panties, socks, boxer shorts, fleeces, baseball caps and logo-printed sweatshirts. Then there were walk-in, undercover emporiums where dusky sheikhs who might have been born in Arabia but probably hailed from Hackney in London, displayed colourful cotton garments with 'Made in India' labels.

Amber was caught up in this jumble of noise and smells. An alluring odour of gingerbread, toffee apples and candyfloss tantalised her nostrils as she passed a confectioner's kiosk. Music blared through the PA and a masculine voice made indecipherable announcements every so often. Babies grizzled, trundled along in push-chairs that resembled racing bikes. Children ran riot, getting in the way, their mothers in nagging pursuit and their fathers sidling towards a marquee bright with bunting. It had a large, handwritten notice emblazoned with the magic words, BEER TENT.

Next to this, flaunting a blue pennant from its flagpole, was the Silver Banner HQ.

Sue made for it, her nose lifted like a pointer's, but Diane lingered, entranced by the trader in the van on her right who was shouting in a Brummie accent, 'Chip, chip, chip! Burger, burger! From the fryer to the buyer! Rainy day prices!'

'That's it!' she exclaimed, transfixed. 'I can do that. He's only here for the public, and I expect the soldiers buy from him, too, but what about in their camp? Let's get the formalities over and start planning.'

'You go on. I'll meet up with you. I must just pop in here and have a reading. You know I'm a sucker for Mystic Megs and their sisterhood,' Amber said, halting at a tent with a fibreboard notice propped up outside bearing the message, 'Madam Tanith. Internationally renowned fortune-teller and medium'.

Snapshots were pinned to it, of Tanith presumably, and a host of public figure. Film stars, TV personalities, politicians and the like were beaming into the camera, apparently inordinately pleased with Madam's predictions.

'For God's sake, Amber! Isn't getting in with the Banner people more important?' Sue snapped without pausing, dragging Diane along with her. 'OK. We'll get the ball rolling. You join us there, when you've done with the Wicked Witch of the West.'

The fortune-teller's tent had few customers. People paused uncertainly, then walked on by. As Amber approached the flap, a voice drifted out, saying, 'Don't be afraid. I can help you.'

It was a pleasant voice, not young, but not old; somewhere in the middle. Amber never could resist a chance to peer beyond the veil, and she now ducked inside. It was one of those old-fashioned bell-tents that had gone out of favour years before, dimly lit by filtered daylight and a few squat, perfumed candles. It was hung with eastern draperies. A Persian carpet covered the decking floor. It smelled strongly of joss sticks, and a faint blue haze drifted on the air. Curious objects ornamented shelves or dangled from the tent-pole. Amber made out a small stuffed crocodile, a dead snake, a collection of feathers and dried herbs, and what looked like bones in a glass jar.

This was not the first time she had consulted one versed in necromancy and she had even dabbled in it herself, but now she felt a stirring of unease, yet the woman seated at the small round table seemed as normal as possible, given the circumstances. She could have been someone's grandmother – she probably was. Big bosomed and stately, swathed in luxuriant gypsy-styled clothing in shades of purple and claret, her fingers were loaded with gold rings, matching the chains about her neck and hanging from her ears. Her wiry hair was half hidden by a scarf of silver-spangled chiffon, and her bright, night-dark eyes regarded Amber with a steady, unblinking stare.

'Tarot, palm or crystal ball, my dear?' she asked.

Amber had a talent for reading the cards, but could never predict for herself. 'All three,' she said. 'What do you charge?'

'A special price if you do it that way. Fifteen pounds the lot, instead of seven each,' Tanith answered.

This seemed fair enough and Amber nodded her consent. She wondered where the woman had come from, half expecting to encounter a charlatan recruited from the ladies branch of the Friends of the Lyncroft Fête, but no,

Tanith seemed to be genuine. She looked like a Romany, dressed like a Romany and had that wily, world-wise ambience about her that put Amber at ease.

'Cards first,' Tanith said, picking up the pack and handing it to Amber. 'Shuffle well, cut into three with your left hand, choose one of them and give it to me, using your left hand all the time. While you're doing it, think about the issues that you want answering.'

Amber tried to clear her mind and concentrate on one question only, but her thoughts were humming like a swarm of agitated bees. From her own limited experience she knew that Tarot reading was part guesswork, part psychobabble, part intuition, but admitted there was something else, too, an unexplained element that existed in all branches of the paranormal.

She did as instructed, cutting the cards, picking up one pile, giving it to Tanith. The fortune-teller laid them out in what Amber recognised as a fifteen-card spread. She was dazzled by the rich artistry of the illustrations.

'I've never seen any like these before,' she said. 'They are so original and lavish.'

'The Thoth Tarot, sometimes called the Tarot of the Egyptians, created by Crowley, and designed by Frieda Harris,' Tanith replied. 'Now, the first card laid down represents the querent, that's you, the second and third card the influences that surround you. You are the Princess of Cups, and look, the Ace of Wands and the Nine of Cups stand beside you. Cups are for emotions. Wands indicate great energy. Discs signify money matters, and Swords disturbances. I can tell that you are muddled just now. You don't know who to choose, and I'm not surprised. There are a number of court cards, now and in your future. I see knights and princes.'

'Men in my life?' Amber already knew what these cards portended if they were in prominent positions. She ticked them off in her head – Camilo, Jason and Ian. Princes, or maybe knights?

'Oh, yes, plenty of men,' Tanith replied with a throaty chuckle. 'Never a shortage of men. In fact, you'll be spoilt for choice. And there's money coming your way ... a six of discs, and here a seven.'

'These men. Do I already know them? Or are they in the future?' In spite of a sensible part of her that insisted this was bullshit, a shiver passed down Amber's spine and connected with her loins. Her panty gusset was damp from that momentary engagement with Jason and the anticipation of seeing Ian. There was the distinct possibility that one or the other would lay her before the day was over – maybe both, though not, she thought, at the same time. Joys to come, perhaps.

Tanith passed her hands over the spread and pointed to cards on the upper right and upper left. 'Let us consider these two potentials for the future. They may complement each other. If they are in conflict, then those on the right may show the direction your life will naturally follow unless you take action, when the left-hand cards will offer an alternative course. As for the knights? You know them, but there are others you don't,' she continued and her voice had become a dreamy monotone.

Amber stared at the male court cards. Those in her right-hand future were the Knight of Cups and the Knight of Discs. Among the ones in the left was a Trump, called the Emperor. A powerful card, as were all those of the Major Arcana. Beside him was the darkly beautiful Prince of Swords, and the enigmatic Juggler.

'The Emperor?' Amber asked, unable to connect him with men she knew. 'He's a heavy old number, isn't he?'

'He can be,' Tanith said, giving her a searching glance. 'He represents authority and power. Is sometimes associated with the father, and with the law.'

Amber shook her head. 'There's only my ex-husband, and he's a plank. Strong willed, but in a stubborn, childish way. No, I don't think it's him. What about the Prince of Swords?'

'He is in your future. Not too far ahead. This is a six-month reading.'

'Will he be good for me?'

'He is a strong leader of men, but no angel. What you make of the relationship is down to you. As for the rest, you have the Juggler, a dancer who adroitly balances creation in his hands, and two loyal female friends, the Queen of Swords and the Princess of Discs. The Wheel of Fortune indicates that you can do anything you want. The Tower suggests that you are about to make great changes, embarking on a venture that will bring you much happiness. Beware of a woman, rich, selfish and spiteful. You have cups in abundance, and fiery wands that give off energy. Let me see your palms to confirm this.'

Amber placed the backs of her hands on the table and the fortune-teller leaned over and perused them. 'A long lifeline,' she said. 'You'll live till you're a hundred, I shouldn't wonder. At least two marriages, and several children. I see two boys, but they are across the water. They will return to you soon. Would you like me to look into the crystal?'

Amber nodded, her mouth suddenly parched. She was angry at her curiosity that had put her in this predicament. Sensible Diane and pragmatic Sue didn't waste their time on such matters. But Amber could not resist seeking answers to the question of life, death and the universe. She wanted to know if there was anything in theories concerning the occult, always curious, her interest reawakened when her grandfather died, and her mother not long after. In the absence of a father, she had been brought up by these two people, relied on them and loved them and their departure had been hard to bear.

With all the solemnity of a high priestess in a sacred temple, Tanith slipped the violet plush cover from the crystal. It stood on a carved mahogany stand and seemed to glow, reflecting the candles and the contents of the tent, miniature reproductions the wrong way up. Tanith passed her hands over the sphere, muttering an incantation.

Amber gripped the edges of the slatted wooden chair beneath her, fascinated by the ball that now appeared to shimmer. 'What do you see?' she demanded.

'I can't quite make it out,' Tanith said, eyes hooded as she stared into the crystal. 'Would you like to look?'

This was an odd request. A fortune-teller asking a client to participate? It was also flattering, drawing Amber into the select circle of sorcerers. She felt light-headed as she gazed into the depths of that fascinating orb. It had turned milky white, but lit from within. Despite the hub-bub from outside, the shouts and laughter, the music and distorted announcements from the public address system, the tent was pervaded by silence, yet filled with invisible things.

Amber could see nothing except cloudy swirls, and suddenly wanted to leave, impatient with Tanith. Why didn't she just get on with it and give her the usual old crap? Sue would be waiting, discussing important issues with the Banner worthies. She should be there, taking a firm hold of her destiny. But just when she was about to stand up and call it a day, Tanith spoke again.

'I can see the figure of a dancing man ... and what dancing! Passionate, filled with fire. He claps his hands, stamps his feet and gyrates. The Juggler himself.'

Amber closed her eyes, and let her imagination or, if it existed, her third eye, supply a picture of Camilo. It was deep within the cold blue flames of the crystal, then it cleared and she saw someone with him. As the mist parted, leaving a tiny flaming heart in its centre, she realised that it was herself. Camilo wore his flamenco suit, head held at a haughty angle, spine straight, taut buttocks and the long finger of phallus pressing against his tight, tight trousers. He was leading her through the steps. Then they were naked, writhing in a sacred dance of desire. She was looking at herself being relentlessly fucked within the core of the crystal.

'He plays a part in your future,' Tanith was saying, breathing deeply, her cheeks flushed. 'But look into your thoughts again. Let me guide you. Pick up on what you see.'

Amber drifted into reverie once more. Camilo had vanished and the mists drifted and changed, now white as clouds, now blue, now black, but always with that hidden light illuminating them. Horsemen appeared and the fog cleared, They were led by a tall, dark man with a saturnine expression. He was splendidly dressed in bright blue, and she distinctly saw his regimental colours – two quarters – black field, gold lion rampant. Two quarters – white and blue Palatine lozenges. Gold fringe. Such a man! Such a star!

'The Prince of Swords,' whispered the fortune-teller.

A surge of longing swept Amber. She wanted him with a madness that leaped through her blood. Then she caught sight of Ian riding just behind him. Her heart lightened at the solid reality of him.

'The Knight of Cups,' Tanith said, nodding sagely.

'I want to know more,' Amber shouted, greedy to know if the other knight foretold by the Tarot might be Jason.

'No,' the necromancer said, closing her eyes wearily. 'This is enough. I am tired. I need to rest.'

'But I have to know. Look. I'll give you more money,' and Amber pulled some notes from her purse, along with a heap of small change.

'Come and see me another time. I shall be here all the weekend.' Tanith covered the crystal in its velvet shroud and moved away from the table stiffly, as if her arthritis was painful.

'Goodbye, then, and thank you,' Amber said, scooping up the money and heading for the tent flap and the next stage of her quest.

'A word more,' said Tanith, igniting the Calor gas ring beneath a battered, aluminium kettle. 'Your mother wants me to tell you that she is proud of you. "Well done," she says. And she adds that she's met up with your father and he's just as much of a dork as he always was. He's due to reincarnate again shortly.'

'I never met him. Does he know I'm his daughter?' Amber asked, getting a quick flash of a photograph album and her mother explaining that the remote young man with long hair and beard, a flowing caftan, beads and flared loons, was her father. She had said that he was dead and that was why they lived with Grandpa and she wrote for newspapers to keep herself and Amber.

'He does,' Tanith nodded, popping a tea bag into a mug. 'And he says, "Hi there, babe. Life's a gas and death is even better."'

Sue didn't usually feel nervous when confronting authority. She amused herself by imagining the persons in command naked, or masturbating or rolling around having sex. This almost, but not quite, worked as she stood in front of a long table, at each end of which were seated several people, mostly male, some wearing flamboyant Royalist regalia and the others more soberly attired, presumably Parliamentarians.

She and Diane were not the only applicants. Several visitors stood around self-consciously, studying the recruitment posters and those announcing forthcoming Silver Banner events. The tent was large and warm; the crushed grass sent out an earthy odour and the administrators rustled papers and talked to those who had already reached their Mecca, the table. One of the Cavaliers was punching data into his laptop. Another was busy with his mobile. The treasurer, a lady in men's clothing, took the cheques or credit card details. The Roundheads were poker-faced and devoid of bonhomie.

'"Life is serious, life is earnest",' Sue quoted, and Diane gave a grin.

'I wish Amber would hurry up,' she said. 'All this rushing off chasing fortune-tellers.'

'That's Amber, ever impulsive,' Sue replied, fixing her beautifully made-up eyes on the portly gent seated in the centre of the King's Men group. She hardly favoured the Roundheads with a glance, though they seemed to be attracting a solid section of the enquirers. 'Watch what you're signing, Di,' she warned. 'You don't want to wind up on the wrong side.'

'Absolutely not,' Diane answered staunchly. 'They look dull as ditch-water. Besides, I mean to be with Colin,' and she made sure to stand in the Cavalier queue.

Their turn came. 'I'm Bernard Fletcher, Public Relations Officer,' said the stout man, confirming Sue's conjecture that he was someone in authority. He stood up, bowed and shook hands with her and Diane across the table. 'How can I be of help?'

Sue did not answer straight away, fascinated by his ruddy complexion, full moustache waxed into needle-points and long, straggly hair of that brownish-black, rusty colour usually associated with fifty-year-old swingers who used Grecian 2000.

She pulled herself up with a jerk, for he was waiting, a politely expectant smile on his face. 'Oh, ah ... yes. I want to find out how to join your organisation. I'm Sue Tucker and this is Diane Wexford. We're expecting another friend. She wants to enlist, too.'

'I see,' he replied. 'Well, that's good news. Not Round-heads, then?'

'No,' they chorused. He smiled even wider and his eyes twinkled.

'Sit down,' he said and indicated two plastic-coated chairs of the easy storage variety. 'Now then, tell me all about it. How did you hear of us? What makes you want to attend our musters? In what capacity do you see yourselves?'

Within a quarter of an hour, he had filled them in and armed them with information packs. They were told how to find a suitable regiment within striking distance of Lyncroft, what to wear, how to comport themselves, and given telephone numbers of the chief cooks and bottle-washers of various brigades. They were not obliged to attend every muster, but it was a good idea to do so if possible. Once they had paid their fee of thirty pounds for a single person, they would then be registered and automatically receive the *Orders of the Day* magazine. This gave details of skirmishes, sieges, musters and battles throughout the campaigning season.

'Phew! You're nothing if not well organised,' said Sue, aware that Bernard was stroking his moustache, puffing out his chest under the splendid red and gold doublet and generally behaving as one would expect a dashing Cavalier to do. A little mature, maybe, but never mind. There was obviously life in the old dog yet.

'Have to be, m'dear,' he said, and his companions on either side nodded. 'The Banner has been running for forty years. We've raised thousands for charity and, I hope, helped to widen the public's interest in this part of England's history. I don't mind telling you that most of us are dedicated to it, but that's not to say we don't know how to enjoy ourselves, too.'

I'll bet you do, Sue thought, imagining him slipping away from his neat detached house and Mrs Fletcher at weekends, dressed in his best and riding a spirited horse on to the battlefield then, winded but triumphant, swaggering back to his caravan, changing into fresh finery and going to the nearest pub, there to quaff ale and pick up a scrubber. She might be a local girl out for a lark, or a member of the Banner who had also escaped into a dream-world where she was a busty, lusty whore or maybe a grand lady in silks and satins who had decided to rough it among the soldiers for the night.

Good for him, Sue concluded. It's got to be better than golf, and I expect Mrs F. finds her own amusement among younger men or even women, meeting them in clubs or at the sports' centre, glad to see the back of him for a few days. She probably labels him a boring old fart.

He had obviously taken a shine to her, and Diane's voluptuous form pleased him no end. It shouldn't be difficult to get what they wanted. Sue scanned the list of suggestions of what part they might like to play. There was plenty of scope: pikeman, musketeer, artillerist, medic, drummer, cavalry person.

'I'd like to become a horseman,' she remarked, 'but was wondering if it would be possible for me to bring a stall along, selling costumes and accessories? I know a lot about the period. Studied it at college and have my own shop selling dresses.'

'I'm sure this can be arranged,' he said genially. 'There's usually a Traders' Corner at most events, and they are all members of the Banner and will lend you a hand. Of course, you will have to contribute to whichever charity we are supporting at any particular muster.'

'No hassle,' she said winsomely, giving him a big smile, while her inside clenched as she imagined nights under canvas with Prudy. She could feel her fingers brushing the dark curls of her lover's snatch, and then wickedly, insistently, dividing the plump cleft as if her finger was a dagger, sinking into soft and deliciously juicy fruit.

'And what about you, Mrs Wexford?' he asked, roguishly. 'D'you fancy yourself in breeches and doublet astride a sprightly nag?'

Diana, who had freed her hair from its restraint, now feathered her fingers through her fair curls and, wearing a demure look, said, 'I don't think I'm brave enough for that. What I'd really like to be is a victualler, selling food to the troops from a van. I'm experienced. Have had my own café in Lyncroft for several years. Everything would be above board. I know all about health and safety and food inspectors. What do you think?' and she paused, as if waiting with bated breath for him to pass judgement on her case.

'Well, I don't know. Let me consult with my colleagues,' he answered, and went into a huddle with both those of his own side and the opposition, all of whom listened solemnly and put forward one or two suggestions.

Diane and Sue waited, aware of the barely contained impatience of those lined up behind them. 'You're in OK,' Diane said. 'Nothing complicated about costumes. Catering is different, and so it should be. The last thing they want is an outbreak of food poisoning. What one does for love, eh?'. She rolled her eyes dramatically.

'Don't you mean lust?' Sue retorted, but she was well pleased with how this interview was going.

She felt like rushing out and spouting poetry over the hills. An ode to Prudy. There was nothing like a new love to get the blood pumping through the veins, to invigorate and fill with optimism. It might be unfounded, but was great while it lasted.

Bernard won the day, of course, bringing the weight of his position to bear on the committee's decision. 'We've talked it over,' he announced in his booming voice, 'and, providing you can give us a written report on yourself, your reputation as a restaurant owner and the condition of the vehicle you intend to use for catering, we see no reason why you shouldn't become a victualler. Wearing of costume for the duration of the muster is essential, and all the other regulations of the Silver Banner apply to you and those who assist you.'

'Thank you so much,' Diane said, jigging up and down with excitement, her breasts bouncing in such a way that his eyes were nearly popping out of his head. 'And may I hope you'll come and see me when I'm set up at the next muster, and I'll give you a free hot dog! I'm an expert with all things sausage shaped.'

'What's all this? How are you getting on?' Amber said behind them, and Sue turned, forgetting to be annoyed at her lateness.

'Fine. Just fine. I'm to ride with the cavalry and have my clothing stall and Di can be a victualler. This is Mr Fletcher. He is head of PR,' and she introduced her to Bernard.

Amber seemed unsure of her role as a Banner member, but then Diane jumped into the breach and said that she could work with her on the catering. This appeared to satisfy the committee and they left the tent fully paid-up members of the Society.

'Right. That's it. Now we go to get a good spot from which to watch the drilling. It starts in half an hour,' said Sue.

A frumpy, big-boned girl was stomping in their direction. She had pale hair, straight as pump water, that fell from a central parting, giving her the appearance of a mournful spaniel. She wore horn-rimmed glasses through which she peered about her with a vague air of disapproval. Two equally unprepossessing girls were with her, giggling and subjecting passing lads to come-on glances and stringent one-liners.

'Oh, shit! There's Karen!' muttered Diane. 'If she sees me I shan't be able to get rid of her without it costing me deep in the purse. She's a lump with attitude. And she doesn't resemble me in the least. She favours her father's family, particularly her "Nan" as he insists that she calls his mother. If I ever have grandchildren and they give me that name, I'll boil them in oil.'

They hid in the lee of a tent, then ran for it. Sue was in the lead, feeling the sun on her face and the breeze in her hair. She couldn't wait to pass through the uniformed guards at the gate and head out across the plain where soldiers, artillerymen and cavalry were posturing and gathering and lining up at the orders of their sergeants. Gunpowder flavoured the air. There were brisk commands, the rolling of drums and the clarion call of trumpets. The Silver Banner was massing in all its splendour, and the pageantry, the colour, the pride of being British and a part of this heritage brought tears to her eyes.

5

'Mr Frobisher, sir. Have you got a minute?' called his secretary, sticking her toffee-coloured head round the door that bore his name.

She caught him as he swept along the corridor, black and chromium stethoscope a rosary round his neck, his long white coat flowing like a surplice. His entourage were in tow, trying to keep up with his stride, earnest women, also in white, with sheaves of paper in their hands and under their arms: files and patients' records. Every one of these loyal acolytes wore expressions amounting to worship. As indeed they might, Mr Rupert Frobisher being the most highly skilled and highly paid plastic surgeon that side of the Atlantic.

The clinic was a private one and had it been a hotel would have achieved five stars. It was fiendishly expensive, and monumentally exclusive. Movie stars of both sexes went there to plunge into the Fountain of Youth, having their faces restored and their bodies revamped.

'What is it, Michelle?' the great man asked, his deep, cultured, masculine voice enough to give a saint an involuntary orgasm.

'Captain Barrett rang and wants you to call back,' Michelle announced, a superior look on her heart-shaped face as she stared at his nursing staff. As personal secretary she was privy to various aspects of his life to which they had no recourse.

'All right. I'm due a lunch break anyway. Carry on, ladies. Tell the patients that I'll be on my rounds p.m., including Miss Myra Zerner. I can't be at her beck and call,' and so saying he dismissed the most famous actress of the day, and entered his splendid, white-walled, white-draped and white-carpeted consulting room and closed the door.

This was his retreat, where he could relax, take a shower and change his clothing. The Osbourne Clinic was part of a large Edwardian mansion that stood foursquare in its own grounds on the hills overlooking Bath. Every fitting, each sumptuous suite with its own bathroom was of the highest standard, and many of the original features had been retained. Rupert had shares in it. He was satisfied – for the moment. He could hardly climb further up the ladder of success, unless he took the gigantic step of transferring to America, or even more specifically, Hollywood.

Michelle served coffee and he lounged in the leather swivel chair at his Napoleonic desk, and stared at the portrait hanging over the ornate fireplace opposite. It was of himself wearing magnificent black armour and a dashing coppery-red cloak in his role as Prince Rupert of the Rhine, his famous namesake and – he fervently hoped – ancestor. This would be on the wrong side of the blanket, of course, for the prince had never married, but the story went down through the family that, during the Civil War, he had dallied with an Oxford bookseller's wife, and she had produced a son that she claimed to be his, her husband being in his dotage and impotent.

I'm like him, Rupert mused, comparing this life-sized, head-and-shoulders photograph printed on canvas to look like an oil painting with ones of the prince on the wall beside it, particularly a reproduction of that executed by Gerard van Honthorst in the 1640s. Rupert Frobisher had copied the pose, hair style and manner of dress for his own picture. The resemblance was uncanny.

There must be some truth in the tale, he thought. I feel like him inside. I've read so much about him and his struggle to save his uncle, Charles I, that I'm perfectly certain I carry his genes. Always have been interested in this period of history. Didn't want to be a modern soldier, preferred medicine, but the Silver Banner gave me the opportunity to show off my skills at swordplay and to pretend for glorious weekends spent walloping Roundheads and engaging their cavalry that I am indeed the Devil Prince.

Rupert glanced from the portrait to the Venetian mirror in its gilded frame. He stared at himself critically, putting up a hand and untying the band that kept his long, wavy hair under control during working hours. He gave his head a shake, and the peat-black locks covered his shoulders and coiled round his face. His dark eyes flashed under the straight bar of dark brows. His nose was strong, giving him a hawklike appearance; his cheekbones were pronounced and his mouth was firmly sculptured, the lower lip full and sensual, the upper decidedly disdainful. He was in his early thirties, but chose to forget this when he was campaigning. The real Rupert had been General-of-Horse for the entire Royalist army by the time he was twenty-one. But then his mother, the Queen of Bohemia, had dispatched him into foreign wars when he was thirteen. Education was different in those days and, an impecunious widow, she had had ten children to fend for.

Michelle hovered and Rupert smiled. Unlike his abstemious forebear who, though a flash dresser, neither drank to extremes nor fucked all and sundry, he enjoyed the flesh-pots – not so much the booze, but the sexual adventures. He could almost smell Michelle's arousal, envisaging her panties stained round the seam where it pressed up and into her cleft. She was attractive and her breasts were naturally well developed, a refreshing change from silicone implants, but her most engaging attribute was her adoration. He was in the enviable position of being able to choose from half a dozen willing females, and this was only at the clinic. When he was in costume, armed and mounted up, the female camp-followers were practically queuing at the door of his luxurious caravan, each yearning for the right to have 'Prince Rupert was here' branded on her bottom.

He made a point of refraining from screwing his staff. Hospitals were so inbred. Word got around like wildfire – who was humping who, when and where and why, and it wasn't confined to heterosexuals either. Smiling at Michelle, but in not too encouraging a way, he indicated that he needed to make that phone call, and she disappeared into the next room.

Ian answered, and the line was crackly. 'Hello,' Rupert said, slumped low on the base of his spine, legs straight, feet crossed at the ankles and resting on the desk's surface. 'How's it going?'

'Fine,' Ian replied. 'Pretty good turnout. I thought I'd catch you before we start drilling. Put on a show for the punters. You know how it is.'

'I do indeed. I wish I was there, but elected to be on duty this weekend. That way I'll have a few days owing to me for the Mayday bash.'

He did indeed regret it, visualising the parade, the grandeur, and his horse, Corsair, trotting beneath him. He recalled the rise and fall of his body in the saddle, and the way the silk lining of his velvet breeches chafed against his balls and cock. He was hardening at the thought, almost smelling the trampled grass, the sweat of horses and men, and women, too, experiencing the blood-stirring feel of a sword in his hand.

'It'll be a big one,' Ian said, and Rupert could hear the rattle of drums in the background. 'A considerable muster. We'll be using at least ten acres of ground to re-enact the battle of Dorrington Hill. We're expecting a strong turnout. This one is smallish, but the crowd are enthusiastic, and we've several new members signing up.'

'Any decent totty?' Rupert was well versed in every aspect of the musters, including the social activities. He wasn't PC, and had never embraced feminist policies, a trait that endeared him to some of his concubines and infuriated others.

'Well ... I've met someone already. I don't know how it's going to work out. I'm busy with the troop anyway. Don't know if I can be bothered to start another relationship. Divorce is a pain in the arse. Thank God we never had kids or I'd be paying for my mistake for ever.'

'Stay single, like me. I've never been tempted to take on the snaffle. I suppose I'll have to one day, if it's only to keep the Palatine line going.'

'You still believe that?' Ian sounded dubious and rather bored. 'Don't you think the blood would be diluted by now?'

'Throwbacks are not uncommon,' Rupert said with considerable dignity, though wondering why it meant so much to him. It was as if, the only child of a brilliant surgeon and a magistrate, he had been desperate, eclipsed by them and seeking to find a role model that was even more charismatic. 'My father is a tall man and so am I. So was the prince, and his cousin, Charles II, the one who became the Merry Monarch and messed around with Nell Gywn. They inherited their height from their great-grandmother, Mary Queen of Scots. Rupert's interred in her tomb in Westminster Abbey.'

'So you've already told me ... several times. I must go. It's very nearly the off.'

'Come to dinner next week and fill me in.'

'Where?'

'At the town house. Thursday, about eight.'

'OK.'

'And bring your latest woman.'

'I don't know about that. There's nothing settled. Goodbye, Your Highness!'

Ignoring Ian's ironic use of that title, accustomed to sarcasm for many people thought him at the best obsessive and at the worst barking, Rupert put down the phone and drank his cooling cup of coffee. He was hungry and quickly demolished the salad and quiche that had arrived for his lunch. The cuisine was also five star. His mind darted ahead. He had several operations to perform in the clinic, as well as his NHS commitments and, a dedicated as well as ambitious practitioner, he worked long hours to see as many patients as he could. It was not just a matter of money. His parents had retired to the Bahamas. They left him a house in Bath's major tourist attraction, the Circus, John Wood the Elder's eighteenth-century architectural marvel, where Rupert resided in the ground floor apartment and let the rest out as flats at extortionate rents. He also owned a bijou Regency abode, Adelaide Lodge, not far from the clinic. There he stabled his horse and rode and kept his caravan and his cars and entertained sometimes when he wanted to get away from the city.

It boasted a swimming pool, too, and hedonistic bathing parties were not unknown.

Now he dialled his home number and said to his housekeeper and general factotum, 'Hi, there, Otto. I've invited Ian to dinner on Thursday.'

'Right-ho. And what about this evening? Are you coming back or will you be operating, or examining your posh tart's boxes, or even shafting Myra Zerner?'

Rupert took no notice. Otto Clarke looked after him and his domestic arrangements impeccably. Muscular, hard featured and shaven-headed, he insisted on going to the musters as Rupert's valet, though he fussed so much he was more like Juliet's nurse.

'I've nothing planned,' Rupert said.

'Bell me if you're not eating here, because then I shall take myself down to the Saracen's Head,' Otta replied in his acerbic way. 'Speaking of which, reminds me that I've a new brand of fruit-flavoured condoms to try out. How's Myra Zerner? The papers are full of it. They say she's suffering from exhaustion and has been ordered to rest in a private hospital, destination unknown. What have you really been doing to her? Giving her liposuction?'

'You know I can't discuss my patients' treatments,' Rupert said a little uneasily, though he trusted Otto. An important aspect of the Osbourne Clinic's service was its absolute confidentiality.

'Well, if you took it from her hips to enhance the shape of her mouth, that really would be a case of kiss my arse,' Otto remarked. 'Did you do her brain at the same time? She's terminally untalented.'

A tap on the door and Rupert ended the conversation and called, 'Come in.'

'Rupert, darling. They said at reception that you were here. The girl wanted to call you, but I told her not to bother and came straight up,' said the lovely, leggy and frightfully upper-class member of the English brat pack who now stalked across the floor towards him. Rupert stood up. It was as natural to him as breathing to stand when a female entered a room.

'Sarah, how nice,' he said so smoothly that she would never guess that he wasn't over-pleased to see her. Bang would go his afternoon's schedule if he wasn't careful, for Sarah Smythe-Jones was an aristocratic harpy, used to getting her own way.

'It's been an age, hasn't it? Have you been avoiding me?' she said, poppy-red lips pouting.

'I've been humongously busy.' Rupert was expert at wriggling out of the direct answer. 'Would you like a coffee?'

'I'd prefer something stronger, a teensy glass of wine, maybe?' As she spoke, Sarah wound her arms round his neck. He could feel her pliant body pressed against his, all the way, her pubis seeking his cock, rubbing against it as she strained upwards on tiptoe.

'I don't drink when I'm on duty,' he said, staring down into her wide-spaced, pale blue eyes hedged by lashes dark at the base and gold at the tips.

'How very professional and proper,' she teased, the pointed tip of her tongue passing over her lips suggestively. 'But I'm sure there are other things you do, aren't there, doctor?'

She dropped her snow-washed denim jacket on a chair. Beneath it she wore a most unsuitably short, stretched-twill ra-ra skirt with front fly button fastening, and a faded V-necked top with 'Cheerleader' embroidered across the bust. Her mop of pink streaked hair was twisted into tiny beaded plaits, or clamped into bunches. Her legs were bare and her feet encased in sandals with wedge heels. All calculated to make her look like under-age jailbait when, in reality, she was 23.

Sarah had been his patient, was still so in fact, for he made a half-yearly check on the small birthmark that he had treated on her left buttock. Many women would not have bothered about it, but Sarah went ballistic if anything marred the perfection of her body. Daddy was rich and could never say no to his daughter. Nothing but the best was good enough for her, and the best happened to be Rupert Frobisher.

The inevitable had happened and they had become lovers. She had even joined the Silver Banner in an effort to monopolise his free time. She had not succeeded, for Rupert, the most eligible bachelor around, intended to remain that way. Besides which his life was full and he had a roving eye. To date, one woman had never been enough to satisfy him.

He knew what Sarah wanted. She was one of those screeching, gyrating, pinching, biting, energetic screws, given to wild histrionics in the sack. He'd had her in the consulting room before, but always with that looking-over-the-shoulder worry, lest she be heard or someone burst in on them. This could be exciting, and the daredevil in him allowed his prick to take over, swelling under his loose, softly pleated trousers. He lowered his head and fastened his mouth on Sarah's. Hers opened at once and it was like being swallowed whole by a large sea anemone, all waving tentacles and suckers, drinking his saliva, feeding on the membranes inside his cheeks, slurping at his tongue and teeth. Sarah reverted to the Stone Age when she wanted sex, ladylike veneer slipping sideways.

Not that he was complaining. In company with the majority of men his cock, when roused, blinded him to everything except the compulsion to bury it somewhere soft, warm and wet. He picked Sarah up and sat her on the desk, scattering papers, books and pens. He pushed her legs apart. Her skirt rolled back and the sight of the sparse beige fuzz at her fork proved that, as he had suspected, she had not bothered to put on panties.

'Michelle,' he muttered, jerking his head towards the interior door as Sarah undid his flies.

'She came out of your suite by the other entrance and was waltzing down the passage as I left the elevator. I don't think she saw me,' she replied, and her face took on a vulpine slant as she licked her lips and looked hungrily at his cock.

He wanted to lock the doors, but was too far gone already. Sarah's fingers were divine, rubbing his shaft, pulling the loose ring of skin back from his helm, then squeezing it up again, the friction sending jism bubbling from the tiny eye. His balls felt huge and full, and he held them in one hand, lifting them towards her, resting them on the desk top, his trousers unbuckled now and halfway down his thighs. If Michelle should come in, the only thing she would see would be his shoulders and hips, covered by his white coat, and Sarah's legs jutting out from underneath.

Sarah: so rabidly wanton, yet such ideal material for a debutante, had they still existed. Sarah: 'finished' in an exclusive college for young ladies, a member of the pony club and, later, playing polo with royalty. Sarah: daughter of an MP, who would have been equally at home in a brothel. And she was here, now, and she was his.

He pushed up her jersey top. It was tight and had long sleeves and the hem gave easily under his agile fingers. It lay like a band above her breasts. No bra either. Sarah had certainly come prepared. She was built like a stick insect, so worried in case she put on an ounce that she dieted continually and had her own trainer who made her exercise every day, but her breasts were firm handfuls and her nipples stood out from them, pinkish brown and sharply pointed. Rupert paddled his fingers over them and Sarah yelped and gripped his cock possessively.

'Harder,' he said. 'Harder. Harder.' And his thighs trembled as she worked on him, and he could feel the surge in his loins that heralded orgasm. 'Stop,' he commanded, and her hold slackened. He fished in a desk drawer for a packet of condoms, took one out and rolled it up his cock.

'Gosh, do you have to buy extra large?' she asked, in her most ingenuous voice.

This was flattering but he didn't answer, pushing her back till her shoulders and head touched the desk and she sprawled there, resembling a blow-up doll inflated for his pleasure. But she wasn't a doll, she was a real woman, with a woman's needs and he must meet them. It was a point of honour. Being a medico meant that he could not hide behind the mantle of ignorance. There was no escape for him, and he wouldn't have had it otherwise; one of his greatest thrills was that of bringing his partner to climax, be the relationship never so ephemeral.

He stood between her spread thighs, then wedged a thick book under her hips, lifting her cleft high, its secrets laid bare. It never ceased to amaze him how different every woman's cunt managed to be. Sarah's labia, swollen with lust, were rose pink and hair-fringed, and guarded the pearl that now protruded like the head of a miniature penis. Rupert wetted his middle finger at her lubricious entrance and then drew the moisture along her avenue and across her clit. Sarah heaved upwards against his fingerpad, thrusting vigorously.

'Oh, yes,' she gasped. 'Yes, yes, bring me off. I'm ready for it! I've been touching myself for hours, making myself wait, wanting to come in front of you.' Somehow, hearing those crude words spoken in her la-di-da accent acted on him like a powerful aphrodisiac.

'All right. So you shall. I'll watch you,' he whispered, and leaned closer, spreading her folds and concentrating on that tiny knob which was the seat of her sensations. It was engorged and shiny.

Using one hand he stretched her cleft upwards towards her navel, making the clit protrude even more, then he rubbed it on either side, massaging the pencil-thin stalk, raising the feelings, knowing how to do it as only a doctor who enjoyed women could. Sarah stiffened, her body tense, moaning in short gasps. Rupert bent over her breasts and breathed on her bare nipples, the light passage of air eliciting another groan from her. He wanted to prolong masturbating her, but his cock was throbbing and he needed relief. He concentrated all his energies on Sarah's clit, making sure it was wet and then rubbing it lightly but steadily.

'Oh ... oh!' she cried as she came, and he felt her bud twitch under his thumb and her vagina clench round the fingers he had inserted into her.

His hand was drenched with her juices and he kept it

there, bringing her down slowly, just clasping her mound and putting no pressure on the ultra-sensitive nub. She sighed and opened her eyes and smiled at him, then lifted her legs till her heels rested on his shoulders, gripped his pulsating cock and guided it. He felt it brush against her perineum, then the firmness as the head penetrated, the sensation out of this world as he slid further and further into the darkness that was still mysterious to him, even after all his research and studies and medical experience.

Now every other consideration slipped away as he was borne along by the age-old force. Here was a pussy, and here was his rod. He needed to put it somewhere and she was waiting. His cock tingled, his balls crimped, and that powerful urge to relieve himself of his spunk was all consuming. It was coming. He could feel it sweeping through him, the serpent fire that rushed down his spine from his brain and exploded in a mighty avalanche. The feeling was cataclysmic. He spurted several times then, shuddering, supported himself on his hands laid flat on the desk.

His pulse slowed, his heart stopped thundering and the consulting room righted itself. He withdrew from Sarah, unrolled the condom, the teat heavy with his emission, and wrapped it in a tissue to be disposed of down the loo. There was no way he wanted Michelle to find it during one of her irritating bouts of tidying up.

Seated on a grassy knoll overlooking the action, Diane could hardly contain her excitement. 'Oh, look! There's Colin!' she squeaked, spotting him among the musketeers.

'Which one?' Sue said, peering through the field glasses she had had the forethought to pack. 'Oh, him, that little guy you were chatting up in the pub.'

'He's not little,' Diane returned smartly. 'No shorter than Ray. Let's have a go with your glasses.'

'I want them,' said Amber from her other side. 'I've a lot of men to look for, according to the palmist, knights and princes and I don't know what-all.'

'Crap!' said Sue, fighting them off and hanging on to her equipment, searching among the dozen or so heart-stoppingly gallant Royalist horsemen who were controlling their skittish mounts, and arrogantly riding up and down, taunting the Roundhead cavalry. Where was Prudy?

'You want to give Tanith a whirl,' Amber advised. 'She even gave me a message from my mother.'

'Creepy,' Diane said, icy fingers crawling down her spine.

She much preferred the here and now and didn't want to think about anything else, especially when there was romance in the air. All right, so this was prettying it up. Colin was after a shag and nothing else. She wanted this, too, but clung to the thought that maybe, just maybe, this might be the beginning of something deeper, stronger, love eternal. He hadn't tried to kiss her or touch her up, but had seemed genuinely interested and caring. But isn't this what all the buggers do in the beginning? she cautioned herself, fearful of disappointment.

Her spirits rose as Sue relented and shared the glasses and she watched Colin taking his men through the routine of handling a matchlock. He placed his weapon on its support, primed it with gunpowder and applied the cordite. He barked out an order, raised the heavy musket in unison with his fellow infantrymen, and fired. All over the field there were flashes and bangs as the cannons and carbines blasted off. The pikemen formed a square, facing outwards, practising how to withstand attacks from enemy footsoldiers. There was uproar all around and Diane had to remind herself that this was only a drill. What would it be like when they came to the real battle tomorrow? She noticed that the ambulance men were on the alert, although no one, it seemed, had been hurt. The spectators loved it, cheering and clapping and wanting to surge forwards, restrained behind the chain-link barrier by several policemen.

'There's your bloke, isn't it, Amber? What's his name? Golden Bollocks?' said Sue, standing up and pointing.

'Yes. It's him. Captain Ian Barrett.'

They all took it in turns to squint down the glasses at him as he led a posse, which included Prudy and Jess, in a gallop that covered the field in a short time, hooves flashing, standard bearer in the lead, prepared to sacrifice his life rather than let the flag be captured. Fine horses and even finer riders in the full panoply of war. Proud paladins in plumed helmets or feathered hats, lace and velvets and finely chased armour, they hallooed as they rode, mocking the enemy in their steel lobster-pot morions, their functional back-and-breast plates, dark clothing and grim mien.

Diane was eager to view the camp, fired by her plans. Once the demonstration was over and the soldiers marching towards base, she ran alongside, keeping up with Colin and shouting, 'Can I come in? Are visitors allowed? We've already enlisted. I'm going to be a victualler, and bring a hot-dog van.'

'A vintner would make more sense,' he said, a smile lighting up his smoke-blackened face, little white lines, sharp as incisors, at the outer corners of his eyes. 'We work up an almighty thirst.' He winked at her, looking positively roguish, becoming ever more like his weekend persona, a swaggering musketeer.

'That, too,' she agreed, and stepped back out of their way, though making sure that he met her at the five-barred gate that separated the camp from the general public. She couldn't wait to get into costume, or rather out of it and into Colin's bed.

She was aware that Amber and Sue were somewhere behind her, but branching off in pursuit of their own soldiers, both heading towards the enclosure where the cavalry kept their horses.

'Well, I'm impressed,' she said, as Colin joined her and they started to walk through the camp.

It was amazingly tidy and well organised. 'Like a real-life leaguer,' he explained. 'That's where the American settlers got the idea when they formed the wagons in a circle to repel Indians. Armies always did this, especially if they were in for a long siege. Small townships sprang up, with the usual hangers-on: whores, tinkers, hucksters, sharp-dealers, sutlers ... which is what you want to be ... seventeenth-century soldiers depended to a considerable extent on the traders who followed them.'

'But here you're mixed up, Roundheads and Cavaliers on the same site,' she said, seeing a little gaggle of more sober figures who lacked the Royalists' free and easy manner.

'Only because this is a small muster. When we do a big one, like the Mayday weekend, then each of us will have separate camps. No fraternising with the enemy.'

'You know your subject,' she said, gazing at the tents that had been neatly erected round the bivouac fires. Behind them were the caravans, well out of public sight, along with cars, campers and motor bikes.

'I should do. As well as teaching for a living, I'm an amateur archaeologist, specialising in battle sites. That's my Volvo and trailer-tent over there. I must lock my gun and ammo away. It's too heavy and awkward to lug about unless strictly necessary.'

'But you'll stay in costume?' Diane wanted to retain the illusion for as long as possible.

'Of course. We have to. No one is allowed in camp wearing modern dress, apart from guests like you. We're even ordered to leave our mobiles at home. HQ has a telephone service, if it's essential to phone or there's some emergency message from the outside world. Come in.' He unzipped the rear of the tent, folded down a step and assisted her inside.

The touch of his warm fingers on her arm, the solid, undeniable reality of him, caused a major seismic shift in her loins. She thought of Ray and felt herself tottering on the edge of despair, the heat of tears behind her eyes.

The tent had everything a single man might need. Colin ignited the oil lamp, moved a pile of tidily folded shirts from the settee-cum-bed and said, 'Welcome aboard. Sit down.'

'This is cosy,' she ventured. 'I feel out of place in this outfit. I should be wearing a skirt and stomacher and a sacking apron or something, if I'm to be a food seller.'

'You look champion as you are,' he answered, taking off his felt hat, his straggly, honey-hued hair darkened with sweat. Then he loosened the lacing of his leather jerkin. 'Would you like a Coke?' he asked, and went to the miniature fridge and took out two cans.

'All mod cons,' she quipped as he snapped the ring-pulls, his every movement delighting her, so confident and precise, unlike the dithering, short-tempered, lack of co-ordination typical of Ray.

'We don't have to keep to the book, not in private.' He smiled, lowering his lean body on to a stool. 'No need to be too uncomfortable, though some of the younger element like it, sleeping rough, dropping down where they fall when they've had a skinful, convinced that this makes them tougher, rougher soldiers. It doesn't. Just turns 'em into prats.'

'I have a daughter. She's nineteen and home from uni for half-term,' she said, bringing this out almost defiantly, telling herself that there must be no secrets between them.

'I thought you might have ... children, I mean. You look the type,' he said slowly, studying her face seriously. 'And a husband, too?'

'Yes ... well, we don't get on,' she blurted, not wanting to scare him off. She had the feeling that he'd turn her down if he thought she was happily married, but then, he was bright enough to realise that she'd not be encouraging him if she were. Women rarely strayed if they were content with their men.

'That's a pity,' he said. 'I've never been married myself, but have seen the devastation it can cause. Is it really that bad? Have you thought about going to Relate?'

'Ray wouldn't wear it. He doesn't hold with what he calls stupid counselling and such, bloody do-gooders sticking their noses into other people's business. Reckons that if he has any problems then he can sort them out himself, not that he admits that there's anything wrong, of course.'

Somehow, the question of Ray and the farce that had become her marriage seemed unimportant, but before she burned her boats irrevocably, there was something she had to do. Ray was in the motor trade. He had set his heart on the London taxi. Right, he should have it, but on her terms.

'Can I help you? If there's anything I can do ... anything at all.' Colin's sincerity was overwhelming. Diane wasn't used to it, having lived with a devious person for so long.

She put down the can, and rested her hand on his shoulder, her fingers touching his curling hair. In the lamplight, strands of it shone like gold or the sun or all the happy, sparkling things she associated with Christmas, and this was ridiculous because it was Easter. She ached inside with wanting him, ashamed to remember the last time Ray had taken her, that episode in the kitchen. So crude and loveless.

'I would like us to meet sometimes,' she whispered. 'We mesh. We can have fun together. I'm so tired of always being in charge, the sensible, responsible one. Good old Di. She'll sort it. Ray thinks like that, too. He's never paid a household bill in his life. I see to it all ... the mortgage, the insurance, water rates, gas and electric and telephone, to say nothing of the café, council tax and income tax. He copes with those to do with the garage. At least, I hope he does, but he is clueless with money and other things. Sometimes I think he doesn't know shit from shampoo.'

Colin laughed and she, her mood lightening, laughed with him. Now he was seated beside her, and she slipped her hand into his. It was warm and dry, not a wet, clammy paw but a palm and supple fingers that she wanted to feel caressing her all over. He put his arm round her and drew her head down on his shoulder.

'You're beautiful,' he said, and she bit back the 'bullshit' comment. 'A sad, lovely lady,' he went on, 'and I'd like to make you happy, but at your pace. I want you ... am having trouble with my dick ... it won't behave, but I don't want to rush you or do anything that may spoil what I'm sure is going to be a solid relationship.'

She was glad he hadn't said 'meaningful' when he came to the relationship bit. She didn't want him to do trite. 'Oh, Colin,' she sighed, perking up at him. 'Are you for real? It's too good to be true. I'm not used to being treated like this.'

'Treated like what? With the respect that each person deserves?' His brows lifted comically and his eyes twinkled in his fine, clean-cut face.

'I'm afraid,' she said, feeling like a silly schoolgirl on her first date, though only someone as disillusioned as herself would have been racked with such soul-destroying doubts.

'Can you stay with me tonight?' he asked, looking at her as if her answer meant all the world.

'I can't,' she said, and placed her fingers over his lips as if to say, don't ask me again or I shall weaken. 'There's Karen. She's here somewhere with her mates. Probably at the funfair ... I need to get home, and then there's Ray. There are things to arrange, most important of all my getting my hands on a halfway decent catering van. He can help me, but he won't if I antagonise him.'

'I understand.' He held her face between his hands and kissed her lips. 'Shall I drive you there?'

She clung to him, braid and leather under her fingertips and a different male skin – not Ray – purely Colin. If the gods were kind, she might never have to touch Ray again. 'Thank you. It might come to that. I came with Sue and Amber, in Sue's car, but she's keen on a lieutenant, another woman; she's bi, you see, so I don't know what she'll be doing. And Amber is falling for a cavalry officer,' she burbled.

She could feel herself melting, sensible thought disappearing like permafrost under global warming. And Colin held her and took off her pink belt so that her jacket flopped open and her ecru lace, underwired bra hardly contained her full breasts. She was glad she had worn so glamorous a thing. Deliberately? To be honest – yes. And her panties matched it, but she was alarmed that they might reach the stage where he saw these, too. It might be too late to turn back if this happened.

He feathered a finger over her nipples, and the lace added to the exquisite friction. He did not attempt to bare her to his sight, merely admiring, as he said, 'Lovely breasts. Do you mind me doing this?'

Mind? She wanted to scream with delight. 'I like it. You're so kind and considerate,' she murmured, and wondered if she dare grab his cock – well not grab, perhaps, but make some gesture towards it. 'You seem to understand women very well. Have you had many?'

'A couple. I was engaged once, but then my sister was widowed young, and left with three kids to bring up,' he answered quietly, and slowly, sensually, dipped a finger between the round globes of her breasts, the deep valley accentuated by the cut of the bra. 'I moved in with her and helped her. What with my job and other interests, this didn't give me much time for dating. But, in recent years, she's found herself a decent chap who wants to marry her and take on the children, too. I've bought a house of my own.'

'By the sound of things, it's high time you thought about yourself and what you want,' Diane said, frantically hanging on to the mundane as a lifeline against the tumultuous sea of lust that was threatening to engulf her. He was such a lovesome man – if what he said was true, and she had no reason to think him a liar.

'I've not met anyone I fancied, not seriously, until yesterday,' he said, and kissed her on the lips.

It was a lovely kiss, its very restraint much more exciting than the meeting of tongues. It held promise, and Diane received it gratefully. There was no need to rush things. If it went according to plan, they had all the time in the world – getting to know one another, their interests, their tastes in music, entertainment, expectations, hopes and dreams.

She pulled back, holding his gaze and saying, 'I've never been unfaithful to Ray. I've thought about other men, naturally. Used their images while I played with myself, but have never been with anyone else. I've known him since we were teenagers.'

His arms tightened comfortingly. 'I'm glad,' he said, and she could feel his hands on her back under the jacket, fingers sliding round the fastener of her bra, but not trying to undo it. 'I wouldn't like the idea of lots of men taking liberties with all this lovely flesh. I'm feeling greedy. I want it for myself.'

'We'll work something out,' she promised, and then they kissed mouth to open mouth, and her resolution was slipping, just like the elasticised waistband of her trousers that yielded to his persistent hand as it eased between her buttocks. 'Oh ... ooh!' she exclaimed against his lips, as he circumnavigated the edge of her fancy panties and slipped beneath her, till she was sitting on his palm.

Then, so smoothly that she questioned his statement about celibacy, his fingers explored her, entering her wetness, probing and intimate and knowledgeable. She settled down on them, but the pressure wasn't where she wanted it. She wondered if he was one of those unenlightened men who were ignorant of the clitoris, its position and its purpose. He wasn't and, just at that moment, she was so breathless that she couldn't ask him where he had learned how to lavish so much pleasure on her swollen little organ. He played her perfectly; a connoisseur, a master of clitoral technique. Where did he get his degree?

She closed her eyes, reeling on the narrow bed, head back, dazed with desire, his finger moving with sure command, bringing her on – on – onwards and upwards. 'Oh, yes ... please. Please!' she squealed helplessly, heat spreading through her thighs and belly. Heat and embarrassment and what about him? She was going to come, as selfishly as when she achieved a solitary climax, and she was a nice woman who had been taught not to put herself first, but to consider the wants of others, especially men.

'Go with it. Enjoy it. That's right. Do it for me ... ah, that's wonderful,' he muttered, breathing fast.

Too late for repining. Nothing could stop the huge orgasm that shook her and tossed her and carried her to the very top of the rollercoaster before plunging her down into repletion.

'Oh, I'm sorry,' she gasped, spasms convulsing her.

'Eh? Sorry? I hope not,' he said tenderly, his magical fingers continuing to caress her, but with just the lightness needed. 'Didn't you enjoy that?'

'Yes ... yes ... but what about you?'

'You can do the same for me sometime soon. Stop worrying, Diane. This is only the start.' He helped her to rearrange her clothes before they went out to find her friends.

It was dusk, and the Banner members were relaxing round the fires, drinking ale, dicing, playing cards, their children running in and out. There was the noise of the fair in the distance and the glimpse of coloured lights. A ceilidh was in progress, with singing and dancing and storytelling put on to impress the public who leaned over the fences, determined to get their money's worth. Some of the women, the more earnest and less slatternly, gave demonstrations at the spinning wheel and distaff and made bread and cooked over camp fires.

Diane, on a high, clung to Colin's hand and tried to imagine just where she would pitch her van at future events. Should she have an awning outside, with rustic stools and tables so that customers could eat there? The possibilities were endless. She spotted Amber strolling with Ian, and waved frantically, unwilling to leave Colin just yet, but needing to get back and talk to Ray.

'Where's Sue?' she demanded, and it was difficult to get Amber's attention for she seemed every bit as cock-struck as herself.

'Off with Prudy somewhere. I think she intends to stay the night. I want to get back, same as you. I haven't even brought a toothbrush. Ian wants to come with me, but it's a bit awkward as he's got a camper van.'

'I've already offered to drive. I can unhitch my trailer,' Colin said, convincing Diane even more that she had made the right choice. He was a thoroughly lovely man.

It was hard to let him go when they reached the café, harder still to say goodnight without even a farewell kiss, and to see Amber disappearing into Collectibles' side door with the captain of her choice.

'I'll be there tomorrow,' she promised Colin. 'Amber and I will drive our own cars and be independent of one another.'

'She'll have to leave early,' Colin reminded, incongruously attired but wickedly sexy in her book, seated at the wheel of his car. 'Both Ian and I will be up at the crack of dawn. There's a castle to be won.'

'I know. But I can't come till the evening. Saturday is one of the café's busiest times,' she said regretfully. 'I'll have to see you in action on Sunday.'

She waved as he drove off and, knickers damp and heart aglow, let herself in and went up the stairs to the flat. She could hear the telly before she opened the lounge door, and there was Ray in all his glory, sprawled on the couch, circled by empty cans and greasy takeaway curry cartons, snoring in front of the football match replay.

6

'I need a shower,' Ian said, wrinkling his nose as he stared at his reflection in the long mirror.

'You certainly do. I'll scrub your back,' Amber agreed, wondering if she'd ever get used to seventeenth-century lack of personal hygiene. Though she was so hot for him that she could hardly put two words together, he smelled pungent. 'When did you last wash, and change those clothes?'

He grinned sheepishly and said, 'Must be about three days ago now. You lose track of time when you're mustering. No radio, no telly. I'm missing out on the soaps ... and it's not really right to wear a wristwatch. My beard's coming on a treat, but I'll just trim it, if I may. It's quite a relief not to have a sword banging against your side and getting tangled up in your legs. Don't tell my colonel, for I'm officially on duty all the bloody weekend. He'd consider it damned sloppy.'

She stared at this genial giant who filled her sitting room to overflowing with his bulk and larger-than-life personality. He was fine as he was, but she was sure she'd like him even better once he had showered. 'Make yourself at home,' she said, more nervous than she had expected. 'We could put your dirty stuff in the washing machine, if you like.' She hoped she didn't sound too pushy. There was no way she wanted to wash his clothes on a regular basis. She wasn't that smitten.

'I didn't come here to take advantage of your facilities,' he protested, but dumped his kitbag on the chesterfield.

'Though I brought along a change of underwear, just in case.'

'Why did you come?' she asked, guessing the answer but wanting to hear him say it.

'What a question? Don't you know that Cavaliers have a reputation for being gallant to damsels in distress.'

'I'm not in distress,' she said, laughing as she walked into the kitchen, wanting something to do with her hands other than strip off his clothes and explore all that promise of muscle and tanned skin and a cock that would be upstanding for her. 'Not now I can use a civilised toilet,' she added. 'Those Portaloos are grim. Even the ones inside your camp.'

'Give 'em a few more hours and they'll be grimmer still, and the ones in the public sector ... yuck! Still, it's better than it was in the olden days, and adds a touch of realism.'

'I never did pop festivals for that very reason ... the state of the bogs,' she said with a shudder.

He followed her, hat thrown aside, doublet undone and grubby shirt open to the waist. His chest was smudged with russet fuzz. His breeches were part unfastened, too, and his navel showed, circled by a ring of hair with a finger pointed downwards like an arrow, disappearing into the flap that concealed his genitals.

'I can see that. You seem to have a nice little set-up here. So, there's no husband?'

'There was ... once. He's in America with my sons. They're grown up now. My shop is below us. I deal in antiques.'

'Do you, indeed?'

'And what about you? Are you married?'

'Divorced. No kids. I could murder a beer,' he said matter-of-factly, and she got one out of the fridge for him.

'What do you do when you're not galloping round the countryside playing soldiers?' she asked, though thinking, what the hell does it matter? We're not making any commitment here, are we? Just a couple of people seeking a way to forget their loneliness for a moment, kidding themselves that the communion of the body is as valuable as the meeting of souls. Like Camilo and me, that's all, and he taught me once again that even the best sex doesn't guarantee that the guy wants to see you long term.

'I'm a chartered surveyor, and I live alone in an old cottage across the bridge in Pensford-on-Avon. Just me and my horse, Billy, and he's stabled down the road.'

That's the details sorted, she thought, leading him back into the lounge, a lager in her hand. She didn't really like the taste, a wimp when it came to drinking, but hoped it would relax her. She wanted to show him that she was made of stern stuff, a suitable candidate for a leaguer bitch. She had heard him use this expression and found it much more arousing than 'camp follower', which some-how made her think of Alastair – or Lily Savage.

He swigged his beer, standing with an elbow on the fireplace. She had already lit the gas under the mock-logs. He was assessing her through those thick lashes, wonder-ing perhaps, as she was, if it was wise to get involved. That's the trouble with maturing, she thought, visualis-ing a round of ripe Cheddar cheese, the spontaneity goes. Though it didn't with Camilo, I must admit. Then why am I hesitating now? It is because there are other issues here? I've joined up and shall be seeing Ian on a regular basis, albeit maybe only at musters. So in a way I have already committed myself to something in which he is involved.

He put his empty glass on the overmantel, strode towards her and said, 'What are we waiting for?'

Amber jumped, staring up at him. She wasn't used to being confronted by a Titan in her own home. 'I don't know. You tell me,' she managed to croak.

'Steer me towards your shower. I can't make love to a lady while I smell like a drain.'

'Who said anything about love-making?' She stood up shakily, leading the way down the corridor to where the bathroom stood behind one door, but was connected to her bedroom by an adjoining one.

He stopped just inside, tipped her chin up so that she couldn't avoid the brightness of his eyes or the beer on his breath, and said, 'We didn't have to. It's a foregone conclusion.'

'You've got an ego the size of a house,' she retorted, pulling away from his grasp and reaching for clean towels in the linen cupboard, but inside she was wet and willing.

'So I've been told,' he replied, and grabbed her round the waist from behind. 'Put those towels down and concentrate on me.'

It was impossible to do anything else. He turned her and started to take off the rest of his clothes. Shirt first and, my God, but he's hairy, she thought. It'll be like shagging the shagpile.

He sat on the side of the bath, hitched the toe of one boot behind the heel of the other and pushed. 'Bloody thing,' he grumbled. 'I didn't bring my jack.'

'Let me,' she offered and backed up to him, bent over, took his leg between hers and tugged. The boot gave and she almost fell forwards. It flopped in her hand. She did the same with the other. Both had mud on their thick soles and heels, and butterfly-shaped leather fasteners that were chained to spurs, keeping them in place. 'D'you use them on Billy?' she asked, setting the boots on the bathroom floor, less gallant looking now, wrinkled and saggy, despite the lace-edged lining.

'Hardly. It's more for show. Spurs aren't encouraged any more, like fox-hunting and deer-hunting ...'

'And bullfighting,' she added. 'But that's a national institution and won't be affected ... not yet, anyway.'

He shot her a surprised look. 'Don't hold your breath. So you are the fan. I wondered when I saw the posters in your hall.'

He peeled away his dirty socks, then dropped his breeches. 'These will wash,' he vouchsafed. 'Nylon velvet instead of cotton. Not authentic but easier to keep clean. Just show me your machine and I'll see to it.' With that he took off his boxers.

Amber, nerve ends sizzling, tried desperately to steer her eyes in any direction but his crotch. It wasn't possible. They kept returning. His cock got larger by the second, as if encouraged by her glance. It rose like a pillar from a thicket of coarse curls, and his balls hung low, one slightly larger than the other.

'Come on,' he said, his hand closing round his tool, rubbing it up and down, making that already stiff appendage bigger still. 'Get your kit off. I've shown you mine, now I want to see yours.'

This is what you've been after ever since you clapped eyes on him, she reminded herself. Now go for it. She stripped, not giving herself time to wonder if he'd be disappointed. The last man who had shared her shower and her bed had vanished months ago, after they'd had a row. She remembered Duncan as she hooked her thumbs in her panties and eased them down. A striking, intelligent individual, but with a core of ice, he had wanted to take over her life and tell her what to do. Dominating, and she had quite enjoyed that when it manifested during sex, but had soon told him to fuck off when it went beyond the bounds of fantasy. She hadn't seen him since and was uncomfortably certain that he had taken umbrage.

Ian seized her hand and pulled her into the tiled stall and shut the glass door. He flicked on the shower, and she shrieked as warm water cascaded over them. He hooted and laughed and grabbed at her as she fumbled for the gel and rubbed it all over his chest. He was strongly built, and her hands explored every inch of him: the pectorals, the wine-red discs of his nipples that peaked at her touch, the navel that dimpled his gut. No problem yet, but she had seen how his beer went down without touching the sides, both in the White Swan and just now.

His cock jumped in her hand and his balls were weighty. She picked up the condom she had brought in with her.

'You going to put that on for me?' he asked huskily, and she nodded, rolling it up with ease, assisted by the slippery state of his shaft.

'Now let me wash you,' he insisted and poured a puddle of gel into his palm, then started to anoint her in return.

'Ah,' she sighed and, as she had been that night in the pub, was elated because he wanted her. She knew it was pathetic; why couldn't she be sufficient unto herself? But there it was; she glowed and felt fulfilled when a personable man expressed desire for her, and Ian was very personable indeed, and as for well endowed? There was no question about it.

The water gushed over her like tropical rain, and she clung to him, her arms wound round his neck, and he soaped her thoroughly, his big hands as gentle as a woman's, and her knees weakened and she wanted this to go on for ever, just her and Ian in the shower together. His soaking hair dripped on to her breasts, and her own dribbled down her back, and his soapy hands were everywhere, coaxing her nipples into hard cones, tickling her belly button, before diving down to lather her pubic bush, then open her cleft and massage between the swollen lips. She came without realising that she was so close, and Ian lifted her while she was still convulsing, and impaled her on his cock, then moved her up and down, rocking his hips and filling her with his hugeness.

He exploded, grunting with pleasure, and then set her on her feet and took off the condom and washed his genitals. They left the shower and, wrapped in bath towels, trailed into the bedroom leaving wet footprints on the Axminster.

'Ah, a TV! What luxury! I'm getting withdrawal symptoms,' he said, drying himself, before using a body spray, top of the range, she noticed, and then settling down under the duvet, remote buttons to hand, and a battery-operated razor smoothing his cheeks and trimming his goatee. Amber was glad about that.

'I'll get rid of these and bring us something to eat,' she said, wandering towards the kitchen, a bundle of soiled clothing in one hand.

She felt like a cat that had had its fur well and truly stroked. Ian knew what to do. Was he experienced? All those women at the musters, attached and unattached. A shard of jealousy shot through her. She pulled herself up sharply. Don't be ridiculous. He's not yours, neither are you his. This is the twenty-first century and personal freedom abounds. It's silly to hanker after a time when if a man was serious about you, then he somehow took on the responsibility for your life. You wouldn't want that. And it didn't even happen in the Civil War days, not really. Marriages were arranged between families, wealth and religion of prime importance, but should a man fuck a maid outside of this strict regime, then he owed her nothing and she could be labelled a slut.

She stuffed the clothes into the washing machine and switched on, then, wrapping her green silk kimono round her, tried to focus on the fridge contents. Bugger, she thought, and was tempted to send out for a pizza. What she really wanted was to hop into bed with Ian. Once wasn't enough. She was feeling horny, not hungry.

'That looks great,' he said when she returned with a cold collation, and he started to demolish it.

Amber watched the way his fingers tore the garlic bread, and how he munched at the cheese and tossed green olives stuffed with anchovies into his mouth. He attacked eating in the same way that he performed sex – with one-pointed immediacy.

'You must meet my Commander-in-Chief,' he said at last, washing the meal down with a large glass of red wine. 'Not only mine ... everybody's. The General-of-Horse for all of us cavalry people. He's a mate of mine, Rupert Frobisher. He claims to be descended from the Prince Rupert who led the Royalist forces.'

'Ah, yes. It rings a bell somewhere, but I get him mixed up with the villain in *The Prisoner of Zenda*.' Amber was prepared to listen and indulge him, but she placed the tray on the bedside table, leaving the field clear for action.

'Not a chance. You're way off track. Anyhow, if you turn up at the battle of Dorrington Hill, that's in Gloucester, on the other side of Bristol, you'll see him. It's a massive gathering of troops from both sides. Will you be ready by then?'

'When is it?' She idled her fingers over his chest, making patterns in the foxy hair.

'It starts on Beltane's Night. That's when we've been ordered to arrive and set up, and it'll go on over the Mayday weekend.'

'What's he like, this friend of yours?' she asked, while he cupped one of her breasts in his hand and fingered her bush with the other.

'All the women go mad over him. He's very tall ... taller than me even, and has this quality about him ... sort of royal, if you know what I mean. But he's a regular bloke, too. No side to him when we're down the pub. You should see him fight. I go to fencing classes with him and he's shit hot. Brilliant with épée or sabre. I don't stand an earthly. As for horses? If he wasn't a surgeon, then he could ride in the Horse of the Year contest.'

'A surgeon?'

'A whiz kid when it comes to plastic jobbies, but you wouldn't guess this when you see him in his Cavalier dress.'

If I was superstitious, I might hook on to this, Amber thought. A prince, a fighting man. The Prince of Swords foretold by Tanith? As it is, it seems to be coming out right, for Ian fits the bill as the Knight of Cups. And I shall meet Prince Rupert at the Beltane celebrations, the first day of summer. It could hardly be cooler ... or perhaps more catastrophic. Tanith told me to beware of him. And this makes it all the more exciting. Oh, dear, I really should try to grow up.

I'll start tomorrow, she resolved, too absorbed in what Ian was doing to bother with anything else. His finger was inside her, thrusting and withdrawing, aping the action of a cock. And his mouth closed on hers, successfully blotting out the last remnants of thought, as he took her on an erotic trip right through the solar system.

Prudy's tent defied logic, small on the outside but expanding once you stepped in, rather like a sci-fi space machine. It was home for not only her, but Jess and a couple of other she-soldiers as well.

Its green canvas walls were disguised by throws and eastern prayer mats, and the double airbeds had also been draped, giving an impression of decadent luxury. It was more like a Bedouin desert abode than a shelter for soldiers. The saddles and horse equipment were a give-away. That and the coat hangers holding doublets and cloaks, hats and helmets, while the candlelight glinted off rapiers and daggers and body armour. That it was a male-free zone was obvious by the lack of strong odours: stale socks, grungy underpants and junk food. Sue picked up on a trace of cigarette smoke in the air.

'Do you?' she asked.

'Fags normally, but a clay pipe in front of the spectators,' Prudy said, and Sue lit up. 'This is Megan (I-like-cocks-as-well-as-eating-pussy) Jones,' Prudy went on, introducing Sue to a lithe, dark urchin whose crotch was outlined by the tightest of tight breeches.

She looked up from her supper and smiled. 'Take the piss as much as you like, but I reckon I've got the best of both worlds. Welcome to our jolly band of pilgrims,' she said, popping a potato crisp into her mouth. 'You going to join the Society?'

'I already have.'

'This is Carla, by the way,' Prudy said, drawing another girl into the circle.

'Hello there. I'm off down the pub,' she said, a stocky girl whose shirt strained over her big breasts, the lacing at full stretch. 'I'll round up Jess and take my car. Who's into it?'

'I'll give it a miss tonight,' Prudy answered, kicking off her riding boots and sitting cross-legged in the middle of her bed.

Both women looked from her to Sue, but made no comment, simply picked up their jackets, swords and hats and ducked under the tent flap. Warmth and intimacy, a stillness during which Sue was certain Prudy would hear her heart beating. She was alone with this dashing, fearless and beautiful young creature who had asked her there for one purpose only. The tension had been building for hours. Now was the time for release.

'Pull the curtains,' Prudy murmured, and pointed to the drapes that hung around the bed. 'We need to be secluded. I've given my orders. No one will disturb us. This is what you want, isn't it?'

Sue slid the curtains along, enclosing them in the subdued glow of scented candles. 'Of course I do,' she replied.

She could smell Prudy from where she stood. The scent

of her long dark hair mingled with that of leather and horseflesh. She had not only ridden her mare, Thirza, for hours but tended her, too, rubbing her down and making her comfortable for the night in the field with the others. And Sue had envied the horse. Lucky Thirza, not only to have been gripped by Prudy's thighs all day, but subjected to fondling afterwards.

'Sit with me,' Prudy said, holding out her hand. Her eyes were compelling, golden brown with tiny jets of flame in the pupils, reflecting the candles. She leaned forwards a little, her smile alluring.

Sue met her halfway and, eyes closed, found her lips. They were soft and moist and the kiss deepened as their tongues probed and explored. Sighing their pleasure into each other's mouths, their hands met, then sprang apart and Sue found Prudy's shirt and pushed it open, feeling the swell of her breasts and caressing the nipples that rose sharply at her touch. She thrilled to the feel of Prudy's hands on her back, intrigued by her new lover's tongue in her mouth and the taste of her saliva.

They broke away momentarily, and Sue undressed, watching Prudy do the same. Both wore male attire, though with over three hundred years between styles. Sue had on a pair of jeans designed by herself, boot-flared, with pink rhinestones and silver stud detail down the outside seams and round the pockets. She undid the straps of her chunky shoes and divested herself of her knee-highs. Neither of these was particularly exciting, donned in anticipation of a day of walking, and she hadn't been wrong. But it was better to get rid of them first; in fact impossible to remove her denims till they were off. She had made an effort to look attractive, but now promised herself a more romantic, floaty ensemble when Prudy visited her flat.

All fingers and thumbs, she pulled off her ruched, sleeveless top. It was one of her latest creations and had a plunge neckline and a sequinned rose corsage. Her breasts were lifted high by an embroidered bra, and the matching thong was forging its way between her swollen pussy lips. New garments both, and she sighed over the inadvisability of wearing anything for the first time if one was embarking on an important mission, like getting laid. Better by far to give them a try out in the privacy of one's own home.

'Don't rush. I want to look at you,' Prudy said, in that stern tone with which she issued orders to her comrades-at-arms. A frisson of excitement shot through Sue. Good grief! This one had the potential to be a dom; maybe she already was!

Prudy stripped off the rest of her clothes, and Sue was floored by the sight of her shapely legs with their long, pure lines, and the supple waist and narrow, boyish hips counterbalanced by firm breasts. Best of all was the dark bush that covered her mound and lower belly. It was curly and crisp, her labia poking between the slit, pink and swollen, begging to be touched.

Sue reached out and caressed Prudy's furrow, seeing the hard knob of her clitoris rising from its cowl. Prudy helped to provoke it, kneeling over Sue and holding her folds wide apart. 'You're so beautiful naked,' she whispered, with a catch in her voice. 'I knew you would be. I've been longing for someone like you.'

'But surely ... you can take your pick?' Sue gasped, overcome by this and only half convinced. 'These soldier-girls.'

'They're not all of the same persuasion,' Prudy said, smiling as she rubbed each side of her clit, while Sue teased the slippery head. Then Prudy threw back her long hair, eyes narrowed in ecstasy. 'Oh, that's so good. But I don't want to come yet ... let's try it this way.'

Sue was beyond speech, and lay with her head between her lover's thighs, while Prudy angled herself so that she, too, could use her lips. The first touch of Prudy's mouth on her clit was exquisite and Sue returned the caress, finding her lover's core, tasting her and smelling her juices.

She sipped and licked and clasped her hands round Prudy's dark head, keeping it at her crotch, her hips rotating against that agile tongue. Now she was in the magic circle, where nothing mattered but the spiralling vortex of pleasure. They were locked together in the closest possible intimacy, and Sue was on the very brink. Another stroke of Prudy's tongue, another suck, another tweak of Sue's nipples that seemed to vibrate in harmony with her clit and she was caught up, whirled high and swept into a mind-blowing orgasm.

Prudy yelped and bucked wildly, then pressed her pubis into Sue's face as if seeking out the very last spasms. She sighed explosively, then turned on her side, freeing Sue's body. She kissed her, long and deep, and Sue could taste herself on her lips. She looked up into Prudy's eyes and saw her smile.

'That's so much better than any man I've had,' Sue said, wanting to talk, pour out her life history, forge links that could never be broken. 'I tried one called Gareth, not long ago. He was hopeless. I knew when he stuck his cock in me that I didn't stand a hope in hell of climaxing.'

'I was engaged once,' Prudy said, cuddling her and pulling the padded quilt up over them both. 'Dear God, what a mistake! I'd rather put my head in a blender than go to bed with a man. I should have known better. I've always preferred women. Toys are fun, too. I'll bring mine along when I come to your place.'

'I've already got some,' Sue confessed. 'Including a Tongue-Tickler and a dildo. Though I'd rather have you make love like just now. I'm not much into penetration.'

Prudy chuckled and hugged her, saying, 'That's OK. You might like it if I was the one on the other end, wearing a strap-on. Whatever lights your fire. Dildos are a fine old institution. The best thing since sliced bread. Why did God make men? Because she realised that vibrators couldn't dance.'

'You can have your taxi, but only if you fix me up with a halfway decent catering van,' Diane said at breakfast next morning. Karen was still in the pit she called her room, and her parents were alone.

Ray had come to bed late and, though Diane had heard him, she had pretended to be asleep. It was useless trying to talk to him at that hour. She had turned on her side, away from him – so far away that she almost fell out, avoided the arm that he flung over her and the broom handle that was trying to roost between her legs and he soon gave up and started snoring again.

This had become a nightly ritual. More often than not he fell asleep on the couch and she was always careful not to disturb him, tiptoeing around, leaving a reading lamp alight and the TV on, talking away to itself, before creeping out and closing the door very quietly behind her. She always cursed if he did wake after she had reached the safety of her bed, put on her reading glasses and found her bookmark. Then there were two courses open to her: (a) she quickly closed her eyes and feigned sleep; (b) she acted jolly and pleased to see him thus avoiding his sulks and her own guilty conscience that told her she was treating him meanly.

Last night she would have been more than just thankful to sleep alone. She had much to think about, mostly concerning Colin. Ray had brought her up a cup of tea about seven. She had risen quickly, lest he might decide to burrow under the duvet with her and have another go at planting the purple sausage, and had successfully kept him at arm's length till she had poured more tea and served up toast.

He was clean and bore no traces of the evening's overindulgence. He had shaved and wore a fresh T-shirt and jeans. Although Diane fell short on ironing, his mother could never complain that she didn't look after him. Now he stared at her across the kitchen table with the expression of a child who has just got his own way after much whingeing and been offered a new toy.

'Really, Di? That's bloody marvellous! I'll give Trevor a ring pronto. Why d'you want a van?' This came as an afterthought, his horizon filled with dreams of glory where he was admiral of a fleet of London taxicabs.

Now for it, she thought, glancing at the wall-clock. She had an hour before she opened the Honey Pot. She spread marmalade on her toast and bit into it. White sliced bread, cooked to a turn, crunching pleasantly under her teeth, delicious with melted butter and the sharp, sweet tang of lime conserve. Would that all things were so easy to contrive as buttered toast.

'I went to the fête at the castle yesterday,' she began, crossing her legs under her overall. It rose above her knees and she was very aware of her cunt and how it had felt when Colin stroked it. 'Amber and Sue came with me. We've all joined a society called the Silver Banner, and I've decided to go along to weekend rallies, feeding them all from a hot-dog and chippy van.'

'You what?' Ray's jaw dropped.

Diane sighed. It was going to be like pushing a huge boulder uphill to get him to understand. There was one thing that might click, however. 'It'll be a nice little earner,' she said brightly, and, going slowly as if talking to a remedial child, she went carefully through the pros and cons.

'Can I come?' he asked at last, grasping the possibility for making money and purloining a share.

Damn, she thought, wishing a hole would open in the floor and swallow him up. 'These musters may take place at your busiest time for cab hire,' she suggested sweetly. 'Weekends and bank holidays and that.'

'Don't you want me along? I'm not booked up tomorrow and could have a dekko,' he said, and there was a suspicious gleam in his little porcine eyes.

Just for an instant, she questioned the advisability of using piggy parts for transplants. If, as was rumoured, organs had memories, then supposing you had a heart or liver donated by a porky animal friend and had the urge to wallow about in the mud and go oink?

She pulled herself together. 'If you want, but you'll be bored, I expect, though there is a beer tent,' she added nastily. 'In any case, Ray, I'm going to do it whatever you say. And it's the only way you'll get your taxi. Is it a deal?'

'OK,' he muttered, then cheered up. 'It's a little belter, Di. You'll love it.'

'And you'll find me a van. No rubbish, mind,' she said sternly, knowing of old the crap he could be talked into buying by wily associates who called themselves his mates. 'It's got to be in working nick, with an MOT, a reliable engine and a new set of tyres, and the inside must be spotless. I want stainless steel everywhere, a fridge, a fryer, a cooker, a microwave, a water tank and a generator, and maybe a dishwasher, although I'll use throwaway plastic cutlery and polystyrene mugs and plates.'

'It'll cost.'

'Leave that to me. Just see to it.'

A working day and a busy one. Amber woke Ian early and drove him back to camp. He looked so heart-stoppingly handsome that she could hardly bear to leave him, but duty called on both counts; he to lead his men to siege a castle and she to open the doors of Collectibles. They arranged that she should join him when she closed. By that time the dastardly Roundheads would have been driven from their hideout, taken prisoner and marched away under guard by the triumphant Cavaliers.

She would miss the fun, but they'd be doing a repeat on Sunday. Ian had talked her into putting the GONE FISHING notice on the door, or getting Alastair to 'hold the fort'. It amused her when he used military terms, adopting the character of Captain Barrett, cavalry officer of the King's Horse.

'I'll ask him, but I can't promise,' she had said, not even bothering to get out of her car as she had to drive straight back. 'He may want to take a butcher's himself. All these magnificent men in costume flaunting their weapons and prancing about. They're enough to turn a young queen's head.'

Home in time to open up, and a quick call to Sue and another to Diane, checking. Sue wasn't there. Did she stay the night with Prudy? Amber wondered. 'Do you know what happened, Di?' she asked. 'Did she say she wasn't coming home?'

'No, but I'm not surprised,' Diane's disembodied voice spoke in her ear. 'She seems keen. The first girl for a while, isn't it? She's told me it's not too easy to find partners, unless you're into clubbing, which she isn't.'

'Looks like we're better off with straights, then,' Amber commented, knowing she should be about her work. Alastair was casting a reproachful eye in her direction and a couple of customers were coming in at the door. 'Ian and I went to town last night.'

'Is this for real or a flying fuck?'

'I don't know,' said Amber truthfully. After so many letdowns one became wary, not counting one's blessings, or even one's screws, leaving it to fate to decide. 'I rather hope so,' she added.

'That's how I feel about Colin. We've not done it yet ...

well, not it exactly, though he did make me come. I've spoken to Ray and he's looking out for a van. Will you be a sutler, too? Or d'you want to fight?'

'I'm quite happy to help out,' Amber said, keeping the receiver glued to the side of her face and turning her back on Alastair. 'Ian's lovely, Di. I really like him.'

'Better than Camilo?'

'Different to Camilo. And Colin?'

'Is a sweetie, but I'm not sure what to do. I'll test the water before I finally burn any bridges. I've a lot to lose.'

'Ray? Surely not?'

'We'll see,' Di said darkly, then added, 'I'll be out there this evening. Are you coming?'

'Oh, yes,' said Amber. 'Wild horses wouldn't keep me away.'

'Ray wants to come along, but I've put him off till tomorrow. Don't want him hanging around. He'll only get pissed and make an exhibition of himself. Fortunately, he's on duty and Saturday night is one of the busiest, ferrying drunks home. So that means I can meet Colin and take it from there.'

'Naughty, naughty.'

'Shut up! Jesus God, we're a long time dead! Oh, Lord, I must go. The zombies have just come in. They look totally out of it after the fair. I didn't think Toyah was old enough to drink. If she is, then I should be paying her more per hour than I do. Good morning, team! Did you have a good time? Fine, then let's have a bit of "hi-ho, hi-ho, it's off to work we go". Cheerio, Amber. Catch you later.'

By lunchtime, Amber had contacted Sue. She went round to her shop while Alastair kept Collectibles open, fortified by a sandwich and a mug of coffee, and Sue hustled Amber into the sewing room at the back. One of the large worktables was awash with patterns, and tomes with titles like *The History of World Costume* and *The Comprehensive Guide to Theatrical Costume Making*.

'Prudy's been really helpful,' Sue said, her voice a trifle shrill and OTT, a sure sign that her hormones were off kilter. 'She's coming to stay next weekend and is bringing the official patterns issued by the Banner, and I'm ordering bales of material from the mills up North and organising my sewing women, and finding a leather factor and a buckle maker and all manner of things. We've barely a month to the Dorrington Hill muster.'

'I know,' Amber said, and marvelled anew at the miracle of life streaming through her, filling her with vitality. It was amazing what a good shafting could do for one.

'I can't wait,' Sue went on, pausing in striding about to grin at Amber. 'I must polish up on the equestrian arts, and take a course in fencing.'

'You're really going to fight?'

'You bet your sweet pussy I am!'

'It's all coming together. Di is on the track of a van, and I'm going to be her assistant. I'll need you to fix me up with the proper gear – of the lower orders, I suppose, though I'd like a posh dress, too. It seems that Ian knows Prince Rupert and I hope to meet him.'

'Prudy was going on about the Devil Prince. Apparently he is the Big Cheese! Numero Uno!'

By the time Diane succeeded in reaching the castle it had long since surrendered, but the camp reverberated with excitement, triumph and esprit de corps, though the Roundheads had retired to their own quarters. It was no fun being on the losing side.

The funfair was going great guns, but she didn't have to bother about Karen being there. She had 'borrowed' ten pounds and taken herself off to behave badly in her friend's house, the parents being absent. Following Colin's instructions, she slowed down at the guard's tent, gave his name and was let through the barrier. She drove straight round to where his car and trailer were parked. He was waiting for her. She got out and almost fell into his arms. It was so long since she had felt so eager to spend time with a man. She knew that she had already made her decision. If Colin felt the same way about her, then she was going to leave Ray. Not leave, exactly – it was essential that she kept the café and her home, but if she offered him a large enough inducement, then she might be able to get him to move out.

'What d'you want to do?' Colin said, his arm about her waist. 'Shall we walk?'

'OK,' she said.

It seemed more appropriate if he made the running. Running? Walking? Walking out? She tingled everywhere, the touch of his hand, his fingers linked with hers, brought it all flooding back – the girlhood she had missed out on, the sense of wonder and bewilderment. But now she was a woman of experience, aware of her needs and determined to fulfil them. Colin was blissfully ignorant of what was about to hit him like a sledgehammer.

It was getting dark, but lights blazed from the fair and shone from each tent and caravan, augmenting the glowing campfires. People were milling about, costumed or otherwise, some heading for the shooting galleries, the bowel-churning rides or the beer tent. Diane slipped her arm through Colin's and hoped she wouldn't meet anyone she knew.

They left the perimeter of both camp and showground, following a path that wound into a copse. It was much darker there and Colin led the way, gallantly holding back brambles and clearing a passage for her. She wanted him to stop, pull her into his arms and take her breath away, along with her doubts. Then she heard a sound in the bushes ahead. She saw the white wedge of Colin's face as he turned to look at her, his finger raised to his lips in a hush gesture. It was too late to go back or do anything but gaze into the space afforded by the thin veil of undergrowth.

'What is it?' she whispered.

'Rather who,' he corrected, and she stepped in front of him to get a better view.

At first she couldn't make much out, except that there was a figure there – no, two figures, one with its back to her, partly covering the other who was pressed against the bole of a tree. She saw the sweeping cloak of the male, recognised him as a cavalryman by the gold braid, the long hair and top boots. At once she guessed what was happening and wanted to back away. She didn't want to watch a couple actually having sex. This was what they were doing. The man, tall and broad-shouldered, had the smaller person penned in; it was undoubtedly female. Diane glimpsed a mane of teased, bleached hair, a flash of bare legs in the gloom that came up and scissored round his waist as he held her under the rump, and pale arms that seized him in a vicelike grip.

They were panting, and the woman gasped out, 'Do it! Do it! That's it, pump me hard!'

Diane was so shocked that she couldn't move. 'Isn't that Ian Barrett?' she hissed, feeling Colin at her back as they stood there, facing forwards, his arm round her breasts, holding her still.

'I think so,' he whispered.

'But that's not Amber,' she said, trying to keep her voice low.

'No.'

'Oh,' was all she could think to say.

'It's not our business,' he reminded, moving his head so that he could talk into her ear, and as the fornicating pair speeded up, so Diane was aware of him hardening against her bottom crack. She had worn a skirt that evening, so much more convenient than trousers when it came to a grope.

'I think we ought to leave,' she murmured.

'Why?'

'I don't want to see them at it. I'm thinking of Amber. He spent last night with her. The bastard! And now he's poking someone else.'

'That's Amber's problem, not yours.'

'She's my best friend.'

At that moment the heavens opened and a thunderstorm broke with the most remarkable and vengeful display of lightning. Diana fled, not caring if Colin was following her or not. If the rain disturbed the lovers, then she could not face Ian without giving him a tongue-lashing. Soaked through, out of breath and disgruntled, she arrived at the trailer tent, at the same time as Colin.

He hustled her inside, lit a lamp and found towels to rub her dry. 'There, there,' he said, and she couldn't decide if he was consoling her for getting wet or for discovering that Amber's lover was a skunk.

Here she was and here she would have to stay, at least until the fury of the heavens abated. Colin opened his sleeping bag and ordered her to get out of her wet things and climb in. She did, too confused to argue, or that's what she told herself, but in reality she knew that the die was cast. Witnessing Ian's perfidy had been a setback but, as Colin had wisely said, it was not her concern. Maybe Amber knew what he was like and didn't care, wanting to be promiscuous herself. Just because he was like that, it didn't mean Colin was the same, did it?

Colin undressed, his body whiplash lean in the lamplight. His hair was wet, and it looked thinner, receding from his brow, but Diane wasn't bothered. She held out her arms and he entered them, slipping inside the bag and zipping it up. It was so cosy, a double version, and as his hands roamed her body, she listened to the drumming of the rain on the tent roof, and embraced him fully, eager to discover all the lovely things he could teach her. A new man. A new experience, different flesh that would react to her in a different way.

It grew hot in there, and she kicked off the covering, opening herself to him completely.

7

'When the victorious young Stag Lord returned fully ant-
lered from the Running, he mated with the Maiden. This
union was the Great Rite, in which the Goddess, repre-
sented by the Maiden and the God, in the person of the
young Stag Lord, brought fertility to the land. That's the
meaning of Beltane,' Amber said, pausing outside her
shop and loading yet another bag into the boot of her car.
She had decided to leave the Bedford for Alastair who had
deliveries to make.

'Thank you for sharing that with us,' Sue remarked
acerbically, raring to go, adjusting the side mirror and
turning the ignition key in her hatchback.

The rear seat was folded flat and full of costumes in
plastic covers, coat hangers, clothing rails and cardboard
boxes of accessories. Amber's roof rack held the poles and
awning, which would cover the stall, and her two-
wheeled trailer contained a tent for herself and Diane,
and an extension for the van. Sue was not troubled by
problems of accommodation. She was sharing with Prudy.

'I thought you'd like to know what it's all about, it
being Mayday Eve and us arriving on site. Expect jollifica-
tion,' Amber went on, ignoring her friend's irritability. It
was very early after all and they weren't at their brightest
and best at that hour.

Diane stuck her head through the window of the van,
nervous and edgy about her catering debut. 'Blimey, I
shall be too busy for that ... at least I hope so,' she
averred. 'Got to make hay while the sun shines or, in
other words, before Ray decides to join me and make

a balls-up of everything. He's threatening to come over, if he can arrange temp drivers. Wish he'd go boil his head.'

'Busy or not, these old rituals sort of weave themselves into the human psyche,' Amber said solemnly, making sure that the shop and flat doors were secure. Alastair was the boss for the next few days, the Dorrington Hill gathering her first muster and hugely important. 'It's said that nubile young women walked in procession to the holy circles and so did the young men. When they reached the centre, they mated and the virgin blood of the maidens fertilised the land.'

'Yeah, yeah, and what has this got to do with the Silver Banner?' asked Sue, in an exasperated tone.

'Nothing, except that the battle is intended to enliven the holiday weekend. There should be dancing round the maypole and morris men and all sorts of primitive junketings that go back to the dawn of time.'

'All to do with King Dick, I suppose.'

'That's right, and what could be better?' Amber said, and a giant hand gripped her core and gave it a squeeze.

A month had passed since the Lyncroft Show. After much dithering and soul-searching, she had phoned Ian several times, but he said he was too busy to see her. He sounded pleased when she told him she was mugging up on the Civil War, being measured for costumes and putting her affairs in order so that she could leave her business ticking over and meet him at the muster.

'If he turns up,' said Diane.

Her attitude towards him riled Amber. She had taken against him but wouldn't explain why. This was doubly irritating. So was the fact that Diane was carrying on a dangerous liaison with Colin right under her husband's nose. Fortunately for her, he only lived ten miles away, and his house was near Anson's cash-and-carry, a mighty, seemingly endless warehouse on a trading estate that provided Diane with stock for the Honey Pot, and now, her latest baby – the hot-dog van.

'Of course he'll turn up,' Amber said frostily, quashing the doubt that wriggled like a maggot inside her. 'Why shouldn't he? Prince Rupert will be there, and they are close buddies.'

'Ah, the prince!' Diane exclaimed dramatically, hand raised to her brow as if swooning. 'His fans think he walks on water.'

'How can you be so horrible?' Amber retaliated, thinking: this isn't going to work. I'm supposed to be her assistant, but there are bound to be fireworks if she's so openly hostile to Ian and anyone associated with him.

'I don't know. Years of practice, I suppose.'

'Stop bitching. Let's get off,' Sue interrupted. 'It's seven already and we don't want to hit the commuter rush.'

They set out in convoy. It was a fine morning that augured well for their enterprise, crisp enough to be invigorating, but with spring spicing the air. Lyncroft was just waking up. They passed a postman on his red bike and a milk float purring along. Amber tried to get her head together. There had been so much to do and excitement had kept her adrenaline pumping. Sleep wouldn't come last night. A leisurely wank hadn't sent her off, not even when Ian was the subject of her fantasies. Now she felt hollow-eyed with weariness.

Sue was in the lead, as always. Amber followed her and Diane brought up the rear. Considering that she'd not been out in the van much she was handling it competently.

'Love laughs at locksmiths', Amber thought irrelevantly, deciding that a woman or man possessed of that insanity, which softens the brain and ignites the body, was capable of anything, be it ever so foolhardy or ridiculously brave. The van was a means by which Diane could get into Colin's knickers. You cynical old bitch, Amber chided herself. Relax. Ian will be there, and you've already steeled yourself to accept that there's nothing serious going on between you. Enjoy the experience, throw yourself into the part of a leaguer bitch. Don't forget, you'll be meeting Rupert. Remember what Tanith said about him. It could be amazing.

Bath snoozed in its hollow, the River Avon winding like a silver snake between green parks and white stone buildings. They drove through and out the other side, heading for Bristol and the bypass and the motorway that would lead eventually to Dorrington town and its famous battlefield below the hill. This in itself bore a question mark. Amber, one eye on the road, had a map open on her knees, puzzling over this blob. Was it a natural mound or man-made, like its counterpart at Silbury? Archaeologists debated and argued, bored into it, took measurements, had geophysics boffins go over it with a fine toothcomb. Still there had been no concrete evidence that it had been a burial site or an Iron-Age fort, or simply a joke left behind by an ancient bigwig with a warped sense of humour.

If that was the case, then it was definitely made by men, she decided. Women were far too sensible to waste everybody's time with silly guessing games.

The journey was going so smoothly that she couldn't believe it. Sue had planned the route, with Prudy's advice. She was the most enthusiastic of the three, and Amber could see what was firing her. It was that slim, dark enchantress who was a barrister by profession and a cavalry officer by preference. Amber had seen Sue infrequently of late; she was occupied in learning to ride all over again, and attending fencing classes. And when she wasn't doing either of these, she was in cahoots with Prudy, getting together a range of costumes and forwarding her sex life. An enviable position, and Amber wished her own love affair would proceed half as smoothly.

Bloody men! Despite what she told herself, her annoyance with Ian kept bubbling up and she was tempted to phone Jason or even try Camilo's number, just to show him that she didn't care.

It was going to be a lengthy muster. April thirtieth fell midweek and the public holiday was from Friday to Monday, a six-day event for the Silver Banner. Rupert had it all planned. He was owed time off, and locked up his town flat and removed himself and Otto to Adelaide Lodge to prepare. When they departed on May Day Eve, he was driving a Freelander with his mobile home in tow, and Otto a smaller FWD, with Corsair in his horsebox hitched to the back.

Before they left Rupert dialled Ian. 'Ah, you're still there,' he said. 'Is everything OK?'

'It is,' Ian answered. 'Billy's in the pink and I'm looking forward to some bloody fierce fighting. Our Roundhead opponents are a right earnest bunch of tossers, so I gather, led by Colonel Corbet.'

'He's a real old Ironsides, one of Cromwell's devotees. He'll have 'em on their knees praying all day. I expect he issues orders forbidding them to fuck before a battle,' Rupert said grimly.

He had come up against Corbet's forces in the past and, although each recorded skirmish and siege was a foregone conclusion, had found him a hard nut to crack, even when it was already ordained that the enemy should lose. Rupert mentally flexed his muscles. The excitement roaring through him bordered on sexual. There was nothing he enjoyed more than galloping off the battlefield victorious, and screwing the first piece of skirt he saw. And this was only a war game. He could well understand how, during the real thing, bloodlust became rape and mindless slaughter, prisoners and enemy women standing no chance.

'What time do you expect to arrive?' he asked levelly, though his cock had risen between his thighs. He put his hand down into his lap and gave it a surreptitious rub.

His heart was thumping, and he glanced in the driving mirror, always pleased to see himself in the cornflower blue, gold-braided doublet, wide lace-trimmed collar, form-fitting breeches and thigh boots that marked his transformation into the prince. Passing motorists might do a double take, but this added to his sense of well being.

'Mid-morning.'

'You're in costume?'

'Naturally. And you?'

'That goes without saying.'

'Is Sarah coming along?'

'I guess. How about your tarts? Is that dirty bit of rough trade ... what's-her-name ... Gina, intending to follow you, presenting her arse at every opportunity?'

'Who knows? She was at Lyncroft Castle. I hope she doesn't show, actually, as Amber will be there. The one I've told you about. She's joined the Banner. A rather tasty piece, who fucks like a fury.'

'Sounds interesting. Can I try?'

'If you want,' Ian said carelessly. Rupert could visualise his dismissive shrug, guessed that he was lying, and smiled.

'But she's your new girlfriend, isn't she?' he quipped, to annoy him and get his reaction.

'It's not set in stone.'

'Right. I'll see you around noon, and we'll take it from there. If the beer tent's up and running I'll buy you a pint.'

This is like trying on clothes for a school play, Amber concluded.

She was standing in Prudy's tent, staring at herself in a pier glass supported on a mahogany frame. She was naked except for her bra and panties, the last links with the twenty-first century, and Sue hovered behind her, offering alternatives.

'That's it,' she urged. 'Get 'em off.'

'But . . .'

'No buts. We've been through all this when you came in for fittings. You simply can't look the part unless your underpinnings are right. Are you sure you want to wear a gown tonight? Wouldn't it be better to get used to trailing a skirt and living in a field in simpler gear? Diane's got the right idea. A country trollop, all ready to serve the soldiers in more ways than one.'

Amber wanted to say that she'd feel better without an audience, but this made her sound like a prat. Paddington station sprang to mind. The tent, though average in size, was the focal point for Prudy's troop, male and female. Modesty was of no avail there. Prudy, after ordering some of her finest to erect Diane's and Amber's tent, to manoeuvre the van into a prominent position near Trader's Corner and get Sue's stall established, had suggested that, as her own quarters were more roomy, they changed in there.

It was high time. Once they had left Dorrington and found the site, they had felt out of place in modern dress. The road had been congested, not only with Silver Banner enthusiasts, but others who had been invited to attend: market traders, showmen, fire-eaters, acrobats and outdoor-theatre performers. In an adjoining field there was a festival celebrating music from all over the world – like a mini Pilton with marquees and a pyramid stage, sound engineers and loud speakers, bands arriving in customised buses and gatecrashers trying to avoid payment.

Sue had been the first to discard her clothes, changing into a keen-hipped, slim-waisted trooper who swaggered around, oozing bravura from every pore. Amber took one look at her and her nipples tightened. It was disconcerting to discover that she found her so attractive that her hormones were responding. She'd never thought about dipping a toe into the turbulent waters of lesbianism before. But now, she wasn't so sure.

Her friend of many years looked so different. It wasn't only the fact that she had grown her burgundy hair longer, still shaggy, still spiky, but somehow period, too. There was no doubt about it, this era in history afforded the males ample opportunity to strut. Not so ridiculous as the Tudors with their ruffs and codpieces: softer, more informal, even looking ahead to later styles, with the tailored doublet and breeches, the wonderful leather riding boots, the emphasis on Stetson-like hats and the fashion for long, sumptuous, curling locks. The rebels might have been forerunners of the skinheads, but the Cavaliers looked like hippies.

Amber was now the only one not in costume so she reached round and unclipped her bra. It fell away from her breasts and she handed it to Diane. No one seemed to take any notice and, emboldened, Amber pushed down her panties and stepped out of them. Diane picked them up and laid them across Amber's jeans and T-shirt on a stool. It was warm in the tent, but even so her nipples peaked, and she wanted to cover them with her hands. She didn't, afraid of being thought a prude.

She had brought several outfits with her; two were plain and had aprons suitable for a victualler, but the one she proposed to wear now was a gown for court, or going to a ball where King Charles and his wife, Queen Henrietta Maria, would lead the dancing. You're losing the plot, she lectured herself. Starting to think all this is real, not a drama organised to amuse people who are fed up with the disposable, computerised, throwaway society in which they exist, nostalgic for a time when honour and loyalty counted for something. When one believed in a cause and was willing to die for it. When one made vows and kept them, faithful to the end.

She was very aware of her nakedness, though the other women in the tent were changing their clothes without batting an eyelid, chatting to their mates, exchanging cracks with the occasional male who wandered in. One of these, a handsome young dandy with an amazing black mane complete with beribboned locks and a mulberry doublet embellished with silver lace, came across to Amber, and looked her up and down.

'You're not one of them, are you?' he asked, and jerked a thumb over his shoulder to where half-a-dozen she-soldiers were gathered, arms round one another, kissing and petting, simply friends or maybe more. There wasn't a lot of intimacy going on, as most of them were preparing to hit the town, giving Dorrington something to remember.

'Get lost, Alan,' Prudy said, patting him affectionately on his taut arse. 'But if you must know, she isn't. Such a waste.'

'Maybe I'll catch you later. Will you be in the pub?' he persisted and his eyes were beautiful, a melting brown, with the most incredibly long lashes.

'Yes, but I'm meeting someone,' Amber replied, thinking how odd it was to be standing there in all her glory without a single, solitary stitch on, talking to a young man to whom she hadn't even been introduced – one, moreover, who was about Andy's age. If this was a sample of what to expect under the Silver Banner, then she was all for it.

'Hop it, Alan,' Prudy said and slipped a fine silk chemise over Amber's head, protecting her from his lewd gaze.

'Can't I watch? You don't mind, do you? I don't know your name.'

'This is Amber,' Sue put in, tweaking the chemise into place. It fell to Amber's knees, a loose shift with billowing sleeves and a low neckline. It was the basic garment worn by all women, rich or poor, though the lower classes had to settle for cotton.

Amber shook her head, catching the raunchy look in Alan's eyes. Now partially clad, she could flirt with him without feeling like a lecherous old cradle-snatcher. She clung to one of the tent poles as Sue folded a pair of boned stays round her, short ones from waist to just under her bust, and strained on the back lacing. It pushed her breasts so high that the nipples poked over the edge, lifted above the frilly chemise. Her waist diminished by what felt like ten inches.

'I can't breathe,' she gasped, and the restriction seemed to force the blood into her lower regions, rousing and inflaming her. She was oh-so conscious of her nipples behaving like pets begging to be fondled.

'It's supposed to be tight. Gives your gown the correct line,' Sue said seriously, wrapped up in her design, obsessed with getting every detail right, wanting to impress Prudy who was watching closely, her eyes boring into Amber's breasts.

'Lovely,' sighed Alan, and he reached out and circled each of Amber's aching teats, first one then the other.

Amber watched herself in the mirror, seeing a wanton stranger in a transparent shift with her bush outlined beneath it and cherry-red nipples standing to attention, and a gorgeous young man flicking and teasing them into even harder points. The mirror woman had languorous eyes, and her hair had been piled high, with a trail of little ringlets covering each ear and at the nape of her neck. She looked well up for anything.

Prudy dropped to her knees beside her and ran a hand up her thigh under the chemise, then fondled her between her legs. 'You're wet,' she said huskily, and her finger parted Amber's folds and dipped into her and returned to hook under her clit-head. Amber jumped and clung to the post even harder.

'Aren't we all?' Diane chuckled. She had recovered her good humour once she had met up with Colin and changed into a brown fustian skirt, a red petticoat and stays similar to Amber's but made of suede. 'I'm about to go crazy with lust. Don't worry about helping me just now, Amber. Colin's promised to do that. He's already got the generator going and we'll make a stonking amount of money tonight, I shouldn't wonder.'

Love among the bangers and chips? Amber thought, visualising a lull between customers, and Diane with her skirts whipped aside and her bare bum offered to Colin amidst the fragrant odour of frying onions.

Amber could hardly get her head round this, distracted by the feel of Prudy's fingers, and seeing the erection distorting the front of Alan's breeches. Spend Beltane's Night serving beef burgers? You had to be joking.

Alan came closer till she could smell his deodorant. Obviously he wasn't sticking to Banner orders that nothing from the present day should be used during the musters. Did he have a mobile phone secreted about his person, too? He was the type to hold up a stiff finger at rules. He put an arm round her bare shoulders and nodded in the mirror.

'Don't we make a pair?' he asked, and bent and placed a kiss on her neck. He was just too beguiling and Amber felt as if she had been drinking, senses heightened, sex clamouring for fulfilment. Was he one of her Tarot knights?

'Break it up,' Sue said, and had Amber step into two petticoats and fastened the ties at the waist. The skirt came next; it was made of rose pink taffeta, pastels being fashionable during the Civil War years. ('All you've got to do is look at your Vandycks, darling', as she was fond of saying). It was full and flowing and actually made that sound known as 'frou-frou'.

'Stand straight,' Sue ordered. 'Bloody hell! How am I suppose to get these points done up.'

The stiff-boned bodice was also laced at the back. It

had a very low square neck, and enormous puffed sleeves that ended in deep lace cuffs below the elbow. They were slashed, the chemise showing, the sleeves held together with pearl clasps. She ordered Amber to sit and Prudy rolled white silk stockings with gold clocks up her legs, keeping them in place by garters ornamented with diamanté buckles. Amber wanted her to go higher but Prudy, though probably well aware, picked up a pair of satin shoes with pointed toes, spool-shaped heels and bunches of ribbons on the instep, and made her put them on.

When the last wrinkle had been smoothed out, the final pleat tweaked into place, Sue stood back and surveyed her handiwork, head to one side, eyes narrowed critically. 'You'll do, Cinderella,' she said at last, and placed a voluminous silk wrap round Amber's shoulders. 'You shall go to the ball.'

'It looks as if you've already found your gallant,' Prudy added.

Alan held out an arm, and Amber placed the tips of her fingers on his velvet sleeve. This was fun, better than a fancy-dress party. Every item of her outfit was as accurate as Sue could make it – no nylon, or press-studs or hooks and eyes. Not even buttons, everything kept together by points – a ribbon with a metal tag on the end. Her shoulders felt very bare, as did her pussy under the chemise. Long skirts did not necessarily keep out the draughts, and what would soak up her juices when, like now, she was aroused? She wasn't sure if she was happy without knickers. It made her feel too vulnerable and this was odd, because hers were so minuscule – tanga briefs or thongs – that they'd be useless as protection.

The evenings were drawing out; soon it would be summer and warm enough to use her back garden. She always enjoyed this, a sun worshipper who believed that with the correct screening factor, one could improve one's image and stay fit and healthy, imbibing a large dose of vitamin D. It occurred to her to wonder if the Banner met every weekend during the season and if she would have to sacrifice her days lounging and basking and dipping into the out-sized paddling pool she had bought herself. I don't always have to attend, she thought, and smiled up at Alan as they left Prudy's tent.

A massive bonfire blazed in the centre of the ground, well away from tents and stalls, and attended by members of the fire brigade. The public were pouring in, drawn by the spectacle and the beer tent and curiosity about the re-enactment society, and wanting to let their hair down at the fair. Schoolchildren were demonstrating the maypole dance, dressed in costume and weaving patterns with the ribbons fixed to the top. Further on, morris men whacked their sticks and jingled their bells and flaunted their leafy cloaks and made obscene gestures to the one dressed as a woman, with big tits and a wig and badly applied make-up.

'They can't wait to get into drag,' Alan commented.

'It was originally intended to raise energy for rituals,' she said. 'The androgynous person is called a Mollie.'

'Fertility, I suppose? A sort of magical Viagra. I don't need it. I can go on all night.' He leaned closer and she could well believe that he was only slightly exaggerating. He'd have testosterone coming out of his ears.

The fire shot sparks into the evening sky; the virile male dancers leaped and pranced and performed their ancient rites, and then there was the maypole. The children had gone now, coercing their parents into taking them to the fair. Banner members had replaced them and suddenly the innocence was gone, their body language plain to read as they wound the ribbons in and out, binding the partner they had selected as their Chosen One. Already couples were leaving the place and disappearing into tents or getting lost in the density of the woods.

'An integral part of tree worship,' Amber said, stopping to watch, aware of Alan and wanting him with a hunger that hadn't been satisfied since shagging Ian. 'It is the earth phallus, the male principle jutting out of the soil, or it can be the fruit-bearing tree of life and is therefore female.'

He gave her a hard stare, his brows drawn down. 'Are you a witch or something?' he asked suspiciously.

She shook her head, smiling at his naiveté. 'I'm not a witch, but I may be a "something",' she said. 'No, it's just that I'm interested in folklore. It's because I deal in antiques, I expect. What about you? Are you working or at uni or what?'

'I'm a student, doing media studies. I want to get into the research department of a television company.'

'Is that why you're here? Doing research?'

'I'm here because it's fun. I like history and riding and sword fighting, and I meet some really fascinating people, like you, for example.'

Oh, smooth-tongued young man, she thought, as they turned their backs on the bonfire and started to walk in the direction of the beer tent. Then she stopped suddenly, her heart doing a mad tattoo inside her ribcage. In the distance, floating above the caravan site, she saw a pennant. It was the vision in Tanith's crystal all over again. The flag of Rupert of the Rhine: black with a gold lion, the white and blue Palatine colours, the gold fringe shimmering.

Alan spotted it, too. 'The prince is here,' he said on a new note, admiration and a touch of awe, laced with envy.

'You serve under him?'

'I'd like to be one of his Lifeguards, but haven't worked my way up to that privileged position yet. It would take too much time anyway, and I can't afford it. He's a rich dude.'

Amber had difficulty in controlling her feet that wanted to rush across the grass and into the caravan enclosure. It was imperative that she meet Rupert. She didn't know why it was so important. A reincarnation link? Did she owe him a karmic debt, or had he to repay her? Where was Ian? He'd be the best bet.

As if conjured by sorcery, he materialised before her, saying, 'There you are. I've been waiting for you. You're late.'

'Did we specify a time?' His assumption that she would be at his beck and call roused her feminist ire.

'A thousand apologies. The fault was mine, Captain Barrett,' Alan said, taking off his hat, its feathers brushing the grass as he made a leg. It was an effusive gesture, but in keeping with the setting. 'I offered to escort this charming lady.'

'Did you, indeed? You impudent jack-a-napes,' Ian retorted. 'I should call you out. Swords, pistols or what you will.'

'Any time, sir. My seconds will meet with yours and decide a time and place.'

'Oh, for fuck's sake!' Amber didn't know whether to laugh or cry. 'What are you like?'

Ian grinned and cupped her elbow in his hand. 'You're living in the sixteen hundreds now, and this is how the hot-tempered, hot-blooded gentlemen carried on. Come on, both of you. A bumper of ale, methinks, and then, Amber, I'll present you to Mr Frobisher, alias Prince Rupert.'

The spirit of Beltane was everywhere, growing stronger by the second as if feeding on the crowd, these old ceremonies energised every time they were repeated. Certainly inhibitions were being thrown to the four winds as villagers and townies, Banner members and open-air performers, mixed and mingled and gave full rein to their deepest, dirtiest desires. The beer tent was full, but Ian succeeded in finding a vacant table and sent Alan off to the bar. There was the overpowering smell of hops and crushed grass, sweat and pheromones. Mine included, Amber thought, as Ian slid a hand on her knee, worked her skirts up and dived unerringly between her thighs, his fingers combing through her bush.

'Oh,' she gasped, casting an anxious look around, sure that someone would see, but the crush was so great and the revellers so intent on their own pleasures that she needn't have worried. Alcohol had been on sale all day. Obese, jovial, vine-crowned Bacchus and a pantheon of other pagan gods ruled supreme.

Men in costume were fondling draggle-tailed sluts and grand ladies alike, patting rumps, fingering breasts, kissing mouths, rubbing wet snatches, dribbling wine down cleavages and bending to lick off the droplets. People in everyday gear were equally possessed by lust. In darkened corners, Amber glimpsed couples on the very brink or already engaged in fornication, and some of these were of the same sex.

A handsome boy, garbed as a musketeer, was on his knees, gobbling at the rock-hard prick of a hairy, bearded pikeman. A wench lay across a beer-stained table. She squealed with joy, her plump white legs raised and hooked round the shoulders of a boy in jeans and sweatshirt, his cock buried to the hilt within her dark crack. A flashily dressed Cavalier was fingering her arsehole. Two men that looked like Roundheads (could this be?) were rolling and roiling the nipples that poked above her corset, while she squeezed their cocks, then kept one in her hand and put the other in her mouth.

Near the main entrance, Mollie, the-pantomime-dame-cum-earth-mother beloved of the morris men, bent over and touched her toes, skirts above her head, sturdy legs apart, fleshy buttocks nude and free for all, balls dangling, cock hard. They leaped round her, skipping and jumping in time to the flute and drum, shedding leaves from their woodland cloaks, bells jangling. Those who weren't shagging were watching, cocks hard and being wanked, showers of milky come raining down to be absorbed by and rejuvenate the earth. It was bizarre, but made a sort of weird sense. If virgin blood could do it, then why not male libation of a different kind?

Amber could not really believe this was happening – an orgy at a showground? Where were the police, or had they, too, been seduced by the witchery of the Beltane Fires? Then she stopped questioning it, going with the flow.

'I've missed your sweet little minge,' Ian murmured, his breath tickling her ear and bringing her out in goosebumps.

'And whose fault is that?' she returned smartly. 'You chose to be too tied up to see me. What are you? Into bondage?' The idea was entrancing; Ian stripped and spreadeagled on a bed, wrists cuffed to the head, ankles tethered to the foot, his dick fiery with need and longing to explode but controlled by her. Maybe she'd let him come; maybe she wouldn't.

'That's a fun idea,' he replied, with a wolfish grin. 'You'd like to try it? Or have you already?' As he talked, he stroked her clit, up and down in a tantalising movement that robbed her of speech.

Alan heaved his shoulders through the crowd, holding a tray aloft. He succeeded in setting it on the table without spillage. Cider for Amber, and thick, peaty, beige-crested Guinness for himself and Ian.

'The ale looked piss weak,' he remarked, sitting down on the other side of Amber. 'This will put lead in your pencil.'

'Nothing wrong with my stiffy,' Ian grunted, sipping the strong brew. 'Amber's been keeping it hard.'

His left hand continued to poke and stroke her, and she

hovered on the edge of orgasm, too repressed to come, too frustrated to thrust him away. Alan glanced down, twigging what was going on. To her horror and unwilling delight, she felt him exploring her crotch, too. She was sandwiched between these flamboyantly dressed soldiers, with their gorgeous heads of hair, their elegance, dash and élan. They were the best-looking men in the marquee and both of them were playing with her. It was like she had died and gone to heaven.

Alan took a long pull at his pint glass, then put it down and half turned towards her. He felt for her hand and said, 'One good turn deserves another.' Her fingers encountered warmth and a rock-solid column of flesh. He had unlaced his breeches under cover of the table.

'Hold her open,' Ian ordered, and Alan obeyed, prising her labia apart. Ian lifted his fingers to his lips and wetted them with saliva. Amber could smell her juices, seaweedy and potent. 'Gorgeous,' Ian added, and Alan nodded, inhaling deeply.

She sank down in her seat a little, pelvis raised towards the blissful sensation, helpless to do other than let them have their way with her, unable to drink even, for one palm was a tube enclosing Ian's penis, and the other a mock vagina wanking Alan. She could feel the rush, heat pouring over her, a tidal wave sweeping her into a most marvellous, shameful, mind-blowing orgasm. She wanted to scream her pleasure, but merely gasped, her whole body tensing, then becoming as limp as a rag doll. Her partners in crime lingered as if loath to relinquish her clit, but their cocks were swelling to the point of ejaculation and first Alan spurted into her hand, and then Ian followed, till it seemed that she was in a lavish bath of come.

They showed no emotion, cool as cucumbers, which was more than could be said of their cocks. When they had spurted the last drops, they produced fine linen handkerchiefs from the depths of their pockets and, with admirable control, wiped their dicks and put them away. No one close to their table was any the wiser.

Ian swallowed deeply of his Guinness, his Adam's apple bobbing, then he ran the back of his hand over his lips and said, 'Drink up, Amber. Mustn't keep His Highness waiting.'

'Isn't one of you going to lend me a hanky?' she complained. 'I don't want to get this all over my new dress.'

'Women!' Ian exclaimed, and he and Alan shared a typically superior male glance that annoyed her profoundly. 'Oh, here you are, but let me have it back. It's one of my best, finished with handmade lace.'

She deliberately took her time, wiping each finger fastidiously and then dabbing her crotch dry as best she could under the circumstances. 'I need to pee,' she said, handing it back to him.

'Round the back and find the Portaloos,' he said, tucking it in his sleeve.

As it turned out, they all went, though, Nature having supplied them with simpler plumbing, Ian and Alan merely found a convenient tree. There was a queue outside the lavatories and, in the end, Amber couldn't wait any more, almost wetting herself. She took Ian's advice and retreated into the bushes. There she realised the advantages of being knickerless. It was so much easier just to lift one's skirts, open one's legs, crouch down and piddle. She really had needed to go, and enjoyed the simple pleasure of it, passing water like a cow in a meadow.

Tents had sprung up like mushrooms all over the site, but the section reserved for caravans and camper vans was roomy, with privacy assured around each. The biggest, sleekest and most luxurious was the one with the flagpole and Palatinate emblem. It was well lit, and had steps leading to a door at the side. A man lounged there, presumably on guard though his attitude was casual, his blue uniform worn as if it was part and parcel of his wardrobe, and not something donned on occasions.

'Hi, Otto,' Ian greeted him familiarly. 'Is he receiving visitors?'

Otto grinned, stared at Amber, then at Alan, and said, 'He's in conflab with Colonel Macarthy and his staff. They're going over the battle plans. He'll be glad of an interruption. Macarthy's a bore. Takes it deadly serious.' He opened the door and then stood aside so that Amber could walk up the steps and in. She was starting to manage her skirts, no longing tripping or getting entangled in them.

The caravan interior was extraordinarily ornate. It looked as if a master craftsman, who was descended from a long line of wagon makers specialising in those ordered by the gypsies, had designed it. Cut glass sparkled, the dark wood bore a high sheen, the lamps had crystal shades and the upholstery was of crimson moquette with a soft, velvety pile. It was quality through and through and had an air of gracious living, though the kitchen glimpsed between sliding doors was as modern as tomorrow. Mr Frobisher did not stint himself when it came to creature comforts.

Then Amber saw him and everything else was eclipsed by the terrible, wonderful reality of his existence. Ian was close behind her, and Rupert looked up from the table that he shared with three older men, all superbly turned out, uniforms bandbox fresh, weapons gleaming, greying locks coiling on wide, lace-trimmed collars, boots cleaned to perfection.

'Your Highness,' Ian said, bowing. 'Is this an inconvenient moment?'

'No. We're just about finished, aren't we, Colonel Macarthy?' Rupert replied, getting to his feet and rolling up a map and passing it over to the senior gentleman. He looked directly at Amber and said, 'Aren't you going to introduce me, Ian?'

He came round the table and stopped in front of Amber, lean and lithe and taller even than Ian, moving with the grace of a dancer. Did he dance? How would it be to have him partner her in the salsa?

She was aware of Ian saying, 'This is Mrs Amber Challonor. Amber ... our commander ... Prince Rupert.' She dropped into an awkward curtsey. It seemed the right thing to do.

'At your service, madam,' Rupert replied, and when he spoke the deep cadences of his voice seemed to invade her as forcefully as if he were fucking her. Suddenly she needed to sit.

A brief smile lifted his haughty mouth; his sombre gaze met hers for a second and his manner was reserved, almost austere and yet she read him correctly: beneath this apparent control lay a fierce temper, and inexhaustible stamina when it came to sex. He was like a time bomb.

What a guy! she thought. He's too good to be true and looks like a film star. He was dressed simply, in a well-worn leather jerkin thonged down the front, a linen kerchief knotted round his neck, plain blue breeches and boots pulled high up his legs, not rolled over into bucket-tops like the other officers. A red silk sash spanned his narrow waist, and she was very aware of the fullness between his thighs, her fingers itching to get hold of his tackle.

Otto saw the commanders out, and, by the time he had returned, Rupert had offered Amber a place on the couch at his side. 'Well? That's got rid of those old duffers. They take it so seriously that I'm afraid to swear and use street-speak. Are you going to tell me all about it? Why you're here, et cetera?' he asked, his dark brown eyes resting on her thoughtfully.

It was disconcerting and she didn't know where to look. All right, so she'd been satisfied by Alan and Ian, yet she was seized by a physical longing that made her pussy ache. She wanted Rupert. It might be a bitter disappointment if it actually happened, but she knew she'd never settle until she had at least tried. Yet she could tell that he was used to and bored by unconditional admiration. She'd have to dream up something challenging. Control, she told herself. Don't sleep with him tonight. It won't be too painful to refuse. I can have Ian instead or, if not, Alan who is as randy as an unaltered tomcat.

'Coffee, sir?' asked Otto, shaven head glistening under the electric wall lights.

Amber could hear the throb of a generator in the background. She had already clocked the expensive vehicles, the horsebox and the small though adequate toilet-tent that was undoubtedly locked to plebs. This was someone who travelled if not light, then comfortably. And the Jeeves person? Where did he fit into the equation? She would have staked her life on him being gay. Alastair would swoon all over him. She made up her mind to engineer an introduction.

'Thank you, Otto,' Rupert replied, and included Ian and Alan as he said, 'Amber's being mysterious. Don't waste your time. My cohorts are loyal and will tell me what I want to know.'

'There's not much to tell,' she said, with a show of frankness that masked the diabolical schemes forming in her agile mind. 'I saw the Banner perform at Lyncroft, where I live. I liked the idea of it and signed up. So did my two friends, Sue and Diane. I'm divorced, have my own business and do pretty much as I like. What about you?'

'Me?' he looked surprised. 'Hasn't Ian filled you in?'

'He said you were a surgeon, and related to the real Prince Rupert. You look like portraits I've seen of him. Don't worry, I've been studying the war,' she said brightly, refusing to allow her body to relax against his, even though he had an arm along the back of the seat and the scent of his hair was making her clit throb. 'But where's Boye?' she added suddenly. 'I've been reading about the prince and his famous dog who was feared by the enemy and credited, like him, with supernatural powers.'

'That's right,' Rupert said and that bored, oh hell it's another besotted tart, expression had faded, replaced by interest. 'Boye was an average-sized poodle, his constant companion who went everywhere with him and was reputed by the Roundheads to be the Wizard Prince's familiar.'

'So why haven't you got a Boye?'

Otto, tray in hand, fielded this for him. 'Dogs are forbidden by the Silver Banner because of their anti-social behaviour and habit of fouling everywhere. People don't mind horseshit on their shoes, but not dog.' He passed the cups around and proffered the silver sugar basin and cream jug. 'Even the prince couldn't pull rank on this one, could you, sir? Not that we want a dog, do we? Even Corsair is a bind, but at least I don't have to follow him around with a plastic bag and a poop-scoop.'

'Corsair is my horse,' Rupert explained, and the smile in his eyes was warm now, making Amber aware that much of his arrogance and lofty cool was due to self-preservation. 'Boye was killed at the Battle of Marston Moor. So, if we're appearing pre that date, we can always pretend that we've left him at home. People aren't all that clued up as a rule, only the history buffs who tend to be picky.'

He's nice as well as tasty, Amber thought. I want to get to know him. A surgeon, one of those big-hearted medical men who devote themselves to the relief of suffering. Oh, yes, I'd like to call him friend, but would be lying if I said I didn't want more. She permitted herself to relax, and felt the pressure as his long leg rested against hers, from hipbone to knee.

Coffee forgotten, she was wondering how to handle the next stage when there was a commotion at the door. It was flung open and a wild-eyed, stunningly beautiful vixen rushed in and flung herself on Rupert. She sat astride his lap, her black velvet riding skirt parting over black leather boots that almost reached her cleft, the high, spiky heels hardly in keeping with her costume.

'Darling,' she purred, and wriggled her bare slit against his crotch. 'I'm here! I got away from that tedious party early, just to be with you. Aren't you glad to see me? You *are*! I can tell. You've got one hell of a hard-on.'

She was blonde and she was gorgeous and she was deliberately ignoring Amber. Her hands came up and undid her jacket that was cut just like a Cavalier's, and beneath it her shirt was unbuttoned to the waist. She sat upright, rubbing herself against Rupert and cupping her breasts in both hands, her thumbs stroking the hard nipples.

'Hello, Sarah,' he said, his eyes hooded as he looked up at her, so brazenly displaying her wares for his benefit.

'Oh, darling, darling ... send these tiresome people away,' she demanded, tugging at his breeches. 'I want cock and I want it *now*!'

8

The sun slanted through windows that were not in the right place.

Amber opened her eyes groggily, totally disoriented. The mattress beneath her was hard, the duvet not right. This wasn't her bed. Then whose was it?

Something large and hairy and all enveloping snuggled up to her. The Abominable Snowman? A real live Yeti from the Gloucestershire steppes? No, it was Ian.

'Morning,' he mumbled.

Amber came fully awake. Then she remembered. She had spent the night in his camper, falling asleep after they had tired themselves with excessive shagging.

'Oh, Lord,' she moaned, groping for her watch. This hadn't been left with her modern clothes: she couldn't exist without knowing the time and had secreted it in her drawstring bag. She peered at the dial, then shot into a sitting position. 'Jesus Christ! It's seven-thirty. I promised to help Diane with the early stint. And I'll have to change first, and wash, if such a thing is possible.'

She was up and struggling into her chemise and petticoat then making for the camper door, barefoot, the rest of her things slung over one arm. Ian watched her blearily, saying, as she let herself out, 'No chance of a quick one, then?'

'I'll see you later,' she said, and ran over the dewy grass to where a queue straggled under the awning and up to the van's serving counter. The unmistakable odour of full English breakfast – bacon and eggs, fried tomatoes and sausages – wafted into her nostrils.

Diane was officiating, hot and bothered. She'd be so cross! There was so sign of Colin. Presumably he was polishing his musket somewhere.

'I'll go and get changed,' Amber shouted.

'Oh, that's noble of you!' Diane retorted with heavy sarcasm, flipping sunny-side-up eggs on to a paper plate. 'Don't put yourself out on my account.'

'Do I smell burning martyr?' Amber asked, holding her own, knowing it was useless to say 'don't get your knickers in a twist'. She dashed off to their tent.

It was then that the whole thing started to pall. Seething, she had sat on her anger about Sarah and flung herself into a bed-rolling session with Ian. Now she'd woken late, there was only a dribble of water in the aluminium container, certainly not enough to give herself a proper wash, and she was still wearing remnants of last night's warpaint and that would have to do for the moment.

Feeling the worse for wear, she took her place with Diane on the business side of the counter. The crush was thinning, and Diane poured two mugs of tea for them and turned down the gas. 'Sorry I'm late,' Amber said, offering the peace pipe.

'That's all right. We did well. I knew we would. Closed shop around one, and they were clamouring for breakfast at six. Colin's on duty. The prince is reviewing the troops this morning. Have you met him? What's he like? Did you fuck him?'

'Yes, I've met him, and he's a bloody knock-out,' Amber said, the tea working its customary magic on body and brain. 'If there was an Olympic event for sexy, he'd get the gold.'

'And? Go on!'

Amber grinned and said archly, 'Give us a kiss and I'll tell you.'

'Fuck off!' Diane returned, and slapped butter on crusty bread and handed her a slice.

'Thanks. Well, I was ousted before I got going on him, by a toffee-nosed bitch who thinks she's the bees-knees but is about as classy as a knitted loo-roll cover,' Amber said, spirits lifting by the second. The sun was out, the camp stirring and humming as the soldiers prepared. There was plenty of time later on for her to have another go at shagging Rupert.

'But Ian was there, wasn't he?' Diane wiped her fingers down her hessian apron, perfectly happy in her victualler's garb, reminding Amber of a buxom Mistress Quickly from the *Merry Wives of Windsor*.

'Oh, yes. I've just left his bed. Jesus, I'm sore all over. I feel as if I've been in a cement mixer or run a marathon. He's so horny, wants to try it every which way. Why are you so cagey about him? Don't you like him?'

Diane settled her posterior on a tall stool, cup in hand and replied thoughtfully, 'I don't want you getting hurt, that's all. All men think through their underpants, and Ian's no exception.'

Amber's eyes cut to her and she pretended to be unmoved, but inside she was breaking up. 'What are you getting at?'

Diane heaved a sigh and put her tea down. 'Look. Don't go into one. The bottom line is that I saw him screwing someone else at Lyncroft.'

'You what!' Amber was livid. She had known Diane for years and had always believed her to be truthful.

'I knew you'd freak! That's why I didn't say anything before, but Colin and I went into the woods . . . it was the night of the thunderstorm, remember? And we saw this couple doing it up against a tree, and the man was definitely Ian.'

'Are you sure?'

'Positive. Do you mind?'

Amber stamped on the jealous reaction that made her

want to rush out and chop off his balls. She was a sophisticated, civilised woman, wasn't she? And hadn't she been seriously contemplating banging his leader, and even the youthful Alan? In a way, this news justified what she was going to do anyway. But it stung, her heart like a piece of raw meat in her chest.

'Mind? No. There's nothing serious going on between Ian and me. In any case, we'd only just met then.'

'He'd stayed at your flat.'

'So what?' Amber did a passable imitation of a free, independent, fuck-you-and-all-about-you woman.

'That's all right, then. As long as you don't mind and haven't started to fall in love with the bugger.'

'*Moi*! Fall in love? Leave it out,' Amber said, too stridently she realised, but it was too late to retract.

'Fine. I'm glad to get it off my chest. I had a lovely time with Colin last night,' Diane said complacently, seeming much happier now that she had come clean to Amber. She beamed down at a pimply lad in a soiled shirt, a battered felt hat and hobnailed boots. He had a staff in one grubby fist, and looked as if he had slept in a hayrick. 'What can I do for you, sweetheart?' she asked jovially.

He took his plastic mug of coffee and sat at one of the rough wooden benches lining a trestle table under the blue-and-white-striped awning. He was joined by a couple of mates, all young, all subject to acne and in a state of semi-permanent erection, dying to be laid. Diane served them, then tidied the interior, washing down surfaces and slinging rubbish into black bin-liners. You never knew when a health inspector might come sneaking around. Amber, super busy to make up for being late and to dissipate the angry energy eating away at her gut, went outside, picking up throwaway plates and cups, empty crisp packets and cigarette stubs.

The madness of Beltane's Night had dissipated, the

beer tent and its environs assuming a decorous air. When Amber returned from reconnoitring, she said to Diane, 'A visit from the vicar would not have gone amiss.'

Amber laughed, but didn't feel very mirthful. All right, Ian, you double-crossing swine, she thought bitterly. Two can play at this game. But you never said, never promised, and neither did he, prompted levelheaded Reason. You swore you didn't want commitment.

'Sod it!' she said aloud. 'Where's that bloody Rupert? I'll show them. Casual sex? Watch this space. I can be as horny as any bloke, more so, as I can come often, whereas they have to wait at least half an hour to get it up again.'

Sue was anxious to have her stall operating, but knew she couldn't be there in person till after the prince's inspection and the opening spectacular. She had left one of her boutique assistants to officiate, a bright girl called Eve, who had pronounced it, 'Wicked!', when Sue mentioned the idea of dressing up for a whole weekend.

Eve had brought along her boyfriend, Darren. They had their own transport and camping equipment and she had made him a pair of brown woollen breeches, a leatherette waistcoat and a plain, coarse linen shirt. He wore thick hiking socks and his own Dr Marten's lace-ups. Though Sue could have done with Eve taking over as boss-lady in the shop, there were a couple of others competent enough to manage in their absence, and it was paramount that she had someone sensible on the stall.

She knew that, being a rookie, she wouldn't join in the battle straight away, but Prudy had organised a horse for her so that she could take part in the rest. She would be allowed to ride in the parade that would take place before the action, and Prudy had promised that, in their free time, she'd teach her how to use a sword whilst in the saddle, and control her mount with the knees, not the reins.

Sue had been introduced to so many people last night and greeted with easy friendliness, all Civil War enthusiasts, mostly Royalists though there had been a sprinkling of Parliamentarians who had strayed across from their own encampment. There were she-soldiers and handsome striplings in abundance, but Sue had eyes for no one but Prudy.

Back in the tent later, Jess had a visitor in the shapely form of a drummer-girl, and Carla and Megan shacked up together under duvets on a double airbed. Sue listened to them making love, the dimness and softness like a warm womb surrounding her. She had begun by removing her garments and lying flat on her stomach with Prudy's face pressed between her thighs, devouring her until she almost fainted with pleasure. They had slept in each other's arms, and Prudy was rapidly becoming not only the one who treated her to exquisite bodily sensations, but also filled the void that had once been her world.

It was different this morning, laxity, levity and sensuality banished, each intent on presenting herself to the prince's eagle eye as near perfect as possible. 'Do I look OK?' Sue nervously asked Prudy, trying to see in the mirror over Jess's shoulder.

'You look just great. Doesn't she, Jess?' Prudy said, adjusting her baldrick and settling her sword at her hip.

'Absolutely,' Jess agreed. 'Don't be nervous, Sue. The prince won't bite you. This will give us a chance to suss out the strength of the enemy. Sir Thomas Fairfax will be reviewing his lot on the other side of the field.'

'Is he really a "Sir"?' Sue asked, fidgeting with her collar. It fastened quite high under her chin, edged with a wide band of point lace.

'Nah! Fairfax was a Roundhead commander,' Jess replied disparagingly, tucking in the ends of her scarlet sash. 'This one's a bank manager from Fishponds, Bristol.

But he's a damn good soldier. Knows his stuff, just like the real Fairfax did.'

Sue realised that she was shaking. It was all very well to don a pretty uniform and prance around in her own showroom, but a different matter indeed to take her place among experienced cavalry and come under scrutiny from the Royalist General-of-Horse and Commander-in-Chief, Rupert himself. In front of all those people, too.

She had tested the gelding that Prudy had cajoled a friend into loaning and delivering. It was a dappled grey who answered to the name of George, and wasn't as docile and well mannered as Sue would have liked. George tended to roll his eyes and flatten his ears, even after she had blown into his nostrils and employed horse-whispering techniques.

'Is he used to crowds and loud noises and gunfire?' she had wanted to know.

'Yes. He's an old hand at musters. There won't be gunfire anyway. You're only going to walk him this morning and in the grand parade.'

This was a comfort, though Sue still had reservations. She was tired of mounting nags who were strangers to her, planning to buy her own and already in conversation with a riding school in Lyncroft where she could keep an animal. A horsebox would be the next expense, and this weekend was a tester to see if it really was worthwhile laying out that amount of money.

'Ready?' Prudy asked, swinging her cloak over one shoulder and setting her hat at a jaunty angle.

'As I'll ever be,' Sue said wryly, hefting up George's trappings.

The paddock looked as if it was a gymkhana waiting to happen. There was a cross-section of sorrels and roans, scewbalds and piebalds, flirting their manes as their owners strove to harness them without soiling their finery or ruining their boots by stepping into fresh piles of dung.

Prudy accomplished the task with ease and, with Thirza ready, helped Sue with George. Then they rode out to join the troop gathering under a massive oak tree. Ian was there, subjecting each newcomer to stern inspection. He was a big man made doubly impressive on Billy who was nineteen hands, mostly Arab with a pale tan coat and silver mane and tail. Billy was skittish and needed firm handling and Ian rode him as if born in the saddle. He stared at Prudy and Sue from beneath his hat brim and gestured to where the cavalry were lining up.

Sue followed Prudy to where Jess, Carla and Megan were already in position, and she recognised Alan, Amber's admirer of the previous evening. She wondered if she had met Prince Rupert, then all other thought was banished as the drummers arrived on foot and the trumpeters on horseback, and then a party of dragoons cantered up, armed with guns as well as swords. The sergeants barked commands and Ian led his troop across the field, towards the foot soldiers, the pikemen and the musketeers.

It was a much larger gathering than at Lyncroft. Not only were the Royalist forces in fine fettle, but the Roundhead army was also well supported and equally fine with their glossy horses, armour and plumed helmets. They, too, had drums and trumpets and Sue felt George quivering beneath her. She fervently hoped he wasn't thinking of bolting.

'Steady on there, old lad,' she said calmly, but couldn't know for sure if this soothed his equine adrenaline that was urging flight. Despite recent brush-up lessons, she had forgotten till that moment just how far from the ground a horse's back was and how much it hurt when you fell off.

It was then that she was aware of that gut-wrenching sensation she'd felt before, a combination of patriotism, romanticism and other sorts of high-flown 'isms'. She

stiffened her spine and kept George quiet with the pressure of knees and hands. She could almost think herself
into this sketch; a solider awaiting the arrival of the
commander. The same sun had shone on the King's men
then as it did now. If there was any truth in parallel
universes, it could still be doing so. She sneaked a glance
at Prudy, wanting to share this with her, but she was
staring straight ahead.

He was coming, magnificent on his great black horse,
his mounted standard bearer a little ahead, and his Life-
guard riding on either side. They all wore vivid azure
uniforms, as did the gentlemen following him on horseback. Known as Prince Rupert's Bluecoats, they were the
crème de la crème of the cavalry.

He came closer, his eyes raking over the officers and
rank and file as he rode slowly down the lines. Lord, Sue
thought, he's an arrogant, handsome bugger. I hope
Amber doesn't get serious about him.

He made comments to his second-in-command, paused
when he came to Ian, had a few words with him and then
passed on. The review was over and the troopers relaxed,
dispersing to exercise their mounts and limber up for their
public appearance.

'Apparently, His Highness was not impressed by the
latest additions to the infantry,' Ian said, taking off his
sword and occupying one of the benches under Diane's
awning. 'He says there'll be problems turning them into
competent fighters.'

'Give them a chance,' Prudy protested, legs spread in a
blokey attitude, hat laid aside. 'This is a first for some of
them. They've never even heard the ordinary words of
command, and haven't a clue about discipline.'

'Ooh, I love it when you talk dirty,' he said with mock
coyness, fluttering his long lashes at her.

Prudy ignored him, following her own train of thought.
'They're needed for the first engagement tomorrow, and

the most the sergeants can teach them will be the basic rules of taking their place in the line of battle. As for the cavalry newcomers, they'll have enough to do keeping their horses straight and advancing to the charge without losing their order. That's one reason why I don't want you taking part yet, Sue. You must carry on meeting regularly with my group in Bath. That way you'll be competent to take part in the next big muster near Oxford in June.'

Sue was not so preoccupied with listening to Prudy that she failed to observe Diane and Amber. Review over, the soldiers had made a beeline for the van. It was so much easier to buy food than go through the hassle of cooking it on camping stoves or slinging pots on tripods over log fires. Diane's idea was a winner. Even a group of Roundheads turned up, wearing breastplates painted black to stop them rusting, serviceable uniforms, buff coats and pot helmets.

'We've got a canteen on site,' they explained, almost apologising for muscling in on a Royalist perquisite. 'But nothing like this. Chips! Excellent!'

'What the hell are these traitors doing here?' demanded the generalissimo, strolling in, so tall that his head almost touched the struts holding up the awning.

'Hello, Rupert,' replied one and clapped him on the shoulder. 'Have you stopped cutting up patients, and started getting ready for us to whip your arse over the weekend?'

'Don't count your chickens, Dirk,' Rupert replied, straddling a chair, his arms folded across the back, as he smiled darkly at his old protagonist, Dirk Corbet, who admired Oliver Cromwell above all men and was even writing a biography about him, in between running a highly lucrative computer company.

Amber saw Rupert and her heart skipped a beat, then went racing on again. She had been wrestling with her suspicions about Ian and was on the point of going over and tackling him, but Rupert's arrival altered the dynamics. Didn't he always? Wasn't he that kind of person? Larger than life and twice as natural.

She pretended to be terribly busy, which, partly, she was: orders for sausages in a bun, beef burgers with onions and a hundredweight of chips coming in thick and fast. 'I'll have to go to the nearest wholesalers in the morning,' gasped Diane in passing. 'We're running out of chips, or shall be after the night-time rush. The freezer isn't big enough. I'll get Ray to bring along another.'

Sweat greased Amber's face and she still hadn't had an opportunity to repair her make-up. It was hot as Hades in the van, and she knew that she stank of frying. She was looking forward to a break when Colin took over for the evening shift. Diane, it seemed, could go on for ever, her batteries charged by the money she was making and the heady assurance of good quality sex.

Ian came up to the counter. 'Two more burgers, Amber, please,' he said, and his face was almost on a level with hers. 'You coming round to my camper later? I thought we could carry on where we left off.'

'Oh, did you? I'm not sure about that. I've been hearing things concerning you, Captain Barrett. You've a wild reputation,' she returned, an edge to her teasing.

His eyes narrowed and he frowned, though more in puzzlement than anger. 'Have I, by God? We'll have to talk about this.'

He returned to his group and Amber felt in dire need of a break. 'I'm going out for a minute, Di,' she said. 'Can you manage?'

'Sure, I can. Here's Colin.' Diane waved and smiled as her lover came in.

It was warm in the enclosed space between the rear of the van and a hedge bordered by trees. A regular suntrap and Amber took off her white cap and shook her hair loose. Her feet ached in the sensible boots she had worn, and she wanted to fetch her sandals from the tent. Not authentic, of course, but a treat for her corns. If anyone quibbled, she'd go barefoot, but it was hard on sensitive soles. She stretched the neck of her blouse and blew down it. Off-shoulder, it should have been cooler than it was, but the sweat was soaking into her tight, boned stomacher. Uncomfortable bloody thing, she fumed. I shall be glad to get back to Blighty.

She sat on the van step and hoisted her skirts high, baring her thighs and letting the breeze circulate round her bush. She could still smell the feral odour of fucking. Without the blessing of a hot shower it was likely to hang around for days. It excited yet annoyed her. Every time she got a whiff, she remembered Diane telling her about Ian and another woman. This had to be cleared up, once and for all. He could tell her it was none of her business, and it wasn't, providing he practised safe sex. There was no way she was going to risk picking up something with a Latin tag and fatal side effects.

A shadow loomed over her. It wasn't Ian's. It was Rupert's.

'I wanted to explain about Sarah,' he began, running a finger round his collar and freeing it, the lace parting over his tanned throat and darkly furred chest.

'No need,' she said, with what she hoped was a careless shrug.

'I didn't sleep with her. I kicked her out.'

'And is that supposed to endear you to me?' She ventured a glanced up at him, and regretted it. He was the answer to any maiden's prayer, and those of others old enough to know better.

'I rather hoped it would,' he replied, dropping on his hunkers beside her, his face and that delectable mouth too close for comfort. 'I've known Sarah for yonks. There's absolutely nothing going on between us ... well, nothing serious, anyway.'

'She's a convenient orifice, is she? "Any old port in a storm"?'

The angry flash that lit up his eyes rewarded Amber's irony. 'I don't need to resort to that,' he said grimly, and one of his hands came to rest on her bare knee, fingers like talons.

The result was catastrophic. Her sex drive took over, persuading her that what he did or had done with Sarah wasn't worth spit. He was here now bearing, if not the olive branch, then an almighty bough of the fleshy kind that was tenting his breeches. All she had to do in order to bury her face in his crotch was slide forwards a smidgen.

'You're a conceited bully,' she croaked, losing control of her speech as well as her libido. 'I don't think she cared. She ended up with Alan.'

He smiled, and his bridgework was immaculate. Obviously, being in the medical profession he had mates who were dentists. Amber wanted to put her tongue where they had been.

'Let's try again, shall we?' he said with practised charm that didn't deceive her one jot, but neither could she resist it. 'Come back to my caravan.'

'I'm smelly. I need a bath,' she protested, as he stood up and drew her with him.

'I like it. I spend too much of my life in sterile conditions,' he answered and bent his head so that she was entirely enclosed by him, or so it seemed. The words 'boxed in' sprang to mind.

When he kissed her, it was like a celebration of lust, wanting, needing – something more than sex – so unattainable that it seemed like a battle of darting tongues striving to make the impossible happen. She had never been embraced by so tall a man before, the kinetics of it strangely difficult. Ian was large, but Rupert leaner and six foot five. It will be all right when we're lying down together, she thought. Height doesn't matter then. It didn't now – much – for Rupert picked her up with one arm round her shoulders and the other under her bottom, and plundered her mouth.

He was breathing hard when he put her down and she knew that her chemise was getting wet where it touched her between her legs. They wouldn't be missed, for a half-hour or so. She guessed that it wouldn't take longer, not if he knew what he was doing and he should do, given that he was a doctor.

'All right,' she said, clinging to the front of his doublet. 'But I need the toilet.'

'Use mine. And there's hot water and a shower in the van, but I'm negotiating for an American mobile home that incorporates an indoor flush loo ... like you get on long-distance buses. Can't be doing with chemical toilets.'

He was a man after her own heart, and it was this information more than his charisma and cock size (though this was, as yet, an unknown factor) that swung it – the prospect of a lavatory used by two.

She dropped into her tent on the way, collecting another dress, make-up and accessories. She wouldn't be working tonight and intended to look around, possibly visiting the fairground field and seeing if she could find Tanith. Or perhaps she'd simply hang out with Rupert. With her things in a holdall and her dress in a clear plastic bag, she handed it all to Rupert when they reached the caravan. He took it inside for her while she explored the wonders of the toilet tent. It was spotlessly clean. Otto was obviously a treasure.

In the van Rupert was waiting. No time to take up that offer of a shower or for finesse and niceties. They collapsed on the floor. He was in his shirtsleeves, breeches wide open, his erection all she could have desired, and more. He wasn't circumcised, his foreskin rolled back from a large, purplish helm, the shaft brown-skinned and embellished with a tracery of veins.

Her homespun skirt rode up, chemise no help, though modesty was far from her thoughts. There was a lot to be said for these fashions, she had already decided when screwing Ian. Rupert lay beside her and stroked her breasts that had popped up over the edge of her blouse. He kissed her, shooting his tongue between her lips then, all wet with saliva, licking her nipples. She fastened her fingers round his prick, and he moved his pelvis, pushing into her palm and withdrawing. His hand went down to her pussy. She spread her legs, the newfound exhibitionist in her wanting him to look. She undulated, letting him know her fantasy, making him bring it to life.

He positioned himself between her thighs, and at first she was ashamed that he should see all her secrets. He was a doctor, wasn't he? He must have seen dozens of women's private parts. But it was his expertise as a lover that thrilled her now. He parted her, flicked at her clitoris, smiled when it swelled, and kept on massaging it, bringing her to annihilation. She was tense, panting, crying out, then release poured over her. It was like opening up a hole in the clouds to let the sun shine through. She clutched at his shoulders, tracing his muscles through the thin lawn shirt, his body honed by riding and fencing, not an ounce of unwanted fat on him anywhere.

'Undress,' she whispered. 'Let's take our clothes off and go to bed.'

'Not now,' he answered, lowering himself on her. 'There's not time.'

He pushed his shirt out of the way, took his cock in hand and guided it into her. She moaned and tossed back her head, writhing under him, her inner muscles clenching round the width and length of him. Now he was harsh, even crude, lust taking charge. It was a quick mating, a fusion of flesh and he pounded away, regardless of the way her spine was grinding against the carpet and she did her best to accommodate him, spreading her legs wide and hooking them round his hips, her pubis bearing down on his cock root. But another orgasm was out of the question. She never had been able to come with a man inside her.

'Blame nature,' one lover had said years before. 'It's the design that's faulty, not the man.'

She doubted this, able to come in seconds when masturbating, although it took her longer even with the most accomplished partner. Rupert had demonstrated that he was good at female satisfaction, knowing which button to press, but now he was possessed with the one-pointed urge to rid himself of his seed.

The caravan shook and she felt his final convulsion and heard him bark his satisfaction. He was hers for that precious instant – nothing else was important to him. It only lasted a second, and then, his balls emptied for the time being, he was back to normal.

Someone was tapping at the door. 'Are you there, sir? You should be getting ready.'

'OK, Otto, come in,' Rupert said, without moving. He lay prone across Amber, his face buried in her hair.

She was embarrassed, though Otto took it in his stride. Was he used to finding Rupert in compromising situations? He picked up the blue doublet and shook it out, then placed it fussily over a chair. The sash followed and the cloak. Rupert stirred, rolled off Amber and removed the condom. She pulled down her skirt and hoisted up her blouse.

'Ah, I remember you, though you were better dressed,' Otto remarked, flitting round the caravan, putting it to rights. 'You made it, then? Fulfilled an ambition, did you? To be impaled on Prince Rupert's cock?'

'No,' she said, feeling foolish. 'It wasn't like that at all. I've only recently read about him, when I joined the Banner. This is my first muster.' Otto made suitably big, disbelieving eyes and minced a little, augmenting her first impression of him. 'I'd like you to meet a friend of mine,' she went on, once more in control of herself. 'His name is Alastair, and he helps me in my antique shop. I think you two might hit it off. He's pining for his boyfriend at the moment.'

'Sounds like a marriage made in heaven,' Rupert commented, fully dressed now and taking on the mantle of the Royalist commander. 'Would you like a cup of tea? I could do with one before I spend several hours in the saddle.'

'Yes, I would, and what about that shower?' she asked, bolder now and recovering. Crossing swords with the spiky Otto had put her back on track.

'Be my guest. There's not a lot of water, but it's better than nothing. It filters and recycles itself in a separate tank. The American system will be far superior. Don't you want to watch the parade? Or you can stay here till I come back, if you like, but I may be a while.'

'I'll see how I feel.' With that she reached up and kissed his smooth-shaven cheek, took the towel that Otto presented and went into the bathroom, adding over her shoulder, 'I'll have my tea in here, please.'

Diane was in the doggie position in her tent. Beneath her was a mattress and blankets; above her the canvas roof; each side of her the muddle of clothes and belongings that neither she nor Amber had bothered to put in order. Behind her was Colin, also on his knees and with his cock so far into her that she could feel his pubic hair tickling her.

She was suppressing grunts, and so was he, though the customers had mostly gone, some to rest, others to stroll and the remainder winding themselves into a frenzy about the parade. He held her with one arm to gain greater purchase, and reached round to rub her clitoris with the other hand. She wanted to play with her tits that had escaped her bodice and were jiggling with his every thrust, but knew she'd fall flat if she stopped resting on her knuckles.

Her clit felt swollen and prominent and Colin trapped it between two fingers, pinching it and teasing it until she came, not in a slow build-up, but in one mighty crash. He pushed the last remaining inch of cock into her and his climax rocked her. As if on cue, her mobile bleeped.

Contrary to the rules, she kept it in the tent, so addicted to this link with the outside world that she couldn't do without her fix. Colin withdrew and fell back against a pile of pillows and bedding, his uniform awry, his shrinking cock latex clad.

'Hello,' Diane said, reaching for a towel and thrusting it between her legs. 'Oh, it's you, Ray.' She pulled a face at Colin and mouthed 'my husband'. 'Yes, everything's fine. We're busy. I told you we would be. You want to come over? When? Tonight? What about the business? Ah, so you're closing. No? Leaving Albert to look after the garage and take taxi bookings? Is this wise? Won't he rip you off? Right, if you're sure. Can you bring another freezer? That spare one from the café will do. I keep running out of chips. You've got the address ... know where we are? Right. See you when I do. Bye.'

She sighed heavily as she switched off and slumped down beside Colin. 'Bad news?' he asked, stroking over her hair with tender fingertips.

'I expect you got the gist of it. Ray's arriving later. What a fucking bind! Just as things were going so well.'

'Does this mean what I think it means? We shan't be able to see so much of each other?'

'I don't know,' Diane said, rebellion surging up. 'I don't

really care if he finds out about us. I want him to know, but have to be sure . . .' She trailed off, unwilling to tempt fate.

'Of my feelings towards you? Isn't it obvious?' Colin replied, with a look in his eyes that made her almost certain of his sincerity. 'There's nothing I want more than for us to be an item. What about you?'

'You're so sweet,' she said, leaning into him. 'But when you've been battered and bruised like me, then it's hard to believe that a relationship will last. Happy Ever After seems a dream.'

'There comes a time when one simply has to have faith and take that leap into the void,' he assured her, and sounded so convinced that Diane was tempted to believe he was right.

'I'll may tell him before the weekend is over,' she said. 'But if I do, you'll have to stand by me, for he can be a nasty-tempered little runt who never hesitates to take it out on those around him.'

'He won't try anything with me around,' Colin vowed, and Diane glowed. She had found her Sir Galahad at last.

She rang Toyah, just to make sure that all was well with the Honey Pot, then lay back on the mattress, seeking the solace of one more perfect coupling with Colin, before reality impinged on her Eden in the shape of her spouse.

9

Tanith was nowhere to be seen.

Amber roamed the miniature township of booths and stalls and tents, searching for her. There were several other mystics offering similar services and she was tempted to see if they forecast her future in the same way, but passed by, deciding to leave well alone. Most of the public had gone to watch the Silver Banner parade. The traders were idling and chatting, the roundabouts at rest with their pipe organs silent, a lull over all. Amber could hear the clarion call of the trumpets and the rattle of the drums from the distance. She imagined Rupert riding out, and Ian backing him up, with Prudy and Sue and the rest of the girls and boys of the cavalry jogging along behind him, like a musical comedy chorus.

The outdoor stage was empty of all save a couple of laconic soundmen twiddling with wires and testing the acoustics. Those who had come to see the bands squatted outside their benders skinning up. A Punch and Judy show entertained the children. Next to this, face painting was in progress, the kids emerging as lions with whiskers or stripy tigers or clowns or even sad pierrots with a teardrop. A penny arcade was flourishing, the bleep and clink of slot machines telling of money won and immediately lost. Pinball Wizard, Amber thought. She nodded to people in costume; there was a camaraderie among the Bannerites, even if they were on opposite sides.

She wondered what Diane was doing with Colin otherwise engaged and a hiatus in the feverish demand for hot dogs. Other food sellers occupied pitches here and there, including an organic set-up, but none was as clean, efficient or appetising as hers. I'll go find her, Amber resolved, and then wait to see what this evening brings forth. Will it be Rupert, Ian or Alan? Or none of these? She suspected that the war would have probably taken over by then, with much machismo debate and battle strategies and lofty disregard of the fleshpots in the face of duty – with the exception of ale.

She rounded a corner in one of those makeshift streets and stopped, astonished. There stood a medium-sized white marquee, suitably hung with banners, and with a billboard outside announcing tonight's attraction.

'At seven-thirty. *El Fuego*. Live Flamenco, dance, song and guitar.'

'I don't believe it,' she said out loud, but couldn't deny the same poster that she had seen at Elberry Village Hall.

Of course. This was the sort of venue where they might well appear. A celebration of music from different countries and varying cultures. Camilo. Was he still the star turn? The marquee appeared to be deserted and she walked in. It seemed very large and very empty, apart from row after row of chairs that swept back from the end where, on a wide decking spread, *El Fuego* would perform. And there, all by himself, seated on a stool with his legs crossed and a guitar held high against his chest, his long, supple fingers plucking out notes of Moorish origin, was Camilo.

He was unaware of her at first, and she walked slowly down the centre aisle towards him. His hair fell forwards over his face and he was absorbed in the music. His skin looked very brown compared to his white T-shirt, and his blue jeans were as tight as his dance trousers. He wore trainers, not flamenco boots. He looked up sharply, as an animal will when it scents a stranger.

'Camilo,' Amber said, reaching him. 'Don't you remember me?'

'Amber,' he answered, and placed the guitar on its stand and rose to take both her hands in his. 'Of course. How could I forget? But just for a moment, I thought you were a ghost. It's your dress . . . from another age. Are you part of this pageant?'

'Yes. Oh, it's so good to see you!' she blurted out, the feel of his slim, warm hands on hers making her want to fall down on the decking with him. She marvelled anew at his expressive eyes and fine-boned features, having forgotten temporarily just how handsome he was.

His frowned a little, his face sad, and said reproachfully, 'You didn't phone me.'

'Neither did you get in touch with me,' she shot back promptly.

He shrugged in that special way only achieved by Latin races. 'I was not certain that you wanted me. I'd never upset a lady.'

A fine excuse, she thought, and how well you can toss those balls and manipulate my feelings. And all the time she was seeing the images that had come to mind in Tanith's tent where she had danced naked with him and fucked him till she was senseless. She was tempted to tell him. He wouldn't be sceptical, she was sure. Perhaps he, too, had the 'sight'. Maybe it would be in his Romany genes.

'And you're working here?' she said, trying to make conversation when they both knew where this was leading.

'Tonight,' he answered, still standing so close that his chest pressed against her nipples and his hands clasped hers. 'One performance only. Tomorrow we go to Shaftesbury.'

'You tour so much. Do you have women everywhere you go?'

'I don't want to speak of that,' he said seriously. 'Only of you and me. I knew we would meet again. I mean it when I say I want you to see my home. Come to Spain at the end of the season. Say you will, Amber. Ah, you are so lovely and that dress, cut so low, and that thing that pushes your breasts up. I can see your nipples. I want to kiss them.'

As he talked, he moved back and took her with him. There was a dressing room behind the stage, canvas walls, canvas roof, a mirror and table, a couch and chairs, a clothes rail.

'We can't. Not here,' she protested, but didn't put up much of a struggle. 'Where are the rest of them? Angelita, Juan and the others?'

'Back at the hotel or shopping. I don't know. They won't be here yet.'

'They might come walking in.'

He chuckled, and this made her smile, too. She felt at ease with him, more so than Ian or Rupert. As far as she could judge, he was a simple man. There didn't seem to be a devious bone in his body, whereas Rupert was too clever by half and Ian had agendas of his own.

'If they do, then they'll walk out again,' he said and dropped to his knees and burrowed under her dress, adding, slightly muffled, 'I love these so full skirts. And no panties! *Madre de Dios!*'

Indeed! she thought, hoping he wouldn't smother under there, thankful that she had managed a shower, no matter how frugal, and then forgetting everything as his hands cruised up her thighs and arrived at their destination.

'Oh, Camilo,' she panted, giving herself up to pleasure as his fingers held her open and his tongue fondled her clit. She swayed at each delicious lick and the spasms built. She was too close to coming to care if anyone walked in on them.

He murmured low, his words vibrating against her clit, then he sucked her labia, gnawed at them with little nibbles, and drew her clit into his mouth and sucked. She had wondered how he would be at cunnilingus and now she found that she was in the hands, or rather the mouth, of an expert. He rubbed the sensitive spots each side of her clit, meanwhile using a butterfly wing flutter on the swollen head. She wanted to put down her hands and pull his curly head tight against her, but her clothes were in the way. Even though she pushed herself into his face, he still managed to keep it agonisingly gentle.

Would she come? Of course she would. Nervous, shaking with eagerness, she moaned her need and Camilo responded, holding herself open and exposing her clit to his fast-moving tongue-tip. Climax poured over her and swept her away on a torrent of sensation. Her legs were shaking. She wanted to lie down. She wanted to grab for something to hold on to. She wanted more.

Camilo popped out from under her skirt like a stage magician from a trapdoor. He was smiling, his lips shiny with her juices. His erection was monumental, straining the stitching of his jeans. She felt guilty, wanting to unleash it, take it in her hand, give him as much pleasure as he had just lavished on her.

He held her in his arms, and kissed her, his mouth tasting of her. 'It's unfair,' she murmured. 'What about you?'

He touched his swollen penis proudly. 'Don't worry. It will keep till later. I'm so hot that I shall dance superbly. You will come to see me?'

'I'm not sure if I shall be able to get away. I'm helping my friend with her catering van.'

'We shall finish at ten. I'll wait for you and we can go back to my hotel. You'll do that?'

How could one refuse this beautiful Spaniard with flashing eyes, a fascinating accent, an agile body and cock to die for?

'Yes, I'll do it,' she promised. 'How do we get there?'

'I have a car. We don't travel in a van or one of those people carriers. There's not much equipment. Juan has a car, so has our manager, and I have one also. This gives us freedom.'

'And you like your freedom, Camilo?' she asked.

'I do, but would give it up for you, Amber.'

Oh yes, she thought sardonically as she kissed him then left him. Pigs might fly!

'What a little beauty,' Ray murmured to himself, caressing the steering wheel with the care and attention he never applied to women.

It was his new toy, this maroon taxi which, to him, breathed class. It had to be superior. Hadn't it cruised the West End, Mayfair, Oxford Street and probably passed Buckingham Palace? He had not yet got over the thrill of owning it. To him, it was a status symbol. His mother had been full of praise when he took her to the supermarket in it. This brought a smile to his face, then he scowled, remembering Diane's tepid reaction.

She never encourages me, he thought sullenly. All right, so she agreed that it was smart and might pull in customers, but she's never enthusiastic. I get totally pissed off with her. And I got her that bloody van, didn't I? Just like she wanted. And is she grateful? Is she fuck! Treats me as if I'm something she's scraped off the bottom of her shoe. Her and her stuck-up bloody mates ... that cow Amber, and that holier-than-thou Sue who looks down her nose at me.

But the sheer pleasure of sitting on the leather driver's seat in its own little glass compartment, knowing that in the back there was seating for five plus a generous space for luggage restored his good humour. He applauded the small white metal plaques screwed into prominent places in the interior that read: NO SMOKING. NO DRINKING. NO EATING.

Great! There would be plenty of room for fucking, not by his punters, needless to say, there was no way he would permit them to enjoy themselves, but for him, if and when the opportunity arose. For some time now he had thought of being unfaithful to Diane. The bitch didn't deserve his loyalty, with her cool hostility and continual harping on about his inadequacy in business and, he suspected, her dissatisfaction in the sex department.

One thing stopped him, apart from the fact that he found it difficult to strike up friendships with women, and that was Diane's hold on the purse strings. She ruled the roost when it came to finance, and he had always been relieved to let her do so, too lazy to learn even the most basic book-keeping. It was his proud boast that he had never been to see a bank manager in his life, leaving all this in her capable hands. Should he upset her and she decide to turf him out of the matrimonial home, then he'd be up shit creek with no means of propulsion.

He took the motorway that bypassed Bristol, consulting the scrappy bit of paper on which he'd jotted down Diane's directions. Hell of a way, he grumbled. But I'll make sure I get something out of it. She'd fixed him up with a costume supplied by Sue. He rather fancied himself in it – sort of mein host, the landlord of a tavern – breeches and shirt, jerkin and hose, buckled shoes. He'd popped into Razor Ted's and had a once-over, his scalp showing pink through the Number One stubble. I look like a GI, he had thought, prinking in the barber's mirror. Yes, a Number One was definitely superior to Number Two; that was for pansies. I could be in Vietnam, could be acting in the film *Platoon*. The girls will go mad for it. They'll run their hands over it, say it feels all scrubby and sexy. His cock made its presence felt, swelling behind his jeans zipper.

It was warm in the cab, the carriageway wide and straight, with greenery either side, part-grown trees planted when this mammoth means of travel and communication was first constructed. The miles swept under Ray's cab, and the sun made him randy, shining straight through the windscreen on to his crotch. He wished Diane was sitting on it, despite her nagging and those veiled insults directed at his equipment. He thought ahead. They'd be sleeping together in a tent tonight, just like a couple of teenagers camping out. His cock uncoiled further and he cupped it in his hand. He only needed one to steer, another advantage of an automatic, you could give yourself a feel – plus diesel was marginally cheaper than petrol.

Slow down, he registered, as the signs appeared. Dorrington twelve miles. He took a side road and had covered most of the distance, when he became aware of a vehicle ahead. It was stationary, pulled on to the verge. A woman was bending over the engine, half hidden by the upraised bonnet. Ray couldn't see much of her, only a generous bottom in a long dark green skirt.

He pulled up beside her, got out and said, 'Can I help?'

Surprised, she looked round. 'Depends,' she said, staring at him, her eyes black as boot buttons, the lashes thick with mascara. Her voice reminded him of the loud-mouthed females in *EastEnders*. 'Know anything about engines?'

'It's my trade,' Ray said and took her place as she stepped aside. He was excited and wanting to show off. 'I'm Ray, by the way, Ray Wexford.'

'And I'm Janice Cole. Nice to meet you, Ray.'

'You, too, Janice.'

She was strongly built, with large breasts and an aquiline nose, wide cheekbones and an even wider red mouth. She was a thrusting person, handsome in a hard sort of way, over forty but done up to look younger. Her skin was olive, and her hair, falling below her waist in a long sweep, was the colour of a raven's wing, perhaps too ebony to be natural. Ray didn't care if the whole shebang came out of a bottle. She stood looking at him, hands on her hips, exuding confidence.

'What's wrong with it, then?' she asked, and Ray smelled her perfume as she leaned nearer. It was something sweet with a musky undertone. Body spray, hair lacquer and woman odour. It was a potent brew that made it hard for him to give his full attention to the spark plugs.

'Give us a minute. I dunno yet,' he ventured, though hazarded a guess. Nothing serious; faulty wiring that he could fix easily, but he wanted to impress Janice. He fiddled a bit more, then straightened and said, 'Jump in and give her some choke.'

Janice did so and, after a few fits and starts, the car purred into life. 'Bloody wonderful,' she exclaimed as he leaned in at the window. 'Are you a professional?'

Ray grinned. 'I've my own garage,' he said.

'And a taxi service? What a cab! She reminds me of home.'

'You come from London?' Ray didn't want her to simply drive off, the contact over. She was too attractive and, from what he could tell, up for it. Her body language was saying it all.

'That's right, born and bred in Fulham,' she replied, and her eyes were resting on him with what he could only deduce was interest.

'Then what are you doing in this neck of the woods?'

'Can't you tell by the costume? I don't generally go out looking like this.' She indicted the ankle-length skirt, and the black boned bodice that reduced her waist and exaggerated her breasts. 'Don't get me wrong. I like to dress up, but it's usually in leather gear. No, I belong to the Silver Banner, and we go around the country putting on battles.'

'Ah, yes. You must be going to Dorrington. I'm heading there, too. My wife's running a catering van.' Ray couldn't believe his luck.

'Yes, I'm staying there. Just came out to go shopping and was heading back when I broke down. A catering van, you say? Is her name Diane?'

'That's right, and it's her first time out. I offered to give her a hand. I've got my costume in the back of the taxi.'

'I know her. A blonde lady, very attractive. I thought she was with the chap that's always hanging around. He's a musketeer. They seem very friendly. But then, anything goes at the musters. That's why I like them so much. Why don't we drive back together and you can visit my caravan. Diane can do without you for a while longer. I want to thank you properly. What d'you say?'

Jealousy rose. Di being dicked by another man? But he was really much more interested in getting this one in the sack. There was nothing he could say but yes.

Nothing when they got back to Janice's caravan but Yes! Yes! YES!

'I think you're a naughty boy who needs to be punished,' she said, closing the door and taking off her skirt. Beneath it she wore leather crotchless panties, suspenders and shiny black stockings that were nothing at all to do with the Banner.

She pushed Ray back on the bed and slowly, teasingly, undid her bodice. Beneath it a bra with nipple slits exposed her hard brown teats. Standing right in front of him, she pulled apart the opening in her knickers and showed him the glory of her shaven pussy. Bald as a coot, it glistened pinkly and Ray's cock almost shot its load in his pants when he saw that her labia were pierced by little gold rings. He sat up and stared.

'Let me touch,' he croaked.

'Bad boys shouldn't be allowed,' she hissed and slapped her thigh with a small whip consisting of short leather thongs, each knotted at the end.

'Please,' he whined and extended a finger, the tip

touching her pronounced clit head. A tiny bar from which a diamond sparkled punctured the hood.

Janice drew in a breath. Her body stiffened and she pushed her pubis towards him, her treasures on full view. 'Give it a tiny rub,' she demanded gruffly, and her eyes rolled back as he did just that, flicking the jewel and tickling her clit.

Her lids shot open. 'Stop!' she cried. 'Get your trousers off.'

Ray almost came with fright and excitement. He staggered to his feet and struggled with his laces. Trainers came off, and socks, then the jeans and boxers. His sweatshirt didn't hide his cock. It stood out from his body at an upward angle as if trying to look at him, eye to eye. Janice lifted it in her hand, then reached below and cradled his balls.

'Nice packets,' she remarked, and lifted one foot, then placed it on the back of the sofa bed.

'Gorgeous,' Ray groaned, unable to tear his eyes away from Janice's crotch. He had only ever seen Diane's, apart from that of a sixth-form slut who had offered to show him her fanny at the school disco when he was a youth. That and the centrefolds of porn mags.

'I may let you suck me, if you behave,' Janice replied firmly, then snapped manacles on his wrists and attached them to rings screwed into the caravan walls behind the bed.

'What are you doing?' he spluttered, not knowing whether to be pleased or sorry.

'You dare to question your mistress?' she shouted, her voice as hard as her face. The whip cracked and pain shot through him as it landed across his thighs. He automatically brought his legs together to protect his testicles, but she would have none of this, kicking them apart.

'I'm sorry,' he said, and his flesh glowed hot and his cock was even stiffer, oozing pre-come.

She slashed him again, one of the thongs catching him on the stem. 'Sorry isn't good enough. And what are you to call me? Mistress. Goddess. Don't forget, you shameful toad!'

Ray's mind was in turmoil. He had read about bondage in the top-shelf magazines, had wondered how it would be to have a woman dominate him, but had never expected it to be this good. To be at Janice's mercy made him delirious. He wanted to debase himself, to be her slave. Diane? Who was she? No one of importance any more.

'Mistress,' he whimpered. 'Make me come.'

'Are you daring to ask for a privilege? Come? I might not let you. I might make you wait for hours,' she retorted haughtily, and searched in a bowl on the side, producing a black condom and rolling it over his straining penis. Then, with cruel deliberation, she sat astride him, held her pussy apart through the panty slit, and lowered herself on to his cock.

Ray felt her moist channel engulfing him, and he groaned. His helm butted against her cervix and he could not help thrusting upwards, increasing the pressure. She laughed and sat still, and her teasing infuriated him. He became crafty, moving hardly at all, concentrating on the orgasm that was building up in his balls, encouraging it with small motions, determined to thwart her and come in a blinding rush when she least expected it.

Janice tensed and pulled out. She slid up his chest, soaking his shirt with her juices. Now she straddled his face, saying, 'Suck me.'

Hardly able to breathe, feeling he was dying in the wonder of her fragrant, hairless slit, he felt for the hard nub and licked it. Janice sat upright, pulling at her nipples through the bra openings, her lips slack, her eyes half closed. He could tell she was close, and increased the pace of his tongue. Janice jerked and she gave a sobbing sigh. His mouth was infused with a fresh gush of juice.

'Naughty slave,' she murmured, holding him by the ears to keep him at her pussy. 'I didn't say you could bring me off. But I'll forgive you this time.'

She gave him a playful lash with the whip, then wriggled down till she was once more riding him. Unable to move his arms, Ray made good use of his hips, propelling his cock in and out while she bounced to meet the strokes. I'm there, he thought, rejoicing. No one can stop me now. And release, more exquisite than any he had ever known, sent his spunk jetting into the condom.

Sue was exalted. Never had she felt so excited, thrilled, proud and downright pleased with herself as when, the parade over, she jogged back to camp with Prudy. She was hot, she smelled of George's sweat, of her own body, and the strong perfume of saddle leather. The crowd had shouted and cheered and roared their approval, and this made her feel like a million dollars. They liked them. They liked the Silver Banner. It took them away from their humdrum existences. It was worth all the effort and organisation.

When she had seen to George – the horse's welfare always the first requirement of a cavalryman – she hobbled to Diane's van for refreshments, bandy-legged and stiff, needing above all a strong cup of tea. She wanted to get out of her sweaty shirt, but was concerned about her friends. She had been too wrapped up in her own affairs that day to pay them much heed. The first thing she noticed was Ray. This came as a nasty shock, although Diane had mentioned something about him coming. He was trying to take over and Diane looked annoyed

'So, he's arrived?' Sue said, managing to have a word with her.

'Bloody hell, yes. He's causing chaos already. A walking disaster area. An accident waiting to happen. But at least he brought the spare freezer. I can't quite get his measure.' Diane looked distinctly flustered. She had been much calmer before he showed up. 'He's cocky, somehow, and there's this woman hanging around. She's called Janice and he helped her when she was broken down at the side of the road. I think he may have a fan.'

'That'll be a first.'

'Absolutely. It's gone to his head.'

'You care?'

'Not really. It might prove a blessing in disguise. Have you seen Colin?'

'He's marching back with the musketeers. I shouldn't think he'll be long.'

Sue retired to her seat, mug held between both hands, and watched Diane and her husband and the woman called Janice. Amber came in shortly after, slipped on to the bench beside her and said, stars shining in her eyes, 'Guess who's performing in the next field?'

'I don't know. Elvis Presley?' Sue distrusted that look. It always boded ill. Amber was probably about to do something extremely foolish.

'Camilo,' Amber replied, on a note of triumph.

'*El Fuego*? Here?' Sue was surprised and apprehensive, too. Didn't Amber have her hands full with Ian and Rupert? Did she really need another complication? Apparently she did.

'Yes, just for tonight. He's off again tomorrow. Oh, Sue, he's looking great.'

'You've fucked him?'

'Not yet, though he did spend some time under my skirt. I'm meeting him later and we're going to his hotel.'

'Won't Di want you?' This smacked of trouble to Sue.

'Ray's here, isn't he? And Colin will be about.'

'And you're not going to bother with Ian or Rupert?'

A troubled expression crossed Amber's face. 'I don't know. From what I know about Ian, and from what I've seen of that cow Sarah, I'm not sure if they're worth it. Anyhow, there will be time when Camilo's gone.'

'Wow! All this intrigue. What's happening to you, my friend?'

'I don't know. Perhaps I'm beginning to take charge of my life at last.'

Sue shrugged and ordered another mug of tea, then waited for Prudy who soon arrived with a gaggle of knackered troopers. She sank into a chair while Jess fetched refreshments. Sue thought she looked amazing, hair awry, cheeks glowing, redolent of health and strength and purpose.

'That went without too many hitches,' she declared. 'I can't wait for the battle.'

'Wish I was coming,' Sue sighed. 'I'm sure people must have joined in who could handle a horse but who'd never fought before.'

'I expect they did,' Prudy said. 'There are lots of aspects of the Civil War that we can't reproduce. It wouldn't be practical. We don't bring dogs with us, for example, and in the real armies hounds would have come along, and the officers brought their hawks. It was a matter of foraging on the way. The soldiers had to feed themselves and drove cattle with them, for meat and milk. That's why they raided hamlets, stealing chickens and pigs. By the end of the war, villagers hated the sight of soldiers, no matter who, and fought them off. The peasants formed themselves into a force they called the Clubmen because they had no weapons except cudgels. They guarded their property against all comers.'

'Grim old times,' said Sue, thinking, she's well clued up. Time I did some homework.

'Drink up,' Prudy chivvied her. 'I want to get out of these things and into fresh. Fancy going into Dorrington for a slap-up meal tonight?'

'Fine,' Sue replied, but though Prudy captivated three-quarters of her attention, there was enough left for her to continue fretting over Amber and Diane.

'We need to talk,' Amber said to Ian, bearding him in his camper van. She had almost made up her mind not to broach the subject of him screwing a woman against a tree during a thunderstorm, but her sense of fair play demanded that he was given the chance to explain.

'Hello there,' he said, beaming at her over his spritzer. 'D'you want one?'

'Thank you,' she said and settled herself on the bed-settee.

He came and sat beside her, shirtless, his hirsute brown torso glistening with water. The smell of soap hung about him and wine and a peaceful tiredness as of a job well done. She wondered if it would be better to leave well alone.

'You're being mysterious,' he said, eyeing her and passing over a glass. 'What's up?'

'It's something I heard from my mate, Di,' she began, feeling foolish. 'Apparently she saw you at Lyncroft. In the woods. You were fucking a woman.'

He raised a peaked and puckish eyebrow at her. 'So?'

'So, you'd spent the night before with me.'

'Ah. Do I detect the green-eyed monster?'

'No,' she said huffily, then drank her wine and soda water too fast. It made her choke.

'Come, come,' he soothed, patting her back. 'We'd only just met. How as I to know that it wasn't more than a one-nighter?'

'So you admit it? Di was right.' This hurt and she couldn't figure out why.

His face sobered and he looked her in the eyes, his bright blue gaze robbing her of argument. 'It's true. I admit it. There's this married woman, Gina. Her husband is our quartermaster. She follows him round the musters. I've seen her at several and she's always up for fun. She's taken a shine to me, unfortunately, and it was her who your friend saw.'

'Taking pity on her, were you? How sweet,' Amber snapped, annoyed with herself for minding.

'It meant nothing. Less than nothing.'

'Is that what you'll be saying about me?'

'No,' he answered, and moved closer, a strong brown arm sliding behind her back.

She didn't sink into it. I mustn't, she thought. It isn't wise to take any of them seriously. She looked at him, and smiled tremulously. 'I'm glad about that, anyway,' she said.

'And you'll come out with me this evening?' Ian's smile was almost her undoing. 'We can come back here later, and continue this conversation.'

'I'm already doing something,' she said, and stood up quickly.

'Oh.' He looked disappointed. 'Is it Rupert?'

'No. I have other interests, you know.'

'Right. Maybe tomorrow, then?'

'Maybe. You'll have to console yourself with the quartermaster's wife . . . Gina.'

'She isn't here this time.'

Amber was ashamed of the satisfaction this brought. You're a bitch, she lectured herself. You know damn fine that you're going to shag Camilo, but you want to keep Ian on a string.

'Catch you later,' she said with a passable imitation of a man's farewell, and left him without even a kiss.

Diane was fine about her going to see *El Fuego* and renew her affair with Camilo. Amber got the impression that she was relieved, fearing for her too great involvement with Ian or Rupert. She had enough problems of her own, it seemed, with Ray and Colin fronting each other up and further contingents of Bannerites arriving to swell the numbers, eager for the fray, all lusty, hungry and thirsty.

Amber changed into her second best ballgown, ready to trudge across to the next field and the white marquee wherein she could escape England, the musters and their angst, and lose herself in the music, rhythms and passion of Spain.

She stepped out of the tent, and almost collided with a party of women fresh into camp, wenches and trollops by the look of them They sashayed along, heading for the beer tent, making uninhibited coarse jokes in the wake of any passing men.

'Hey, Gina,' one of them shouted at a woman with a frizzy mass of peroxide hair. 'Where's your old man? You hoping to cop off with that captain again? Ian Whatshisname?'

Amber did not wait to hear her reply, walking away as fast as she could. Otto was outside Rupert's mobile home, polishing boots, and she was just in time to see Sarah arrive, wearing a gorgeous dress and sumptuous silk cloak with an enormous wired hood that framed her head.

'Is he in?' she demanded.

Otto pulled a face and jerked a thumb up the steps. 'He is.'

Amber was glad they hadn't seen her and she set off along the path leading to the brightly lit and noisy showground. She could see a group of soldiers coming in her direction; not Cavaliers by the plain uniforms and short hair. They made her feel a little uneasy though she knew this was only a charade. Roundheads, though, and she'd had little contact with them.

She did not pause, looking straight ahead, when suddenly one of them halted and she heard him say, 'Amber, isn't it? Amber Challonor? Fancy meeting you here.'

She stopped and looked up at him. A stern face, though not unattractive, a thin, upright body and confident manner. 'Duncan Crompton,' she exclaimed, recognising a lover of at least two years ago. 'I didn't know you were interested in this sort of carry on.'

'I joined after we broke up,' he said, and he was staring at her in that way she remembered; a proprietorial way, as if she somehow belonged to him and must obey him at all times. It stirred up old resentments, as well as a certain heat in her backside. He had spanked her on several occasions during foreplay.

'Where are you living now?' she said, making conversation, agitating to get away.

'In Bargate, not far from where you are. I've opened another branch of my business there. Perhaps you would like to come to dinner.'

'Thank you, maybe.'

'How are the boys, Andy and Chris?'

'Well. In America with their father. And you, Duncan? Have you married?'

'No,' he said, then his eyes narrowed as he looked her up and down. 'Why are you in the Banner and which side do you support? Your gown suggests a Royalist, with its low neckline and extravagant ornamentation.'

'That's right. I'm a Royalist, and so are Sue and Diane, who joined with me.'

This is silly, she thought, sensing a sudden hostility in the air.

'I can't believe that you'd link yourself to Charles, that Great Malignant,' Duncan continued, reminding her of a kind of Witchfinder General persecuting herbalists who did no harm.

She wanted to laugh off this uncomfortable feeling, saying, 'It's only a game, Duncan. We're playing at it, aren't we? Rather like cowboys and Indians. A chance to dress up and rush about waving a sword.'

'I take it much more seriously than that,' he said, thin-lipped. 'And so do my comrades. There's too much levity and immorality among the Cavaliers and their trollops. It saddens me to see that you are allied to them, Amber.'

She'd had enough. 'I've got to go,' she answered, hand raising her skirt hem from the damp grass. 'Maybe see you another time.'

'You need saving from yourself,' he announced loudly, and she wasn't sure if he was joking. 'We shall meet again.'

'Right. Fine,' she replied, starting up the track and thinking, not if I see you first. The Emperor flashed across her mind and she went cold.

10

'You're home. Did you have a good time?' asked Jason, his voice caressing Amber's ear when she answered the phone.

'Marvellous,' she replied, though wondering if it had been all that great. Traumatic would be a better way to describe it. 'I've just got back. Absolutely shattered. Looking forward to a night in my own bed. TV and tea and toast and little luxuries like that. You can keep the seventeenth century.'

'Does that mean you're giving up?'

'Oh, no. I'll go to the next one on Midsummer Eve. It's being held in the grounds of Pirton Court, a stately home near Oxford.'

'Flea market?'

'Nothing so common. Maybe an antiques roadshow and auction.'

'Worth a look?'

'I shouldn't be surprised.'

She curled up in a corner of the outsized chesterfield, enjoying a gossip with him about trade, back on her own territory and loving it. Alastair pottered in bearing a tray, as happy as a tail-wagging spaniel to see her again. She signalled for him to set it down.

'Shall I be mother?' he whispered, pantomiming with his hands. She nodded. He really was a pearl without price.

'How about coming round to my place for a spot of nosh tonight?' Jason went on, and didn't wait for her answer, going on blithely, 'I'm a blinding cook. TV chefs ain't got nothing on me.'

'That's one thing I admire about you, Jason,' she retorted, smiling. 'Your modesty. But I'll give it a miss. Too tired. Want to stay in my own burrow.'

'Tomorrow?' he insisted. 'I'm dying to show you my collection.'

'What of?' she asked, visualising china or glass, bronzes, pictures – it could be any of these.

'Wait and see,' he said, and she could imagine his mocking eyes and crooked smile. 'All I'm prepared to divulge is that it's most unusual and you should think medical. Can I go food shopping for tomorrow night, then?'

'All right,' she agreed, and found herself looking forward to it.

'I'll expect you around seven-thirty. You know where I am, don't you?'

'It's that lovely house next to your shop ... the Queen Anne one, with double steps leading from the pavement to the front door.'

'That's it. I've spent a lot of time and money on its restoration, but can't grumble as I got it cheap during the recession. See you then. Bye.'

'Another date? Lucky you.' Alastair pouted. 'My love life seems to have gone up the spout.'

'Never mind. I'll get Otto across. He's Rupert Frobisher's general factotum.'

'Oh, is he of the faith?' Alastair sat forwards, hands between his knees.

'A dedicated disciple.'

She talked with him for a long time, discussing Collectibles and how well it had done during her absence. Takings were up. The bank holiday had brought swarms of tourists into Lyncroft. Then she told him all about the muster, the excitements, the abundance of men, the trials and tribulations due to lack of water and sanitation. This made him squirm. She was frank, needing a sounding board other than Diane and Sue who were pretty much taken up with their own amours.

'You see, there are two Cavaliers I fancy, well, three if you include Alan, though I haven't had him yet. But I don't trust any of them. Womanisers, the lot. I met up with Camilo.'

'The flamenco dancer?'

'That's right, and he's lovely, but are there any men who can keep their trousers up and their cocks under control?'

'Rare as hen's teeth, I should imagine,' gloomed Alastair. 'And you're talking to the voice of experience here.'

When he had gone, Amber checked her answerphone. There were two messages from buyers arranging to call and one from Chris, saying, 'Hi, Mom. We're OK, and planning a visit. I'll ring again and confirm.'

Her boys were coming home. Her sons! The most important males in her life. Screw the rest! Glowing with those warm maternal feelings that had no equal, she unpacked, put things away in drawers and dirty articles in the washing machine and then undressed, while running a bath. A shower just would not do. She yearned for a long, hot soak in water steeped in perfumed oils. She shampooed her hair, pinned it up out of the way, put the mobile handy and then stepped into the tub, giving a sigh of sheer sensual pleasure.

Lying there, head supported against the rim, body covered by white foam, with only her nipples and a few pubic fronds breaking the surface, she relaxed every limb, the aches and weariness slipping away. Little vignettes of recent events passed across the screen of her mind; the flamenco show finished, a car ride and a flight of stairs and she was in Camilo's hotel room and in his arms and all over his bed, legs wide so that his cock could get in as far as possible. He had treated her like a queen, one of nature's gentlemen. Nothing had been too much trouble, her every wish his command. She had hidden away there all night, sleeping hardly at all. There was too much sex to be enjoyed. Sleeping would have been a colossal waste of time.

Back at camp next morning and the soldiers were engrossed in the forthcoming fray. She had worked with Diane on the catering all day, Colin preoccupied with his musketeers. Ray was there, ostensibly to help, but the couple's continual sniping and backbiting nearly drove Amber mad. She had begged time off to see the battle and had found it noisy and exciting. The hundreds of spectators were caught up in the furore: the clash of arms, the boom of artillery and rattle of musket-fire and the dazzling cavalry charges led by Rupert. To her intense relief she had not seen hide or hair of Duncan. Presumably he was gainfully employed with the Parliamentarian horsemen, but his presence somewhere on the site had made her distinctly uneasy.

There had been casualties, nothing serious, but enough to add to the realism and keep the ambulance staff busy. When twilight came and the field was the Cavaliers, the Roundheads skulking off defeated, Alan had cantered in sporting an impressive bandage on his left forearm. He had dismissed it airily as a mere scratch, and done rather well on free booze and sympathy all evening.

Amber had deliberately ignored Ian and Rupert, though they had not been much in evidence, invited to a dinner by the mayor of Dorrington. She had been satisfied to see Gina hanging around the camp and Sarah hobnobbing with several young officers, all big talk, flash and gold braid. These pushy tarts had not been asked to attend the mayoral bash.

She had slept alone in the tent, huffy and tired and

certainly dispirited. Camilo was gone and Ian and Rupert hardly worth bothering about. There was a repeat performance of the battle next day, with an even bigger crowd, and the event had been pronounced a huge success. A large amount had been raised for charity. By nightfall some members were already packing up and heading for home, though the majority decided to leave it till the next day, squeezing in a few more hours of fornication and debauchery. The hot-dog van had still been in demand though Ray and Diane had had a barnstormer of a row. He had been asked to drive to the nearest cash-and-carry for supplies, and Diane had learned too late that he had taken Janice along for the ride.

'Why are you so angry?' Amber had asked, trying to calm Diane who was fuming and fulminating. 'You don't want him, do you? Aren't you glad he's found himself a girlfriend?'

'That's not the point. We're here on business. I won't have her poking her nose in.'

This was unreasonable, considering her involvement with Colin, but nothing Sue or Amber could say made any difference.

As for me, well, I sort of blew it with my swains, Amber thought, popping soap bubbles thoughtfully. They'd gone all laddish anyway. Talk about male bonding, with no time for anyone except their comrades, holding postmortems over the battles, blustering, swaggering and swearing a lot. Did they wank each other off? she mused. I shouldn't be at all surprised. They had been really quite boring and she had even begun to envy Sue a little. The she-soldiers, though into the fighting, amused themselves off duty in a much more civilised manner.

Now it was Home Sweet Home, and her sons would be visiting soon. She went to bed and fell asleep right away

with the stereo still on – guitar music, blissfully passionate. Camilo's CD. For once she was completely satisfied –
satiated, in fact. She didn't even want to masturbate.

Sue had started to miss Prudy even before she'd finished
driving over the rough ground towards the road. They
would be phoning constantly and meeting almost at once,
but she was very much afraid she would find it hard to
live without her. The traffic was congested. I should have
left earlier or later, she thought, but it was worth it! What
a weekend! I'm going for this. Prudy's willing to advise
me on buying a horse. We got on so well, and sold masses
of clothes. My orderbook is full. God bless Eve and Darren.
They richly deserve a bonus, and will get it when I've
sorted out the money.

She was bone weary, having risen early after a passionate night with Prudy. Darren and Eve had been already at
the stall, packing the clothes, what was left of them; it
had been in the nature of a sell-out. Then Darren had
started to haul down the tarpaulin, dismantling the frame
and securing the whole caboodle to Amber's roof rack.

Amber. Sue's thoughts turned to her once she reached
Lyncroft and, with the help of her stalwarts, stowed everything away. They were eager to get off, and she promised
to have their money by the next day. 'No sweat,' they
chorused. 'It was a blast. Wick-ed.'

Amber had been behaving strangely. She seemed
totally confused, torn between too many lovers. As for Di?
It looked as if she and Ray had reached the parting of the
ways. And here am I setting out on a new relationship
that seems set to last. She couldn't help feeling a little
smug, as she picked up her mobile and got through to
Prudy.

'Ray, I'm too pooped to talk now,' Diane said grittily,
filling the kettle and switching it on. 'Stop mithering.

You'll get your share, but give me a chance to work it out ... profit, expenditure, things that it never occurs to you to take into account.'

He stood there awkwardly and his scruffiness offended her. No longer in costume – that had been rammed into a black plastic bag for her to sort out – he wore his grubby jeans, sweatshirt and jacket. Some men would have looked desirable with a three-day growth of stubble, but not Ray – not to her, at any rate. Janice, perhaps?

She automatically put out two mugs and dropped in tea bags. She wanted to go to bed, but her work wasn't over by a long chalk. They had unloaded what remained of the catering goods, and stored it in the Honey Pot. The awning and tent would have to be fetched from Amber's trailer, but not yet. The van had been driven to Ray's garage and given standing space under cover, perfectly safe till it was required again. Diane planned to have it scoured from top to bottom. There was a cleaning firm who specialised in this. They would leave it immaculate for the muster at Pirton Court, so hygienic that no known or unknown germ would have a snowball's hope in hell of surviving.

Wearing fatigue-style trousers and a fleece, she sat at her kitchen table, held the reviving brew between her hands, and reflected. It seemed strange to be in modern clothes again. She wanted to wash her hair and have a bath, yet somehow regretted the absence of her sutler's garb. Her head felt light and bare without the white coif. Not long to wait, she told herself. A few weeks, that's all. What an opportunity not only to make money but also to be with one's lover, night and day.

Ray slurped his tea glumly and an uneasy silence yawned like a protracted scream between them. Oh, God, how I wish it was Colin sitting there, she thought. I wish I'd had the guts to tell Ray. I'll ring Colin tomorrow, maybe before he sets off for the school, if I can get rid of Ray by then. I must get down to the café early, see what Toyah and Co. have been up to. When I rang her, she sounded as if she was doing fine. I must concentrate on this money-spinner during our busiest season. I shall need all I can get if I'm to give Ray the heave-ho and come out of it solvent.

She wanted to bring up the subject of Janice, but had nothing to go on really, only a gut instinct. 'Are you planning on coming to Pirton Court, or have you had enough of real work?' she asked, glancing across the table at him.

'Oh, yes. Sure, I'll come. Anything to help you, pet,' he said in that oily way she knew all too well.

'And your friend, Janice . . . will she be there?'

His face turned an unpleasant shade of puce. 'I guess so. She and her pals support the Banner, and turn up at most of their meetings.'

'I see. So there's nothing special going on between you?'

'No more than you and that guy, Colin,' he returned sourly, starting to bluster, a sure sign of guilt in her reckoning.

If you only knew, she thought. If you're as intimate with Janice as I am with him, then we've certainly reached a deadlock. She hoped he was. This would be the perfect solution, but Ray had been hers for many years and the idea of him fucking Janice was somehow abhorrent. But, you can't have it every which way round, she reminded herself.

'Colin's a friend,' she answered frostily. 'He knows everything about the war. A useful man to have around. Unlike Janice, I imagine. She seems a right ignorant pig.'

'She knows lots of things. More than you can begin to understand. What's the matter with you?'

'Nothing.'

'Mardy mare! If you carry on like this, I might as well go and watch the box.'

Diane scraped back her chair and got to her feet. 'Not till you've helped me tidy up,' she said, firmly thinking, then slump in your trough, couch potato, and leave me to bathe and have the bed to myself – apart from my dream-lover, Colin.

What to wear? It was exciting to go through her wardrobe, and how much less restrictive and cumbersome were the fashions of today compared to those of olden times. All very romantic, I suppose, but not exactly my thing, Amber mused, taking one outfit after another from her wardrobe and spreading them on the bed.

She favoured a floral dress: deep pink background with lighter cabbage roses. The material was flimsy. It was cut to fit from bust to hip where it flared out into swirls reaching mid-calf. The top had a sweetheart neckline and frilly, ruched straps. It was feminine and revealing and raunchy, but not too much. It depended on the mood of the wearer. Beneath it Amber wore a gold lurex underwired bra and briefs. Oh, the bliss of knickers, be they ever so scanty. She didn't bother with suspenders or stockings, going barelegged, her feet thrust into pointed, spindle-heeled, ankle-strap shoes made of the softest rosebud leather. A chain with a pendant, earrings that matched, make-up that was bold, hair backcombed to within an inch of its life, and she was ready.

She added a generous squirt of French perfume, then picked up a clutch bag and a pashmina, and headed for the door when the bell rang. In anticipation of drinking, she had ordered a taxi (not from Ray), and proposed to return home the same way. She congratulated herself on thinking of everything. She even had a pack of three just in case.

She had half-expected Jason to live in bachelor untidiness, if not downright squalor, but his house came as a revelation. Far from it: the red-brick exterior was immaculate, the sash windows sparkling, while the hall into which she stepped had a mosaic floor with scatter rugs, a staircase that curved gracefully upwards, and panelled doors surmounted by foliate architraves. Naturally, given the nature of his occupation, the ornaments were superb and in keeping, the furniture in the dining room a ravishing example of George III craftsmanship. The dinner service was Royal Worcester and must have cost a bomb, but Jason served up on it as nonchalantly as if it had come from Habitat. She was glad that he hadn't gone for that tired old cliché, lighted candles on the table. He preferred to show off the chandelier directly above it, and wall lamps of the same vintage.

'Ante-bellum New Orleans,' he explained, pouring white wine into crystal flutes. 'Rather too late by a century or more, but in keeping with the ambience of the house, don't you think? I saw them when I was down there and just couldn't come home without them. French, of course, but then so are many things, including the architecture in the Deep South. Have you been there?'

'No,' she said, shaking her head and becoming more impressed by the minute. Not only was Jason's home delightful, but so was his cooking.

Salad nicoise: basmati rice mixed with tuna and anchovies on a bed of lettuce that had been previously tossed in olive oil, vinegar, herbs and crushed garlic. This was topped with cherry tomatoes, sliced eggs, grated cheese and a mayonnaise of his own making. Served with warm garlic bread, it was light but filling, and complemented by fine wine.

The conversation was as light as the meal. 'Has the shop been busy today?' he enquired, seated across from her, dressed somewhere between formality and casualness. A raw silk shirt, a tie with a large knot, black chinos, black loafers and no socks.

'It has,' she replied, though with that caution inherent amongst those in the same business. 'I've seen a buyer from Italy. Comes over regularly. It seems that many of their antiques and knick-knacks drifted here with the Edwardian upper class, who loved to travel, sightseeing in Tuscany and Venice. Rather like *A Room With a View*.'

He nodded, understanding her fully. 'I know the firm, I think. Is it Tibaldi and Son? Yes? They visit me, too.'

'That's them. They don't try to beat you down too much. Give a fair price. I like dealing with them.'

'Pudding?' he asked, sweeping away the used plates. 'Try this for size. It's a sensational dessert, even if I do say so myself. It's centre is so soft it will melt your resolve.'

'And which one is that?' she asked cagily.

His smile had never been sweeter, or more seductive. 'It depends on what this may be. To go on a diet? Though you don't need to lose an ounce, or to give up men and concentrate on your work? Excuse me one moment.'

He did a vanishing act through a door that linked with the kitchen, returning almost at once with a silver salver on which stood white china ramekins filled with dark chocolate pudding. He served these with warm mocha sauce and extra-thick pouring cream, finished with a generous helping of vanilla ice.

'Gosh! This is melt-in-the-mouth stuff!' she exclaimed, her taste buds pleasantly titillated. 'Where did you learn to cook like that?'

He reached across and wiped a smear of chocolate from her upper lip with his little finger, then licked it, and the sight of his tongue and the way in which he used it, transformed this simple action into something lascivious. Amber's pussy ached and she eased her bottom down against the brocaded upholstery of the Chippendale chair.

'I took a course,' he said. 'The experts like to shroud it in mystery, but it's all a matter of common sense, really. I like to do everything I undertake to the best of my ability. And this applies to sex. I always make sure that my lover is satisfied. You won't have to fake it with me.'

Amber's cheeks were hot. 'Who says I'm going to do it?' she asked.

He gave an enigmatic smile and answered her question with another, 'Coffee and cognac?'

'Yes, please,' she answered, already a little tipsy and wondering if she could be bothered to say no if it came to the crunch. He certainly was very attractive, different somehow to when he was in the auction rooms. Non-competitive in the privacy of his own home, and he had no partner, or so he maintained. Money-oriented, though. The Knight of Discs, sometimes known as pentacles or coins? If she threw in her lot with him, she'd never be short of the readies, provided she played fair – not necessarily in matters sexual, but when it came to deals.

The coffee was strong and Turkish, the cognac strong and heady. Jason toasted her and then said, 'Now for my collection.'

'Ah,' she replied hazily. 'Intriguing.'

He took her through the hall and opened a door on the far side. 'The library,' he said, standing back so that she might enter. 'It also serves as my den and, on occasions, whatever I decide it shall be. You're into role play, aren't you, Amber?'

'It depends,' she said cautiously.

'Oh, I'm sure you'll enjoy this game.'

The library lived up to its name. It was lined with glass-fronted shelves containing volume after volume; leather binding, gilt-decorated spines. A marble fireplace dominated one side. There were deep club chairs, a wide writing desk and, half-hidden by a screen made up of silk panels thickly embroidered with Japanese scenes, an old-fashioned examination couch.

Jason had brought in their drinks and now placed them

on the desk, then went to one of the cupboards and opened it. 'Whatever are those?' Amber asked, puzzled by the metal objects, large and small, stacked on the shelves, along with a pile of dog-eared magazines and manuals.

'My collection of early vibrators,' he said, watching her as he took down an unwieldy-looking contraption that bore little resemblance to the dildos she knew and loved. 'This dates from eighteen sixty-nine, and was a steam-powered massager, patented by an American doctor. Twenty years later, a British doctor invented a battery-operated model, and by the turn of the century and the advent of electricity, dozens of different styles were available to the medical profession.'

'What did they do with them?' she asked, unable to believe that they could possibly give such exquisite sensations as their modern counterparts.

'Victorian and Edwardian doctors used them to masturbate their female patients back to health.'

'You what? I thought sex was kept under wraps in those days.'

'It was, but for centuries women had been treated for hysteria. Symptoms were anxiety, headaches, irritability and fear of insanity, to name but a few. What the men didn't understand was that their women needed to come, and not through penetration – for it was generally believed that sex wasn't sex without that. So, doctors brought their patients to orgasm, not understanding what it was and calling it an hysterical paroxysm. These days, they'd be struck off.'

'That's incredible.' Amber indulged in a mind scenario in which she went to see Rupert in his clinic complaining of this problem and having him finger-fuck her. 'And where did you get all these?'

'I've picked them up at garage sales, jumble sales, car boots and second-hand shops. Most people don't know what they are and I get them for next to nothing. An interesting piece of history that shows once again how women have been misunderstood, when all they needed was a clit-friendly lover.' He came closer to Amber, and she was now in a highly charged state, her imagination running riot.

'But how was it that they didn't play with themselves and get relief that way?' she asked.

'We're talking the Victorian age here, when even piano legs were covered so as not to offend. Girls were brought up to believe that nice young ladies didn't touch themselves, or get aroused or think about sex.'

'That's bizarre,' Amber said. 'Women trotting off to the doctor to be pleasured, and this was considered to be normal, and them so prim and proper.'

'It was a lucrative business,' he went on, and looked as if he wished he had been in on it. 'But the vibrating machines were forbidden to anyone except a doctor. Things changed with the advent of electricity in the home.'

'I can't believe all this,' Amber said, bemused.

'It's true. There were different types,' Jason enthused, 'supposedly for massaging the neck and joints, but the main purpose was never acknowledged. Once porn movies appeared featuring them and the censors realised what was going on, vibrators were banned. Years later they were sold for what they were, but under the counter.'

'Even now they're not freely available,' she said.

'Let's play,' he exclaimed. 'I'll be the doctor and you can be my frustrated lady patient. This is your first visit.'

He straightened his tie, found a pair of pince-nez and a gold watch on a chain, and assumed a sober expression as he sat behind the desk with his fingers steepled together. Amber, feeling foolish, wrapped herself in her pashmina and assumed a demure air, eyes cast down.

'Good evening. Mrs Challonor, is it not?' Jason began, getting up. 'Your husband has consulted me. It seems you are troubled by head pains, bad temper, fantasies of a – ahem – sexual nature, and excessive vaginal lubrication. Is this so?'

'Yes, Doctor Ansley,' Amber whispered, wanting to giggle and then thinking herself into the part.

'And how long have you been troubled by these symptoms?'

'For years, doctor.'

'Your husband is a patient man, it seems.'

'Oh, yes. He's kind and considerate.'

'And he performs his conjugal rights regularly? Penetrating you fully?'

'Yes, doctor. We have six children.'

'Nothing wrong there, then.'

'No, doctor.'

'I'm going to examine you. Remove your undergarments and get on the couch, please.'

His tone of voice was commanding and Amber experienced that awe she felt around authority figures: schoolteachers, clergymen and doctors. She obeyed, stepping out of her panties and standing on a small stool placed beside the couch, then climbing up on to its hard, slippery, horsehair-covered surface. She lay flat, wishing she had been wearing the correct costume: knee-length cambric drawers, several petticoats, a wasp-waisted corset and button boots.

Jason came across and lifted the hem of her dress, back and back, until it rested across her navel. He stared at her bush, and Amber peeked at him between her lashes. He looked extremely serious.

'Now, Mrs Challonor, I'm going to stimulate your genitals,' he said solemnly. 'I shall use my hands to do this and, later, may try out one of these new devices especially invented for the relief of hysteria. Nothing I'm about to do will cause you any pain. In fact, you will find it a pleasurable experience resulting, hopefully, in the paroxysm that will make you feel so much better. Open your legs.'

Amber's heart was thundering as she let her thighs go lax. Jason went straight to the target, no messing. His fingers parted her pubic hair, and he held her labial lips apart. She could feel them swelling as the air played on them. Jason now concentrated on her clitoris, his fingers each side of it, rubbing the flesh and encouraging the sensitive little head to burgeon like a ripe, sugar-sweet pea. He didn't attempt to storm her pussy, though he did dabble a bit, wetting his fingers and spreading the copious juice up her slit. She would have liked him to touch her nipples, but this wasn't part of the treatment.

He rubbed swiftly and she bucked against his hand. A glance sideways showed her that his penis was distending his black trousers. Had this happened in the old days? Doctors must have got excited. She could smell her female odour, and was now totally abandoned, chasing her orgasm.

'Is it coming, Mrs Challonor?' Jason asked huskily. 'Can you feel the beginning of your paroxysm?'

'Yes, yes,' she panted. 'Oh, I can't describe it. So good ... so good ... go on! Please, go on, doctor. Make me well again.'

'I will! Oh, yes! Don't worry, Mrs Challonor. That's fine. Tell me when it comes.'

His fingertip teased her clit-head and she added her own movements, hips raised against that tantalising touch. This added stimulation took her to the point of no return. She felt the first contraction of orgasm.

'Now! Now!' she cried, and this was enough to send her into the most explosive climax she could recall.

'Well done,' Jason growled, cupping her mound in his warm palm, letting her down gently. 'Very well done indeed, Mrs Challonor. You are an exemplary patient. I would like to repeat the treatment but using a vibrator, something that I and my fellow physicians have found very effective in cases like yours. A second paroxysm will be most beneficial to you.'

'Thank you, doctor,' Amber sighed, and her clit was already tingling again as she realised he was about to fetch one from his store.

Which would it be? There were so many for him to choose from. Jason brought one of the heavy types over and plugged it into the mains. It had wheels beneath it so that it could be pushed along by the patient's side, and an attachment that looked rather like a wand with a rotating knob.

'You may sit this time, legs apart and over the side of the couch,' Jason ordered, and switched on. It buzzed like a bunch of irate hornets and the head whizzed round. He pushed her shoulders back so that she was supported on stiff arms, her hungry clit thrust forwards.

He touched it with the vibrator, and the feeling was intense. She grunted involuntarily, and splayed her legs, pushing herself upwards. He slowed the rotation and allowed the head to rest against her dark crack. It was good. Not as good as the magnificent birthday beauty that Alastair had given her but remarkable for a tool more than a hundred years old. Jason wetted the tip in her cleft then smoothed it over her bud. She came without warning, a sharp, fiery spasm jetting through her, so severe that it was almost pain. She shoved Jason and his machine away.

'Honey,' he said, pulling the plug on it and reverting to himself. 'It's time we fucked.'

'So you see, darling, there's no need for us to camp at Pirton Court. Lord Bramley is a friend of Daddy's. They use the same club, and I was at school with his daughter, Jilly. We called her Silly Jilly, but she was OK. We can stay in the house. No prob,' Sarah gushed as she walked round the side of the terrace and stood by the edge of the pool, looking down at Rupert who, mother-naked, was sunning himself on a padded lounger.

Rupert glanced at her through his dark glasses. 'I don't think so,' he said, and felt not the slightest flicker of interest, though she was all legs and bosom, wearing the minimum of clothing. Summer had come and Sarah welcomed the chance to bare all as often as possible.

'Why not?' She stood over him, legs parted, her high heels making her calves bunch. He could see right up her skirt, and this wasn't difficult as it was no longer than a lampshade. She wasn't wearing panties.

'For one thing we are not a couple and never will be, no matter how much you use "we" and "us". Apart from that I prefer to take my caravan,' he answered, then added moodily, 'Move, Sarah. You're blocking the sun.'

'Pardon me for living!' she retaliated, but stepped aside. Her lips drooped and she added in a wheedling tone that irritated him vastly, 'Spoilsport. We could sleep in a four-poster and have a whale of a time. Lots of baths and showers and bubbly. Lord B. keeps a well-stocked cellar. I know. I've stayed there before and Jilly and I got well and truly sloshed.'

'No, Sarah. I'd rather enter into the spirit of the muster, discomforts and all.'

Her eyes narrowed and she said spitefully, 'It's those other bitches, isn't it? That creature from the sticks ... Amber thingy. You've shagged her, haven't you?'

'That's my business,' Rupert replied, resenting this interruption. He had been half asleep, snatching an hour in the sun, the pool ready to welcome him when he'd had enough, the peace of Adelaide Lodge permeating everything.

'I took a lot of trouble to find you,' Sarah went on, flinging herself on to a spare lounger, but keeping her face shaded under the parasol. 'First I went to the clinic, but they said you'd left.'

'I've been operating all morning,' he answered, though wondered why he was bothering to explain anything to this self-centred bint.

'All the more reason why you should take it easy,' she came back smartly, claws out. 'Will your *mature* married woman be at Pirton Court?'

'I've no idea,' he said, but had to admit that he had been on the point of phoning Amber.

Due to some personality defect, probably because she had made no move towards him since that one occasion when they had screwed, he could not get her out of his mind. The words of a song from John Gay's *The Beggar's Opera* came to mind. 'By keeping men off you keep them on.' Is that what Amber was doing? Deliberately ignoring him. Leaving him in suspense. And did he really care?

Basking like a sleepy cat, his penis had been stiff as he thought about her. He wanted to repeat their intimacy and now Sarah, contrary to her intentions, had brought her to mind even more.

'There'd be stabling for Corsair,' she mentioned cunningly.

'He'll be perfectly fine in the corral with the others.' Rupert did not intend to budge an inch. He was tired of Sarah and her spoilt-brat attitude, and had been going to finish with her anyway, even contemplating passing her on to another doctor so that they did not have to meet.

Sarah jumped up, recognising defeat. 'Oh, you're the most unreasonable man I've ever met!' she yelled. 'All right. Have it your way. Sleep in a field and I hope it buckets down with rain the whole bloody time!'

'Anything you require, sir?' asked Otto from the French doors of the conservatory, keeping a weather eye on Sarah.

'Lemonade, thank you, Otto, made by your own fair hands,' Rupert said, rolling over on to his stomach. 'And see Miss Symthe-Jones out, will you?'

'Damn you, Rupert. Go to hell,' she muttered as she stormed past him.

'No doubt I shall,' he replied, and reached for his mobile phone, flagging up Amber's number.

It rang for a few seconds and he hoped she wasn't out. Then he heard her, saying breathily, 'Hello. Amber Challonor.'

'It's me ... Rupert,' he replied, smiling to himself as he imagined her, hair tumbling all over the place, green eyes wide and questioning.

'Oh. Hi, Rupert. I wasn't expecting you to call.'

'Why not?' He decided to play her a little, like a shining trout trapped on his hook.

'Ah ... well ... you always seemed so busy at the muster.'

'Not too busy for you.'

'There were always people surrounding you. You're the commander.'

'It will be different at Pirton Court. A smaller affair. Anyway, I want to see you before then. I've two tickets for the ballet tonight. Will you come?'

'What? Where? I don't know if I can make it.'

'The Theatre Royal, here in Bath. I've a friend who had taken a box but can't use it. Prior engagement or something. You like ballet?'

'Love it ... mad about all forms of dancing ... and opera ... and classical music in general.'

'Good. That's something else we have in common, besides enjoying the most incredible sex together,' he ventured, throwing this in boldly to test her reaction.

There was a short pause and he amused himself by visualising her absorbing this statement and probably doubting his sincerity, then she asked, 'What's being danced and who is doing it?'

'A new production by an innovative young company from up North. They've dared to choreograph Giacomo Puccini's opera *La Bohème*, using his music but dancing throughout, not singing.'

'It's one of my favourites. This seems almost sacrilegious, though I enjoyed the televised performance directed by Baz Lurhmann for the Sidney Opera House. He set it in nineteen fifty instead of the mid-eighteen hundreds, and it was rather like *West Side Story*.'

'I know. I have the video.'

'But as a ballet?

'Trust me. I've seen them before and everything they tackle is first-rate. Will you come? I'm at Adelaide Lodge at the moment. The weather's too nice to stay in town. I've a pool here. We can come back and swim after the show. I'll bore the pants off you by talking about Prince Rupert.' He didn't add that he intended she should drop them anyway.

'I'll pack my costume, then,' she said, sounding nervous.

'No need. It's very private.' Don't push it, he told himself, and gave her instructions how to get there.

That wasn't difficult, was it? he thought after he had stretched out again to enjoy a final hour of sun before getting ready for her arrival and the theatre.

It was a night to remember. Had it been possible, Amber would have wrapped it up in cotton wool and fastened it with a bow of blue ribbon – Rupert's colours.

Firstly, she had never seen him wearing other than Cavalier clothing. When he came to meet her in the garden of his Regency house, he almost took her breath away. A near-perfect draped suit, made from ivory cotton and silk by an Italian tailor, a crew-necked T-shirt, and terrain sandals. His skin was coppery, darker than she recalled, but he had been sunbathing. His thick hair was swept back and braided into a cue that hung over the nape of his neck. He looked different, sterner, his high cheek-boned features expressionless. Then he smiled and his eyes lit up.

From then on the magic grew and intensified: his behaviour towards her, the wonder of the beautiful theatre, the sheer genius of the performance acting as an appetiser for sex. The box was dimly lit and quite secluded, even though it faced slightly out over the orchestral stalls She was entranced by the clever staging, the mime and dance and the funny, poignant, tragic story of young, penniless students living in a garret overlooking the Latin Quarter, but also aware of Rupert by her side, his hand on her knee, pushing up her skirt ever so gently.

His fingers rested on her naked thigh. She quivered. A glance at his face showed that he was looking at the stage: Act Two outside the Café Momus; time, Christmas Eve. Amber didn't press her legs together or stop his hand from wandering higher. His fingertips passed under the lace hem of her knickers and touched her mound, rubbing the curls lightly. She continued to stare at the action on the stage, a colourful scene with principals and crowd dancing to Puccini's superb music. But her thighs parted and he penetrated further. He's a doctor, she thought, and must know every nook and cranny of the female body.

He parted her lips and drummed softly on her clit. She tensed, gasped and reached into his lap, clutching the bulge straining his zipper as she convulsed suddenly but quietly against his finger. Jesus Christ, she thought, could this be a one-off? A first for this gilt and plush stage-box, though possibly not, come to think of its age and history, but certainly a first for Act Two of this innovative production.

It didn't stop there. After the curtain came down on the distraught hero throwing himself on the body of his dead love, a victim of poverty and consumption, the thunderous applause and bowing and flowers, Rupert drove her back to Adelaide Lodge, where Otto had left supper prepared for them.

She couldn't eat, hot and bothered and aroused, so he carried drinks on to the terrace and undressed, then plunged into the pool, his body cleaving through the water effortlessly. Amber took off her clothes, that best pink dress that she had last worn to visit Jason and was starting to think of as her 'fucking' frock, not figuratively but literally, and lowered herself into the pool gingerly. The night was chilly but the water was heated and lit from underneath. Rupert denied himself nothing, it seemed, well able to afford such refinements. Then what does he want with me? she asked herself. The world is his oyster. He can marry into the aristocracy, I shouldn't wonder, or be snapped up by some American heiress who fancies an upper-crust English husband, a surgeon to boot, and the snob value of sending their children to public school. Why me?

Who cares? replied her alter ego. This is the here and now. One day at a time. Don't project.

She struck out, revelling in the silky feel of water caressing her body. She reached the far side and hung on to the shallow conduit that ran along below the tiled rim, then felt the hard supportive length of him behind her.

'This is fun. A pair of water babies,' he said into her wet ear. His hair was streaming, and so was hers.

'Not quite,' she reminded, feeling the rise and fall of his chest against her spine, and the hardness of his prick pressing between the crack of her bottom. She raised her pelvis, brushing against his erection.

His hands came round her, finding her breasts and pinching the nipples. She lifted her own and covered his, holding him there. His shaft was between her thighs, long and hard, sliding past her anus, the helm hovering at her entrance. One hand left her breast and found her clit. Her head was filled with echoes of Puccini's score, her emotions roused by the dance, her whole being aflame with desire for Rupert. Oh, do be careful, Common Sense reminded. Don't fall in love with him, whatever you do. Dangerous. Perilous. Sheer, unadulterated folly.

She stood still, her body responding to the movement of his fingers. Then she leaned back against him, as he allowed her to find her own rhythm. She came on a glittering wave, and he recognised the signs. She smiled in the midst of it, remembering Jason's lesson on the history of hysterical paroxysms. Then, even as the bubble of laughter joined the convulsions of climax, so he nudged against her and surged inside. His was large, but there was a lot of lubrication – pool water and her own juices.

No more delays. He turned her, lifted her and penetrated her, his cock like a heat-seeking missile. He plunged and thrust deeply, and she hooked her legs round him and went with the flow. She couldn't come again, but this was his time, and she enjoyed every moment, even when it seemed he was just too big. He came with a violence that shook them both, then subsided, his chin resting on her shoulder, the water sloshing around them.

11

Keep in line, keep in line, Sue repeated like a mantra. Her first battle, and she was scared shitless.

The cavalry were moving at a brisk trot behind the Palatine flag. This developed into a canter, then a fully fledged gallop and Sue's apprehension increased with every thud of George's hoofs. Gritting her teeth, she dug her heels into the stirrups and gripped with her thighs, feeling the lift of his withers, and seeing his grey mane blowing round his dappled neck. Her companions pounded alongside, and the enemy charged towards them.

They met with a sickening crunch. The cries of men mingled with the shrill whinnying of horses. Blades flashed, clashed and engaged. Pistols roared. Cannons boomed. There was a muddle of dark uniforms and blue and red and green, of orange Parliamentarian sashes and Royalist scarlet.

'Jesus and no quarter!' the Roundheads yelled their battle cry.

'For God and the King!' roared the Cavaliers.

Sue was in the first wave. She braced herself for the shock of collision, then George dashed through a gap. She raised her sword and thrust at a shouting figure as he thundered past, felt the jar of her blade hitting his breastplate, was aware that he was hacking and slashing. By a miracle, she avoided being hit. Prudy was there, rapier bared, controlling Thirza with her knees. Fighting from horseback required a certain cool, and cooperation between rider and mount. Sue had been in training, and had formed such an attachment to the rather erratic

George that she was negotiating a sale with his owner. She had kidded herself that she was ready for combat. Now she knew she wasn't.

The pikemen were stubbornly keeping to their square. The infantry were engaged in hand-to-hand combat. The drummers marched steadily, though some dropped in their ranks under fire from the opposition's musketeers. Rupert was out front, rallying his troops, and the Roundheads were giving as good as they got, led by their own indomitable commander, Colonel Dirk Corbet, who was once again pitting his men against the prince's.

Wounded and dead lay scattered on the grass. There was a lot of overacting, particularly among the dying, and quantities of very realistic-looking blood. The medics moved from one to another, as did the camp women ready to give succour. Ghoulish creatures hopped about like vultures among the carnage, robbing the corpses. The air was thick with smoke and the smell of gunpowder. The spectators cheered and yelled and applauded from behind the barriers.

George was behaving magnificently. I'll give him an extra feed of oats, and an apple and a carrot and anything else he wants, bless his little cotton socks, Sue thought. Her sword arm was numb, her brain whirling as she strove to make the impossible happen; to live in her world and that of the Civil War. Prudy managed it effortlessly. She leaned forward from the saddle and ran a man through the shoulder, or so it appeared, then pulled Thirza to one side, avoided a sweep from another rider's sword, lunged and sent him crashing to the ground.

'Tallyho, lads! Keep the bastards on their toes. Get 'em on the run!' barked Ian, jogging up on Billy, parrying slashes on either side. 'Up boys and at 'em!'

Several Roundhead troopers charged towards him. Prudy rushed to his defence. So did Sue, blinded by the floating red mist of battle fury. Road rage? Sissy stuff!

She took a blow on the head and another on the arm. She heard Prudy shouting a warning and the crack of a flintlock as Ian fired in the face of a man who was swinging back for another cut at him. The messy crimson dye of the war games missile was spectacular. It looked as if his head had split apart. His saddle miraculously emptied.

Still dazed from the knock that had rammed her hat down even more firmly on her head, Sue swung round to see an enormous man wielding a battle-axe. That's not cricket, she thought. This isn't the Viking Society, mate. She struck at him, missed, seeing the axe falling, falling, its shadow blotting out the sun.

'Fucking hell! Whatever's happened?' Diane exclaimed, alarmed when Sue walked in under the awning, supported by Prudy on one side and Jess on the other.

'It's nothing. A bump on the head. I've been checked over in the first aid tent and they've given me painkillers. No concussion or anything,' she said, pale but smiling.

'You'd have known it if that chap with the axe hadn't decided to pull out,' Prudy said, looking anxious. 'But you did well for your first attempt. It'll get easier. Three teas please, Diane, and make them strong.'

The setting for the muster was breathtaking. When Diane had driven in and pulled up at the space allotted to her, she could hardly believe that such a beautifully maintained and immaculate estate would have been offered for an event like this. Apparently Lord Bramley's heart was as big as his wallet and he thought it his duty to sponsor charity. He never hesitated to open Pirton Court and its grounds in aid of a good cause. Of course it helped put the place on the tourist map and he charged visitors for going round the house and motor museum, getting lost in the maze and being ferried across the lake, but all in all, it seemed that his motives were philanthropic.

'It's great!' Diane now exclaimed as she brought the teas over. 'So clean. Even the toilets aren't smelly, not yet, at any rate, and they're properly built loos that flush, and there's a shower block and a standpipe. Apparently the fields are regularly rented out to the Caravan Club. There aren't any roundabouts this time, just Trader's Corner, and a few stalls and a booze tent and a marquee for the antique sale. Plenty to entertain the punters though, including an archery contest, and they love to see the Silver Banner going for it.'

'There's a falconry display,' put in Jess, easing off her helmet and mopping her face. 'I want to go to that. I've always fancied a hawk.'

'You're busy,' Sue said to Diane, nodding towards the customers.

'Very,' she answered; it was satisfying to know that her enterprise had paid off. The trestle tables and benches were full and Ray was sweating it out in the van, serving a train of warriors and hangers-on.

Best place for him, she thought bitterly. They had set up yesterday and, to her extreme chagrin, Janice had put in an appearance that morning. With Colin fighting, a surly Ray had had no option but to assist, but she knew that he'd seek any excuse to be off, sniffing up Janice's skirts at the earliest opportunity.

'I'll catch the sod,' she had vowed, addressing Amber. 'That will give me grounds for divorce. I'll get him for adultery. I'm certain he's been meeting her on the sly over the past weeks. He hasn't bothered me much, and Ray likes regular sex. If he's not stuffing me, then he's stuffing someone else.'

Colin took over from him for the evening shift and Ray disappeared. Diane was due a break, and said to Colin, 'Can you manage for a while?'

'Sure thing. Take as long as you want,' he said, giving

her tightly laced waist a squeeze. 'Are you coming back to my trailer later?'

'Just you try stopping me,' she teased, reaching her hand down and cupping his balls through his velvet breeches. He kissed her on the lips and went back to tossing chips in the deep-fat fryer.

She passed Amber on her way out and said quietly, 'Keep an eye on things for me. I'm going to find Ray. I'm bloody sure he's off knobbing it with Janice. I haven't told Colin. Don't want him to get the idea that I care.'

'Can I knock off soon? It's Midsummer Eve, when all the sprites and fairies are about ... Puck and Titania and Oberon, and magic is abroad,' Amber replied, and Diane thought how much her wench costume suited her. She positively sparkled.

Was it because of e-mails from Camilo, the attention of Jason and his electrical gismos, or frequent calls from her brace of Cavaliers? Could it be that she was looking forward to her sons' visit? For her own part, Diane found Karen an absolute drag and the lengthy summer vacation a trial. She had forked out for tickets so that she could go backpacking in Europe with a gang of like-minded friends, and now worried herself into a lather every time she heard reports of young people vanishing.

'That's OK, Amber. I shan't be long, and then you can go shag Ian or Rupert or whoever turns you on,' she said and left the well-lit van and entered the twilight zone.

Pirton Court stood rather self-consciously on its knoll as if posing for a picture postcard, its diamond-paned windows a dramatic blood red, reflecting the dying sun. Bats swooped and skittered from ivy-hung turrets, adding a further Gothic touch. Lush green lawns stretched down to the tree-dotted meadows where the Silver Banner had their encampment. A lake glistened, dividing the Round-head tents from those of the Royalists. It was on ground next to this that the battle had been fought. It would be repeated tomorrow. On Sunday the site would be cleared, the weekend heroes returning to their humdrum existences, feats of glory simply memories to be taken out and relished and talked over in anticipation of the next occasion when they'd take up arms.

Diane could see finely dressed participants strolling on the terrace. Not all were camping, then. It seemed that his lordship was host to the more important, and she wondered if Rupert would be sleeping soft tonight. Then she saw his caravan parked beneath a spreading oak, with Otto at ease on the steps. She assumed that Ian would be drinking in the beer tent, but neither of these men were her concern, only in so far as they affected Amber.

She turned her attention to the cluster of tents, bivouacs and camper vans, mobile homes and trailers. She knew which one belonged to Janice. Ray had pointed it out in an effort to pretend that there was nothing untoward in his friendship with her. Diane approached. There was light behind the drawn curtains. She stopped and listened. The van swayed slightly. She could hear the squeak of its springs and someone gasping. She mounted the step, gripped the handle and yanked the door open.

She had steeled herself to find them in flagrante delicto, maybe in the missionary position or with Ray ramming his cock up Janice's arse. What she saw rooted her to the spot. They were there all right, but it took her a second to adjust her thinking to the extraordinary sight of Ray in a pink satin negligee that strained across his back, shoulders and halfway up his brawny arms. His wrists were bound behind him, and he was kneeling in front of Janice with his face buried in her hairless crotch.

She stood there spread-legged, clad in black leather, with big naked breasts and a whip snaking round Ray's backside. The dressing-gown had risen up, displaying his pasty buttocks latticed with fiery stripes. His balls dangled between his legs and he was sporting a massive erection, pre-come wetting his helm.

'What the hell ...?' Janice shouted, staring at Diane with a sneer. Ray abandoned his slavish tasks and looked round. The expression of shock horror on his face was gratifying.

'Di, I can explain,' he began.

'Shut up,' she snarled.

'But, lovey ... listen ...'

'I said shut up.'

She wasn't sure what she wanted to do. Anger raged through her, and indignation and – yes – hurt. He had betrayed her with a scrubber, a tart who was older than her, whose hair colouring came out of a bottle and who was probably grey as a badger. Moreover, he was at her feet as if she was a goddess to be worshipped – her slave – and Diane had never once suspected that this was what he wanted. All those years and I never knew! My God, is it possible to understand what goes on in another person's mind? Will it be the same with Colin?

'Did you invite her here, you bad, bad boy?' Janice said harshly, and snapped her whip over Ray's belly and thighs, catching the end of his cock, making him yelp.

'No. I swear it,' he whimpered, grovelling awkwardly in his bonds.

'You'd better not be telling porkies. You know what happens to dirty little cheats and liars, don't you?'

'Yes, mistress,' he whined.

Even in this fraught situation, Diane was aware of a vein of black humour. If only Ray's mother could see him now. Wish I had a camera or, better still, a camcorder, she thought.

'Do you want him for keeps?' she demanded, thoroughly sickened by the pair of them.

'I might. He needs training to turn him into an ideal sub,' Janice answered, carelessly flicking at his rampant cock that grew harder at every stroke.

He's going to come in a minute, Diane thought, watching it, fascinated. He's amazingly excited by being scorned by both of us. I could join in, I expect. Janice and I could bring one another off in front of him. Then we could both beat him and torment his prick and balls and keep him waiting for orgasm. He'd love it.

I need Colin, she thought suddenly. Though these obscene images had made her wet, she had no intention of carrying them through. She loomed over Ray, shouting, 'The writing's on the wall. I want a divorce. You'll be hearing from my solicitor next week.'

'You can't kick me out,' he protested, flat on his belly now, Janice's stiletto heel rammed into his neck.

'I already have. You'll have to find yourself somewhere else to live. I'll have the locks changed. And don't expect to sleep in my tent. Bunk down here with your mistress.'

'I don't know that I want him full time,' Janice said coldly.

'Tough. Ask yourself, can you afford him? He's very expensive and work is anathema to him.'

'I'd soon change all that,' Janice replied, and trailed the whip down his spine from nape to bum crease.

'Good luck!' Diane fired back and walked out. Then she burst into tears.

Nine o'clock and Diane reappeared, red around the eyes and positively steaming, heaping maledictions on Ray's and Janice's heads. As far as Amber could make out, the gist of it was, 'And he's wearing her dressing gown. She's old, she's fat and she has cellulite, and he doesn't mind!'

'What's that to you? You don't even like him any more.'

'I know. Crazy, isn't it?'

Amber left Colin to cope with her, popped into Prudy's

tent where she had slept last night, and exchanged her working dress for a posh frock.

Ray had shared Diane's tent and though they had invited Amber to stay with them, the prospect of close contact with his feet, bad breath and flatulence had not been encouraging. Sue and Prudy had sheltered her and though it sounded very much as if the breakdown between the married couple was irretrievable and there would now be plenty of room for her with Diane (who'd probably be sleeping in Colin's trailer anyway) she decided to stay put. She had deliberately kept away from Ian's camper or Rupert's caravan. Let them seek *her* out, not the other way around. This brought home to her how much more confident she had become lately.

'Lace me up, Jess,' she said, having got as far as the stays that fastened at the back.

Jess obliged, and then helped her into the slightly high-waisted bodice, straining the laces of that, too. Big sleeves that dragged heavily at the décolletage, strings of pearls, silk stockings and satin slippers (a blessing it wasn't raining), a black lace veil over her hair, a fan and beaded purse and Amber was fit, ready to enjoy whatever adventures happened along.

She had made a tentative arrangement to link up with Prudy and Sue near the main campfire. This bordered the lake, the great flames swirling high, reflected in the water, and people were gathering there, drawn by the age-old magic of fire and earth rites of this most potent solstice. The morris men were dancing and weaving in and out and leaping. Whether they were party to it or not, Amber knew that these prehistoric rounds were calculated to raise the energy and awareness.

She didn't find her friends, walking to the lakeside alone, tickled by the wolf whistles that followed her. It was almost as exciting as the Spanish men's greeting when an attractive woman walked by. These soldiers, young and not so young, appreciated her and found her attractive and would like to give her one. Perhaps she even caused a stirring in their breeches. It gave her pussy power and was a boost to her self-esteem, no matter how much of a feminist she imagined herself to be.

Then her loins lurched; Rupert was lounging on the ground, his back against a log, in conversation with Ian and several other officers. His hat was canted over his eyes, his long legs stretched out, and he was looking so astonishingly tasty that she wanted to go across and impale herself on his prick.

Ian was holding forth, shouting angrily, 'I don't give a fuck who said it. It's bloody bollocks!'

'Get it sorted. Colonel Corbet's brigades are too damn competent. They're taking a leaf out of the Ironsides' book. Solid as a rock in the charge. We've got to beat them again tomorrow, or at least make it a draw.'

'We're not playing bloody football,' Ian grumbled, taking a swig from a stone cider jar that a subaltern handed him. He wiped his moustache on the back of his hand and passed it on, adding truculently, 'This is what we're good at. This is what we do. Can't let Corbet get away with it. No fucking way. There must be no farting about and no cock-ups.'

Oh, dear, he's spitting his dummy out all over the place, Amber mused. What's rattled his cage? Should I go and soothe his ruffled feathers and give that arrogant Rupert cause for concern? Or shall I sit with the generalissimo and flaunt myself?

Sarah stalked into the clearing, wearing a Bluecoat uniform with exceedingly tight breeches. This swung it. Amber sank down gracefully at Rupert's side, saying, 'It sounds awfully serious. What's going on?'

Before he had time to answer, Sarah was on her like a fury. 'Get away from him, bitch' she screeched.

Amber saw stars and heard her neck crack as Sarah's

hand connected with her face. She reacted instinctively, leaped up and kneed Sarah between the legs and hit her in the eye. Then she grabbed a handful of her hair, yanking at it violently. She felt Sarah's nails gouging a pathway down her cheek. She brought up her knee again, became trapped in her skirt and they both fell to the ground, rolling over and over, pummelling each other, with Sarah screaming insults. Amber had no breath left to retort, just stubbornly hanging in there, punching her with a viciousness that had appeared from nowhere.

A crowd collected rapidly, laughing and shouting encouragement. Rupert was the first to put a stop to it. Amber felt his hard hands on her shoulders, prising her away. Ian held on to Sarah who was spitting and kicking. As angry with Rupert as with his nasty girlfriend, Amber lashed out with her foot, catching him on the shin.

'Ouch!' he muttered, but did not let go of her.

Amber glared at Sarah across the space between them. Now that the action was over, people began to drift away, seeking more stimulating amusement, goggling at some of the campers who were already splashing about in the lake, most of them nude.

Amber's face was smarting, her bruises beginning to throb. Blood was trickling from Sarah's nose, and the back seam of her breeches was ripped, exposing her buttocks. The expression on her face was murderous.

'Keep her out of my sight, or I swear I'll kill her!' she shouted.

'Be quiet or I'll have you barred,' Rupert grated angrily.

'You can't do that. I'm Lord Bramley's guest.'

'I can do what the hell I like. I'm the Commander.'

Their rage against one another smacked of a more passionate emotion, and Amber wondered dully if he had been telling the truth when he assured her that Sarah meant nothing to him.

'Are you all right, Amber?' Ian asked solicitously, and

the concern in his deep voice was like balm to her physical and mental wounds. 'Shall I take you to your tent? Your dress needs attention. I love to see so much of your boobs, but so do all the rest. A needle and thread wouldn't go amiss.'

She looked down and hastily drew the edges of her torn bodice together, thankful that her pearls hadn't broken. 'Thank you, Ian. I'd appreciate that,' she said, and gathered her belongings before slipping her arm through his. She didn't once look at Rupert as she limped away with as much dignity as she could manage under the circumstances.

'What's happening to me?' she groaned when they reached the tent. 'I've never been violent like this. Never fought at school, or lashed out at Matthew. As for making a public exhibition of myself? It's horrible, and completely out of character.'

'You certainly pack a punch. I'm glad I wasn't at the receiving end. You've got to let your hair down sometimes,' Ian remarked, lighting up a cigarette. 'Here, let me get at that lacing.' He freed her by the simple expedient of slipping his dagger underneath and slicing through it.

'My gown,' she wailed. 'Sue had it made, and it cost me a fortune.'

'It'll repair,' he said with gruff sympathy. 'Get it done, send it to the dry cleaners and no one will be any the wiser. Are you insured?'

'I guess.'

'Well then, there you go. Put in a claim.'

Amber was gazing ruefully into her hand-mirror. 'I'm a mess. Look at my face.'

He grinned wider than the Cheshire Cat. 'You should see hers. She's going to have a right shiner, a black eye to be proud of. She started it, the silly cow. Thinks she owns Rupert and anything to do with him. She doesn't, and every time she shows him up like this, she lessens her chances. He can't be bothered with her. Likes you, doesn't he?'

This startled her. She dabbed at her face and got out her mascara wand. 'Does he?' she prevaricated. She wasn't sure how much Ian knew about her trip to the ballet and erotic dip in the pool.

'There's no need to pretend. He's bound to have had you. He's that kind of chap. But this doesn't make any difference to what we do together, does it? You haven't fallen for him or anything daft like that, have you? I'm warning you ... don't. He's a confirmed bachelor.'

'Are you trying to teach your grandmother to suck eggs? As if I would!' she blazed back, wanting to show him – what? That she was immune to the charms of these part-time soldiers?

It was a shame that Jason had cried off, deciding to give the antique fair a miss: the profit margin would be too low. And how much she would enjoy it if Camilo came dancing in at the tent flap, castanets clicking. But when Ian put his arm round her and drew her down on the mattress, she was too upset, raw and sore to resist her own urges. She wanted comforting. Why hadn't Rupert stuck up for her? Ian obviously laid the blame for the unpleasant incident slap-bang on Sarah's doorstep, where it belonged. Tanith had warned her about an evil female. This must be her.

Ian crushed out his cigarette and Amber snuggled up against him, getting a mouthful of point-lace, a nose full of aftershave and a hand full of cock, which he had now released from his breeches. It wasn't long before his warm, fleshy organ replaced the lace and she sucked him with relish, closing her mind to any thoughts of Gina or others who might have performed the same service recently. If one was going to start worrying about where men put their pricks, then one might as well join a nunnery.

'You do that so well,' he said, his voice low and gravelly. 'Umm . . . lovely. I'll do the same for you. Back off a bit, sweetheart, or I shall come in your mouth.'

Lust clenched in Amber's belly. She wanted him to do just that, yearned to feel his spunk jetting down her throat. She kept up the pressure, knowing he wouldn't be able to resist, feeling him see-sawing his hips as she crouched over him, nibbling at his helm, running her tongue up and down his shaft, caressing his tight balls, then returning to that relentless sucking, her nose buried in his hairy underbelly. She could tell that he was on the brink, his crisis a heartbeat away, and she showed no mercy. He grunted, his cock grew that little bit harder and he was coming, his creamy libation filling her mouth, and she paid him the tribute of swallowing, not spitting. His semen tasted salty, like a mild yeast extract. She rose up, and took in a long draught of air.

'Jesus! That was something else,' he panted, lying prone, one hand coming down to enclose her mound. 'I want to wank you, and then screw you.'

'Better get started, then,' she said and spread her legs.

She came quickly, but he took longer the second time around. By now, she was getting bored, wishing he'd hurry up and wondering if Rupert was doing the same to Sarah. When Ian finally achieved his goal, she let him rest for a moment and then scrambled out from under him. He groaned and freed his spent cock from the condom.

'I could do with a cold beer,' he said, smiling up at her. 'How about you?'

'I don't think I want to be seen, not with these scratches,' she muttered.

'You must face your public,' he joked. ' "On with the motley", and all that jazz.'

'You go on and I'll catch you up,' she said, mourning over her reflection. 'Shan't be long.'

Still shaken, she didn't feel like hurrying, fishing out

some antiseptic cream from her holdall and dabbing it on the scratches. There was no knowing what unsavoury places Sarah's nails had visited. She stripped, then put on her peasant skirt, a tanga and toe-post sandals, a wench blouse, but no stomacher. She didn't feel inclined to adhere to the costume ethos. She fluffed up the sides of her hair and shrugged on a cloak. It would be chilly later and she intended to stay up and see the sun rise at the mystical dawn of midsummer. She regretted that she wasn't at Stonehenge.

She stepped from the tent. At once, she was grabbed from behind, a hand clapped over her mouth and a coarse voice grated, 'Don't give us no trouble and you won't get hurt.'

Too surprised to disobey, she stumbled along between two armed men, with a further two behind her. It was dark, and grew darker as they left the camp, plunging into a coppice and coming out on the far side of the lake. Amber's mouth ached from the press of her assailant's hand. It smelled of ale and leather and piss, where he had urinated and neglected to wash afterwards. Her thoughts were whirling like dervishes. Was this a not very funny, revengeful trick organised by Sarah?

The black bulk of a building appeared. Her captors hauled her over the threshold. It was a barn, a rambling structure where the candlelight didn't penetrate the gloom of the corners and was lost in the height of the vaulted roof. Ancient as the hills, and redolent of horses and hay, cow byres and farmstock, and now occupied by Roundheads. Her mouth was released and she was frog-marched towards a long oak table, and found herself face to face with Duncan.

The eyes of the officers seated with him were equally hard and unfriendly. 'Well done, Sergeant Jenkins,' he said, addressing the soldier who had been manhandling her.

He saluted smartly. 'Thank you, sir.'

'You know this woman, Major Crompton?' asked a hard-featured man with a hooked nose. Like the rest, he wore his hair short, his doublet was unadorned and his white collar plain.

'I do. She is Amber Challonor, Prince Rupert's whore. Tonight our spies saw her brawling with another of his strumpets. I've had her brought here for correction.'

'Oh, yes. Right. Pull the other leg, it's got bells on,' Amber cut in. 'Have you entirely lost the plot, Duncan?'

He ignored her outburst. 'The Lord has delivered you into our hands. Through you, we'll capture the Devil Prince. We shall send him a message and he'll want to rescue his harlot.'

'This is ridiculous. You should be careful what you're doing, Duncan. Kidnapping is a serious offence,' she said, trying to brazen it out, though fear was leaving a bad taste in her mouth.

'You'd have a hard time proving it,' he returned, and rose, paced round the table and stood close to her. 'No one would take it seriously.'

'You do, it seems,' she retorted and stepped back, only to be brought up short by one of the guards. She could sense Duncan's arousal, and that of his men. It had a feral quality that paralysed her, blood lust and carnal lust combined. This is how a real prisoner must have felt, a Royalist woman who had fallen into enemy hands, but because it was only play-acting and no serious harm intended, the whole episode gave Amber a perverse thrill.

'We shall send a message to the prince letting him know that we hold you hostage. He will come to your rescue and through negotiation, we'll ensure that the battle is ours tomorrow.'

'You think he'll believe it? He's no fool, you know. He'll want proof.'

'And he shall have it.' Duncan nodded to the sergeant

who clamped his arms round Amber's body. It was the work of a second to snip off one of her curls. Duncan coiled it round his finger and put his knife away.

'You're nuts!' Amber squawked. 'If you've ruined my hair I'll ...'

'What will you do? Sue me?' he asked in a maddeningly supercilious way. 'Tut, tut! "All is vanity, saith the Preacher."'

The other officers rose, their spokesman saying, 'We'll leave you to your interrogation, Major. Congratulations, it's very realistic. Perhaps it could be worked into the next display.'

'We could use you, Amber,' Duncan persisted, a fanatical look in his eyes. 'You'll be tried as a witch and found guilty, then they'll drag you to the stake, and burn you alive. You'll pray for death and, by that time, your prince's head will be stuck on a pike on Tower Bridge.'

'I'm fed up with all this. It's time I went back to camp,' she said angrily, but Duncan gripped her upper arm.

'You're not going anywhere,' he whispered, but when he turned to his colleagues, he smiled and said aloud, 'I'll see that she gets home all right. We're friends. Pity she's not on our side, what?'

They guffawed and bade her goodnight and then wandered out of the barn. Duncan dismissed the sergeant and guards.

'Right,' Amber said, mentally girding her loins. 'I'm off. I can't say it has been a pleasure. See you sometime, Duncan, and I'll send you my hairdresser's bill.'

She remembered his strength from the past, and he hadn't lost it – maybe it had increased – whatever, she couldn't stop him as he walked her to the back of the barn.

He stopped and said, 'Raise your arms above your head.'

'No,' she said, looking round for a means of escape. There was none.

He clasped her hands, pulled them in front of her and snapped fur-lined manacles round each wrist linked together by a chain. Her heart was beating fast and her stomach clenched, but more than this was the pulse between her thighs. He murmured in her ear, holding her fast by the cuffs.

'We never went as far as I wanted, but now I'm going to hurt you in a very special way. You're perfectly safe, but you'll belong to me. I'll be your master and the pain you feel will add to the ecstasy. No responsibility, Amber. I shall do everything you've ever dreamed about ... dirty things ... things that would disgust you ... things you've hardly dared think of.'

He picked up a short-handled deerskin flogger and whisked it through the air. The crack of the thongs made the down stand up on her limbs. He pulled on a rope and a hook came down from a beam. He slipped the wrist-chain over it and hauled. Her arms rose, her body stretched taut, her toes scrabbling on the cobbled floor. At first she wrestled with outrage and indignation.

'Let me down, you sod!' she stormed. 'Jesus! You can't get away with this. Now I remember why I dumped you. You're odd ... perverted ... abnormal.'

He ignored her, cutting away her blouse so that it fell open. The chill air teased her nipples and she wanted him to touch them. He didn't. Instead, he slipped a blindfold over her eyes. It tangled with her hair as he knotted it at the back. Her skirt came off easily, and he dropped it to one side.

'Panties? You're disobeying the rules, and wearing sandals, too. But then you always were a rebel, if I recall rightly,' he said, and grabbed her pubis in a firm hand, dragging the tiny G-string up between her lips.

He massaged her clit ruthlessly, sometimes covered by the strip of Lycra, or bare as he pushed it aside. His harsh treatment made her writhe on his fingers, so close to orgasm, yet kept on the edge, the pressure too great to permit that explosive relief.

'You're wet. You want to come? Ask me nicely and I might let you,' he growled, and shook her pussy in a tight-fisted grip and then let her go.

He walked away and this was the worst thing of all; she was throbbing with desire and terrified of what he might do to her next. Sight denied her, other senses came alive, that of hearing, ears alert for the smallest sound, skin tingling in expectation of the first blow, nose twitching to inhale the scent that heralded his approach.

If the girls could see me now, she thought, storing up impressions to recount to them later. She didn't believe Duncan meant to seriously harm her. It was frightening, but then he had always had that air of menace about him, even when wearing a suit and off about his duties – a magistrate among other solid-citizen-type ventures. This is what she had once found attractive, and still did – his ability to make her shiver. He had wound her desire up to such an extent that she was willing to do almost anything in order to be satisfied.

Out of the silence, she heard a rustle and braced herself, but even this was not enough to prepare her for the first blow, the flogger landing on her buttocks with a thwack that echoed round the barn. She yelped and swung her body in an effort to avoid the second blow. She couldn't. This time the deerskin thongs punished her thighs and belly. He wasn't laying them on hard, almost playing with her skin, but they stung nonetheless, and she wanted to scream for him to stop. Now the heat from her stripes was communicating with the heat in her cunt. She longed to come, her hips betraying her, gyrating as if begging for the favour of his fingers or tongue.

He dropped the flogger and caressed her everywhere, pressing against her, and she could feel the surge of arousal in his cock. He let her down and freed her hands, then took the blindfold off. He held her lightly, for she was bruised and sore, both from the catfight and his beating. Now he had become the forgiving master, ready to soothe and console. It was hard to decide which was the most threatening. His thin mouth was soft as if greased with butter, and his air that of a man languid with the thought of imminent repletion.

'You want to come very badly, don't you?' he said softly. 'Shall I let you?'

Amber had enough sense left to say nothing, quickly learning that he would most likely do the opposite if she asked for a climax. He didn't seem to expect a reply, and moved over to where several bales of hay made a makeshift couch. He spread a blanket on the straw and laid her down. She hurt everywhere, but was so aroused that pain and pleasure seemed intermixed. He leaned over her and she opened her legs, his eyes inspecting the red weals marking her belly, and examining the dark bush and waiting slit. He breathed on it, every hair quivering and communicating with her anxious clit. Then he fondled it, watching her face as she writhed on his fingers as orgasm shot from her pussy up her spine to her cortex. She sighed, the ache in her arms and body detracting from the complete bliss that somehow evaded her.

Duncan unfastened his breeches and his cock was as she remembered, long and meaty and circumcised. She did a quick flash back through memory, trying to remember what it had felt like inside her. Good, as she recalled; it was Duncan who had been the problem, not his cock. Did he have any condoms with him? she wondered. There was no way she was going to take it if he hadn't.

'You have such beautiful tits,' he said quietly, and heaved up till he was kneeling across her body. He took her breasts in his hands, his thumbs rotating on the nipples, and Amber felt desire stirring in her again. 'I've often thought of them, and wished . . .'

'What did you wish?' she asked throatily, finding it impossible to hate or even dislike him now.

'That we hadn't broken up,' he said and lowered himself so that his penis lay on her sternum between her breasts. Ah, now she remembered. He had liked coitus à mammilla, a pearl necklace that hadn't necessitated the use of a rubber.

She obligingly pushed her breasts together so that they formed a channel, a mock vagina for his pleasure. He rocked his pelvis faster and faster, his cock slipping between her breasts, lubricated by the tears seeping from its single eye. He was heavy, but braced himself on his arms either side of her head, and she did the work, rubbing him with her breasts, until he fountained a stream of come over her face, neck and hair.

'I'll keep your curl as a memento,' he said a little later as she found her skirt and tucked in her blouse, folding the slit edges over and covering all with her cloak. 'I want to see you again.'

'I don't think that's a good idea,' she said, eyeing him warily, ready to make a bolt for it if he turned nasty.

'Why not? You're single, so am I. My accountancy business is booming. I've always been fond of you, Amber.'

She stood up and went towards the door. Moonlight abounded and escape was at hand. 'I don't want to commit myself,' she said. 'I'm enjoying my freedom now the boys are grown up. Like you, I'm a very busy person with little time for a serious relationship.'

She was outside the door now, skirts bunched up, ready to do a marathon sprint across the clearing to the trees. 'I won't take no for an answer,' he said, and she could tell he was annoyed. 'You'd better not upset me, Amber. I've a lot of influence in and around Lyncroft and Bargate.'

This stopped her in her tracks. 'Are you threatening me?' she demanded.

'Just warning you.'

'And what can you do?'

He shrugged and replied, 'Don't underestimate my influence.'

'You're a magistrate and a Freemason, and friendly with the cops, but what could you possibly do?'

'You have a shop in town, in a narrow street in a congested area. I could make parking difficult, for example.'

'You would, wouldn't you?' She wondered why she felt so let down. She should have known him capable of blackmail. 'I'm not giving you an answer straight off,' she said.

'I'll phone you next week.'

'All right,' she agreed, and scurried towards the Cavalier's camp and comparative safety, half expecting him to follow, but he didn't. A quick glance round and she saw him leaning against the door jamb, watching her.

He *is* the Emperor, she thought. That contradiction who symbolises authority and conventional religion, needing to be socially approved, yet with hidden depths, kinky in the extreme.

The coppice was fairylike, the moon tracing filigree patterns over the leafy ground. Amber hurried along, wondering if Titania was about, blinded by love-drops so that she had fallen for Bottom the weaver who, under an enchantment, had been given an ass's head and that was not all – a donkey's prick, too. Could a woman take a tool that size? Amber had heard of this being done for the entertainment of visitors to eastern nightclubs. I must ask Jason, she thought, he's bound to know.

She went to the lake and washed her face, wanting to get rid of Duncan's emission. The scene was hotting up. Naked women who danced in circles and males with their arms round one another's shoulders moving in lines reminiscent of the Greeks had replaced the morris men. It was getting rowdy, most of the participants ending up in the water. The bushes were alive with rutting lovers, rustling and gasping. Amber did not stop to see which gender they were – it didn't really matter just as long as the force was released to add to the solstice power.

She found Ian arguing with one of the corporals who had really got up his nose on the battlefield. Prudy was acting as arbitrator, and Amber slipped into the seat beside Sue, her bottom stinging.

'Are you all right? I heard about the fight,' Sue said. 'Your face. Let's have a look. What a bitch! That would do it, if it was me. I'd go flat out to get Rupert, just to spite her.'

Amber nodded, unsure whether to tell her about Duncan, yet thought, why not? Sue, Di and herself kept few secrets from one another, three heads being better than one when it came to decisions. But nowadays Sue's concentration wavered when Prudy was about. Di was not in evidence, coping with dozens of hungry mouths, so she kept quiet, keeping it till later.

Ian bought her a drink, but was too preoccupied with the cares of captaincy to do other than check on her recuperation. There was no sign of Sarah or Rupert. Then Otto came in, a predator on the hunt. He looked hard, even brutal, with his shaven head and piercing, but she knew better.

'Come to Lyncroft and meet my friend, Alastair,' she suggested, catching him as he sauntered up to the bar. 'Next week, if you like. By the by, where is Rupert?'

'Not with *her*, if that's what's worrying you,' he replied. 'He's on his own, in the caravan. I think he's really pissed off about what happened. Go and see him, and, yes, I'll pop over on Friday, if that's all right.'

Rupert opened the van door, his frame filling the aperture, silhouetted from behind. 'Come in,' he said, standing back.

'I'm sorry,' she began, overwhelmed by the feelings he engendered inside her. 'About earlier. I shouldn't have lost my temper with Sarah.' She had drunk enough to be bold. 'The thing is, Rupert, I really like you very much. That night at the ballet was out of this world.'

'We'll do it again,' he promised, and stood so close to her that he was almost too tall, making her feel like a dwarf. 'I want you to come to dinner soon. I've stacks of videos and CDs, and don't find many people to share them. Most of the women I know are airheads, and the men into macho sports. I need a music lover, in more ways than one.'

Tempting, oh so tempting, to mix her metaphors, dive in at the deep end, lose her head, fall headlong. She was enjoying her sexual freedom, but there was something missing. Awful to admit it, but she needed to fuss over someone, to buy him birthday presents and remember anniversaries, and do all those things that had gone sour when she was with Matthew.

'Let's make love, Amber,' Rupert said, and took her into the bedroom. It was furnished to resemble the cabin of a seafarer – the captain of a pirate ship – filled with sumptuous drapes, coverlets and trinkets.

'Rupert,' she said, having the urge to confess about Duncan, but he snatched her up against him and the moment was gone.

He opened her cloak and the sight of her torn blouse arrested him. 'Sarah hasn't attacked you again, has she?'

'No. It wasn't Sarah. It's nothing. It doesn't matter.'

He gave her a quizzical look, as if not quite believing, then took her to the canopied bed, laid her down and took off what remained of her clothes. 'Have you been playing S and M?' he asked, frowning at the blotches on her skin.

'Something like that,' she replied, and made no attempt to explain.

He seemed to accept it as her business and stripped off

his shirt and breeches, his feet and legs already bare. The mattress sagged as he sat on one side of it, then lay down and pulled the duvet over them. It was an intimate gesture of greater significance than the joining of flesh. The first time she had shared a bed with him. After the affair in the pool, he had stayed up late with her, listening to music in the drawing room, then she had driven home.

She put her arms around him, trying to ignore the slow-fire warmth spreading in the region of her heart. Instead she let her body take over, and this wasn't difficult. He attended to her breasts and her nipples rose like corks on water. She slipped her hand down and fingered the satin smooth column that rose from his glossy black thatch. There was no hurry. Otto was otherwise engaged in finding himself an orifice and Ian, de-spunked by her earlier on, was expending what remained of his energy on a row. Peace fanned down over her, and she permitted herself to admire Rupert and allow that melting, strawberry mousse feeling to swamp her.

They took their time, exploring slowly. He used his surgeon's skill, tracing every muscle and bone and sinew, leaving no inch of her unturned – mouth, sex, the tiny pucker of her anus. Inside and out, scars, warts and all, till there was nothing left and she belonged to him. He put on a condom with a ridged surface.

'You'll like this,' he said. 'It grazes the pussy with every movement.'

'That's not the important bit. It's the clit that matters.'

'I know,' he said and his lips brushed between her legs and his tongue flicked over her bud.

He sucked the fat little organ, and reached up, his fingers scratching over both nipples, giving her triple sensations. She climaxed violently, gasping for breath, pulling him down on her and scissoring her legs round his waist. His cock slid into her. She could see it as he pistoned in and out. Then he speeded up, and grunted and thrust deeply and stayed there, eyes closed and sweat beading his face. She felt him twitch inside her and guessed that the fancy condom was now filled with his come.

12

'It's ages since we've had a girl's night in,' Sue said, having just fetched wine from the fridge and brought it into her comfortable lounge. It was knee deep in feather cushions, couches, a television set with a 28-inch screen, ornaments, curtains and throws that gave a clue to her eclectic taste.

'I know. We've all been so busy, since becoming Bannerites,' Amber agreed.

'Looks like I'm going to get busier,' Diane put in. 'No wine for me, Sue.'

'No? You're usually up for it.'

'Not any more. I did a test this morning and it's positive. Colin and I are going to have a little musketeer.'

'Stone the crows!' Sue couldn't think of anything else to say.

'You're a dark horse. How long?' asked Amber.

'Six weeks.'

'And you didn't let on? Didn't say a dicky bird?' Sue was wondering why she was so astonished. Pregnancy happened, and Diane and Colin were at it like mink at every opportunity.

'I wanted to be sure first. At my age, well, you never know. It could have been a false alarm, though I've been careless with the Pill and given up condoms since we both got the all clear. I'll go and see the doc, just to make sure, but I've missed a period and my tits are sore,' Diane said, and she was beaming and obviously tickled pink.

'What about Karen?'

'*What about her*? I've spent years bothering about her. She can like it or lump it. She's hardly speaking to me anyway since Ray went. It's all my fault, of course. She's found herself a boyfriend at last, and is talking about getting a flat with him. He's a student, too. So she won't be worrying about me having a baby.'

'I'll bet she will. Any excuse to give you a hard time. She'll be so jealous. Think of the money she won't be getting if you spend it on a rug rat,' Amber said, lounging full length on the settee, wearing twill combat shorts with zipped pockets and eyelet details. Sue thought she was looking great, with an enviable tan accentuated by a white knitted camisole top with appliquéd lace and a tie-through front.

'You'll model for my next fashion show?' Sue asked suddenly.

Amber smiled and said, 'Sure. What is it for? Hell's grannies?'

'About this baby. Is it selfish of me to keep it?' Diane said, her expression a touching mix of pride, longing and anxiety.

'Do you want it?' Sue said.

'Oh, yes. It's Colin's and I love him. He's so pleased. Like a dog with two tin tails. It won't be easy. I shall have to do a balancing act between the café, Colin, next year's musters, as we intend to keep the catering van going, and a new child. It's due around April, by my reckoning.'

'I wish you all the best, but don't expect me to knit anything,' Amber said.

'I shan't. I've already been browsing through the Baby Gap catalogue, but I do want one of those great big coach-built prams. You know the ones, mid-fifties vintage. Will you keep a look out at auction sales? I can always have it refurbished. I didn't manage to have one when Karen was born, had to make do with a horrible little buggy. I know you can get them new in Harrods, but they'll cost hundreds. I'd rather have one with a history, anyway.'

'I'll see what I can come up with,' Amber promised. 'Get Jason on the case.'

'Does Ray know?' Sue could foresee difficulties. The divorce was in hand, but he was greedy and demanding and hadn't liked packing his belongings into the maroon taxi and leaving the marital establishment.

'I haven't told anyone but Colin and you two,' Diane answered earnestly. 'What can he do anyway? He might countersue if I press the adultery plea, so I'll change it to incompatibility and the complete breakdown of the marriage. He's kept the garage and that will be his share of our mutual assets, and he's well in with Janice who is a widow with her own business and a bob or two in the bank. Ray always falls on his feet. His mother likes Janice, by the way. Thinks she's much more capable of looking after him than I ever was. My name's going to be mud when she hears about the baby. One day, I might give myself the satisfaction of telling her that Janice is a dom and he's her submissive. Colin and I plan to tie the knot once it's all done and dusted. Will you be my bridesmaids? I want a proper do with a reception, and a blessing in church with Colin in uniform and musketeers making a triumphal arch with their firearms.'

Sue laughed, and said, 'Bet your life we will. Shall we wear daffodil yellow taffeta, with bows and puff sleeves? Seriously, I'll organise your wedding dress for free; costume, I presume? But I think we'd be better off as matrons-of-not-much-honour, don't you?'

'You're right. What's honour anyway?' said Amber thoughtfully.

'I think it's being loyal to your friends,' Sue replied, handing round the crisps and peanuts. 'Prudy agrees with this, but also says it is never turning your back on a fight, or letting an enemy get away with it. She's into duelling, as you know. You should see her. She's brilliant, should be fencing for England.'

'So it's not a sexual thing, like keeping oneself pure?' Amber mused, and Sue topped up her glass.

'Not any more,' she said, 'and that's just as well considering what we've been up to this year. You, Amber, more than us. You never did tell what happened on Midsummer Eve.'

'I did. I told you that I was kidnapped by Duncan.'

'And got off on it. And then?'

'I went to bed with Rupert.'

'Ah, this is the bit you left out. Why hide it? We know you shag him. Are you afraid of losing face because he's such a stud?'

'OK. You can have the whole story, not that it's very exciting,' Amber said, sitting up and reaching for her wine. 'I went to his caravan and we made love, and I call it that deservedly . . . one doesn't simply screw with Rupert.'

'Oh, yawn,' groaned Sue. 'He's so Mr Cool, is he?'

'Do you want to hear about it or not?' Amber said tetchily.

She used to be even-tempered, Sue thought. Not any more. 'Right. Keep your hair on.'

'Well, I went to sleep when we'd finished. I was dead beat, what with the fight and Duncan and all. I woke about twelve and heard Ian and Rupert talking. Then they came across and started to kiss me.'

'Both of them?' Diane said, round-eyed.

'Yes. One on my mouth and the other on my pussy. I'd never had two men at the same time, but this is what happened.'

'So you let them carry on?'

'More than that. I thoroughly enjoyed it. Imagine being in bed with the most dishy men on the block. They are yours for hours and no one else's. You're all lit up with this excitement inside, breathing in male . . . more than that . . . wallowing in male.'

'It wouldn't appeal to me,' Sue said with a shudder.

'But I've joined in with the girls. That tent of Prudy's becomes a veritable paradise for women pleasuring women, and I guess the same applies to you when it's more than one bloke.'

'I'd like to hear more,' Diane murmured, and her hand dropped down into her lap, fingers pressing her crotch through her dirndl skirt. She seemed younger, brighter, happier and more sexy than ever. 'Not that I'd ever be unfaithful to Colin, you understand, but this does sound amazing, Amber. Prince Rupert and Captain Barrett, the leading lights of the Silver Banner. I'll bet there are women who'd scratch your eyes out if they knew.'

'No doubt,' Amber replied dryly. 'I must admit that it made me proud. And they are both good lovers ... none of this "you've got to come when we put our cocks in you" nonsense. They were gentle giants, and concerned about the marks of the flogger. They wormed the story out of me and were furious at Duncan's colossal cheek. They leaned on him next day, and he left me alone after that, but it hasn't stopped him ringing me since.'

'And they weren't jealous? Didn't mind sharing you?' Diane asked, cupping her breasts in both hands as if they were already heavy with milk.

They are bigger, Sue observed mentally. Funny, I didn't notice it before.

'I think they got off on seeing each other doing it,' Amber said, totally unrepentant. 'It backs up my theory that most men have a homosexual streak somewhere.'

'What? Tough guys like Ian and Rupert?' Diane exclaimed. 'Well, say what you like, but I'm sure there isn't a gay bone in Colin's body.'

'No? Make him a castaway on a desert island with several men and no pussy and see what happens,' Amber went on. 'Think of prisons, and the navy in the old days when they were months at sea. Cabin boys were called "sea-wives", and Jason told me about a rubber woman the crew of one boat made and used regularly. I don't know what she was like, nothing more than a pair of boobs and substitute fanny, by the sound of it. At any rate, she gave all of them syphilis.'

'Trust Jason to know that,' Sue remarked. 'Him and his collection of thingumajigs. He's twisted, Amber.'

'Not at all ... just interested in matters antique and what makes human beings tick,' Amber returned.

'Serves those sailors right, the dirty beasts,' Diane said firmly. 'Go on, Amber. Tell us some more about your night with double lovers.'

'What can I say? It was exhausting. I came over and over again, whereas they only managed it a couple of times each.'

'Did you sleep like that, with Ian on one side and Rupert on the other?' asked Sue, rather tired of the subject and wondering if she might phone Prudy. This evening wasn't proving as enjoyable as she had expected. Sadly, she accepted that the three of them were growing apart.

'I did, and I've spent more comfortable nights. The bed was small, a double whereas I'm used to a king size, and they are large in every department. I was squashed in the middle with Ian on one side like a hairy teddy bear, and Rupert on the other, all leanness and angles. But I managed to doze off, wakened by Otto bringing in morning cups of tea, and freed myself from the entanglement of muscular legs, hands that were all over me and cocks that rivalled one another in length and girth, both upstanding and ready to perform again.'

'And did they?' Diane asked.

'Of course. "One for my baby and one more for the road."'

'Weren't you sore?'

'I walked bandy all that day.'

'And you've seen them since then? You weren't at the August bank holiday event in Bridgwater,' Sue said, remembering the muster and how much she had improved under Prudy's tuition.

'Yes, I've seen them, but individually. Ian's been over here and I've stayed in Rupert's house. We've a lot in common ... music being one. I couldn't make it because, as you know, Andy and Chris were home, and I wanted to spend quality time with them. I barred boyfriends, but now they've gone to Cambridge to find accommodation as they're taking their degrees there, starting in October, I shall resume play.'

'I told you they'd get fed up with their father, didn't I?' Sue said, having enjoyed meeting them again, two handsome young men with minds of their own and careers firmly in focus.

'There's nowhere like an English university to give that extra polish,' Amber said. 'I love having them with me, and am so glad they will be in this country now, but I relish my freedom. They'll visit me during the vacs, but will soon fill up their lives with new friends, work and the golden opportunity to reside in a city that's a seat of learning.'

'Right. Enough about babies and men. How about a game of Scrabble?' suggested Sue. This was getting just too much for her. She had to engage her attention on something challenging, rather than thinking about Prudy all the time.

We'll meet tomorrow, she thought as she got out the board and markers and tiles. We get on like a house on fire. Not only in bed, though that is the most beautiful of experiences, but in daily life, too. She wants to become my partner as a costume designer. She manages the website and can liaise with Banner commanders and folk who need advice on dressing. In her occupation as a barrister she meets influential people, and some of them are war-gamers. We've discussed expanding the business to include other periods.

Her flat had become Prudy's second home, and they worked side by side in the sewing room downstairs. Sometimes, she had time off and went to stay in Prudy's house, enjoying the club scene and nightlife of Bristol. But always, they were together, and Sue dared to let her guard down and believe that this might go on for ever. As for progeny? Thirza and George were their family.

It was extraordinary to see Rupert in a dinner suit, his shoulder-length hair tied back in concession to the formality of the occasion.

He strode across the tiled hall to meet her as Amber entered the imposing front entrance of the Osbourne Clinic. 'You look stunning,' he said.

'Thank you,' she replied nervously, her stomach a skating rink for a dozen butterflies.

'There's this rather tedious dinner party,' he had said to her over the phone a few days before. 'It's at the clinic. I wondered if you'd care to come.'

'Crikey Moses!' she had said, gobsmacked. 'What's it in aid of?'

'That's just it,' he had continued, his deep voice rippling down her spine into places where it had no right of entry. 'We, that's my partners and me, are entertaining some wealthy Americans and their wives, hoping they'll be so impressed by our facilities and service that they'll donate generously. It's not only the rich who need us. We could do so much for people on the NHS desperate for treatment, but unable to afford to go private.'

Aw, bless! she had thought, half cynical of, but mostly admiring, his altruism. 'Why do you want me?' she had asked. 'I'm sure you know dozens of women far more suitable.'

'On the contrary. You are perfect,' he had murmured so smoothly that she expected him to metamorphose and dribble through the earpiece as a spoonful of honey.

'You're intelligent, well read (and they won't be, if I know my friends from over the Pond). You can talk about music ad infinitum, and literature and antiques...'

'But not medicine,' she had reminded him.

'Leave that side of it to my colleagues and me. You'll come?'

'Yes.'

So there she was, in a dress chosen in close collaboration with Sue. It was long and sleek and black. It had spaghetti straps, the skirt was cut on the cross, the bodice practically non-existent and she'd never, in her entire life, paid so much for an article of clothing. Sue maintained that it was a snip, and marched her off to Maison Armand to have her hair fixed.

'You're looking fab and groovy,' he had commented, whisking a gown round her shoulders and ordering one of the juniors to shampoo her. 'Getting plenty, are we?'

She had refused to be quizzed, wondered why so many people were interested in her private life, and given herself over to his ministrations, the guru of perm lotions, colour baths, highlights and lowlights and scissor points. She had come out feeling fantastic, but with a hundred pounds less in her bank account.

It had worked out. Despite her misgivings, she had found it inspiring to stand at Rupert's side, listening to his groupies, and realising that he was a most respected and important surgeon indeed, way ahead of others in his particular field. When she slept with him that night, it was with an added sense of his worth, and the regret that she wasn't a tiny bit younger so that he might seriously consider proposing. She could tell he was very fond of her. But there would be the question of heirs, and she didn't know that she could take this on with Diane's readiness. Having just got shot of two, she was dubious about occupying the sacrificial altar of motherhood again.

Ian was her next date. He wanted her to dress up and

go with him to a Silver Banner 'do', as he put it. A boozy celebration as the end of the season was approaching, where they'd be entertained at a hotel that specialised in medieval banquets. This had been fun, too, and she loved Ian's sense of humour. Her ballgown had been repaired, as he had suggested, and she wore it with ease, used to managing the tight stays and sweeping skirts. He had paid for her ticket and booked a room and they had retired there in the small hours. He had imbibed deeply, suffering from brewer's droop, and she had begun to realise that drink might pose a problem. She wasn't going to get deeply involved with a serious boozer, be he ever so jolly and funny, handsome and loving.

Autumn was almost there, chilly dawns and warm Indian summer days, but the sun was low now, and birds were migrating and leaves starting to spiral from the branches, covering the ground with red-gold magic carpets. There was a trace of melancholy in the air, a regret for the passing of heat and languor. Winter was on the horizon. Everything was so much more of an effort when it wasn't sunny.

'But you don't have to stay in a cold climate,' Camilo said, at home on Amber's chesterfield. He had rung politely (he really did have lovely manners) begging to say goodbye before he went back to Spain. 'Come with me.'

'I can't,' Amber said regretfully. She hated winter, watching her tan fade, having to put on layers of clothes, central heating bills adding to the cost of living. Some people raved about the crispness of snow, the invigorating frosts and sentimentalised about a white Christmas, but all she could think of was months of grey skies and rain.

'Why not?' he insisted, rising with feline grace, going to the stereo and putting on a CD. The music of his country evoked scrubby hillsides banded by orange groves, dryness and heat haze, blue seas and golden beaches.

He took up a stance, back straight, tight bum tucked in, chin at a haughty angle. He was wearing jeans and a T-shirt, but this didn't detract from the classic line as he raised his arms, elbows flexed, and clapped to the rhythm, feet stamping, heels clicking on the parquet for, yes, he was wearing flamenco boots.

'I can't leave the shop,' she said, the elegance of her Spaniard, his timing and seemingly effortless movements making her heart ache with sheer joy at such perfection. 'I have to make a living, you know, just as you do with your dancing.'

'Then come for a holiday,' he insisted, his hands forming graceful arabesques, castanets reverberating. 'It is still fine in Seville through October. We have bad weather sometimes, more lately, which some say is the fault of world warming, but never, never cold, like here.'

'I'll think about it. I've said I'll find Diane a pram,' she said and the more she watched him, the more spellbinding the idea seemed – to leave foggy England and journey to Seville, and Triana where the gypsies lived and where Camilo had been born.

He shook his head, black ringlets bouncing. 'I don't understand. What is "pram"?'

Oh, dear, she thought. Why is it that foreigners don't get the English sense of humour? 'I only meant it as a joke, but it's true anyway. She's having a baby. A pram is to wheel it out in.'

'Ah, so your friend is to be a mama again,' he said, his face clearing, then. 'Dance with me,' he added in dusky, enticing tones.

Knowing he was coming, Amber had chosen an asymmetric cotton skirt in patchwork stripes, teamed with a lace vest. Her nipples poked through, peaking even more as Camilo advanced towards her, like a bantam cockerel showing off to his hen, strutting, posturing, stamping his feet. She responded, remembering steps he had already shown her, remembering all the women flamenco dancers she had every seen. Tits to heaven, spine straight, feet as if rooted deep in the earth. Proud, oh so proud, the pride of an oppressed race who had survived through thick and thin. Pride in the family, the bloodline, the *canto* – the dancing.

'That's it,' he murmured encouragingly. 'Beautiful. The spirit of the dance is in you. I could make you into a performer.'

'But I'm not a gypsy,' she breathed, delighted.

'You have the soul of one,' he said, touching her at the waist, then parting again, swirling round her, reappearing. He was so quick, so light on his feet. Not dressed as he had been in her crystal vision, but the scene was so reminiscent of it that when he approached her again she stopped. So did he. And, while the CD played on, he pulled her close to his hot body and kissed her with a dizzying sweetness.

She slid her hands up under his T-shirt, feeling the sweat, finding his nipples and tweaking them. He groaned, and they collapsed on to the couch. Then it was haste, clothing off, cushions on the floor, both of them following suit, needing more space for their energetic coupling. He was wiry and slim, much smaller than Ian or Rupert, but his very agility made up for lack of bulk. And his cock was as large as theirs. It was another one of those old wives' tales, or more likely old husbands', that said the bigger the man's feet the bigger his penis. Amber hadn't found that to be so.

He caressed her wonderingly, as if she was the first woman he had ever had, and she returned the fondling boldly, holding his cock while he ventured the length of her body, leaving a trail of kisses all the way. She had showered in anticipation of this, but was always a little afraid that the man going down on her might find something offensive in her female smell. Not so Camilo. He sucked her with relish and, with those compelling rhythms pounding in her blood, she could feel herself rising on a wave of euphoria, and reaching a blissful, uninterrupted crisis.

He rubbered up and entered her vigorously after making sure she was satisfied, and did not pause till he, too, had reached his apogee. Later, when they had moved to her bed, for he intended to stay the night, he said to her, idly playing with her damp pubic curls, 'So, that's decided. You will visit me in October. *Si*?'

'*Si*,' she replied, letting sensible considerations gallop off at a tangent.

She was sorry to see Camilo go, wishing that she really was free as a gypsy, but then, she reasoned, he probably wouldn't want me. It's only because I'm unobtainable, but I will honour my promise and go to him in Triana. I'll look forward to that when the North winds blow and All Souls' Night is upon us, Hallowe'en, the winter solstice, Samhain, when the dead return and visit the living.

Meanwhile, there were auctions and house clearances and Alastair and the shop. He was a happy bunny these days, since the advent of Otto. So far so good, Amber thought, and kept her fingers crossed. Her sons came home and went again; they had found a house-share and seemed all set to become Cambridge undergraduates. Jason was an infrequent visitor; he was obviously keeping it cool, and they met in their line of business more often than socially, but she had the feeling that he wanted their friendship to develop into something deeper.

One September evening she was waiting for him to drop in to discuss an important sale at a manor house whose owners had fallen on hard times. When the buzzer went, she pressed the security button, saying, 'The door will now open. Come on up, Jason.'

But it wasn't him whom she greeted in the hall. It was Duncan.

'Good Lord! I thought you were someone else,' she said as he stepped over the threshold, giving her no time to shut the door in his face. It clunked behind him, trapping her.

'This "Jason" person, I presume? Whoever he is,' Duncan replied, looking round him and adding, with a sardonic, disparaging smile, 'The place hasn't changed. You've not done much to it, Amber.'

'I like it as it is. Can't bear the upheaval of decorating,' she answered, flabbergasted by his rudeness.

'You always were lazy, as I remember. Liked nothing better than lying on your back and roasting in the sun,'

'So? It has nothing to do with you how I conduct my life. I didn't invite you here, so please leave.'

'We've spoken on the phone and I thought it would be better if we talked face to face,' he said, making no attempt to move.

He was dressed in a tailored suit, and had probably come straight from a business meeting or a council fest in the town hall. She couldn't deny that he was distinguished looking and, had it not been for his behaviour, both at Pirton Court and in the past, she might have considered taking it a stage further. She had experienced a dark, perverse excitement when he flogged her, and had used the memory to add to the tension when she masturbated. No matter how many men she had or how often, there was nothing quite like the private and very special contact between her own fingertips and her clit.

'I should have thought it was obvious that I didn't want to,' she challenged, though she was feeling threatened, and this was annoying in her own home.

'Too preoccupied with the Cavaliers,' he grated. 'If you wanted to join in, why didn't you become a Parliamentarian?'

'I don't like the way they dress,' she said flippantly, and still hadn't invited him into the sitting room. They were standing in the hall.

'Typical. Haven't you studied the Civil War?' he snarled.

'Not in any great depth,' she admitted. 'I joined on impulse . . . for fun, if you like.'

'And ended up with Rupert Frobisher, who likes to fancy that he's descend from the Devil Prince. Change sides, Amber. Come with me to the musters. I'll teach you to respect the Roundheads.'

'Go away, Duncan,' she said recklessly. 'I'm expecting a guest.'

'You don't have to answer the door to him.'

'I want to. This is my place. Now please get out.'

'Amber, Amber, calm down,' he murmured and, taking her by the arm, led her through the hall and into the bedroom. 'There really is a lot of unfinished business between us.'

'Let me go.' She felt inclined to kick him, but this wasn't a civilised thing to do. Come to that, neither was entering a lady's boudoir uninvited.

They reached her bed, with its tester draped in lace and satin, her pride and joy that she had acquired by bidding far more than she could afford at a saleroom in Devon. Unfortunately, Duncan had slept in it before, and this gave him a kind of precedence, a familiarity with her territory that she found deeply disturbing. It was as if her ex-husband was there, an alpha male who she was not prepared to receive. Or was she?

She'd never felt more undecided. There was no doubt as to Duncan's intentions. It was in his eyes, the slant of his mouth, the way his erection spoiled the cut of his trousers. He pinned her between himself and the mattress and took off his jacket. Now, in shirtsleeves, he pushed up her jersey crop-top and reached round the back and unclipped her black bra.

Holding her a little away from him, he looked down, admiring her, and saying, 'You've always had gorgeous breasts. I love coming all over them. It was good that night in midsummer. You enjoyed it, too. Don't even try to deny it.'

His eyes were heavy-lidded as he watched his fingers flicking across her nipples, rolling and kneading till they were stone hard and brownish red. He lowered his head and sucked each in turn. She wasn't sure what to expect next, and the uncertainty was exciting. She didn't particularly like Duncan, and had been relieved when he had been out of her life, yet he was unpredictable, subject to mood swings, cruel and selfish, powerful and ruthless. An irresistible combination to someone of her temperament.

He sat on the bed and, with one quick movement, had her across his lap. His thighs felt rock-solid beneath her. He had unzipped and his cock stuck out, pressing into her side. He lifted her skirt and tucked it way up above her waist. Then she felt his hand inside her panties, caressing her buttocks, then the short, sharp tussle as he got them down and round her ankles and off.

'What are you going to do, you idiot?' she shouted angrily. His cock was jerking against her bare skin, leaving a trail of wetness.

'You need discipline,' he muttered, and strange emotions were churning in her, making her recall the flogger, the pain and the pleasure, the humiliation, and tingling anticipation. Years ago, too, he had experimented with her, but it had been a tepid venture.

Now his breathing was ragged and his dick like a battering ram, as he parted her bottom crease and moved between her tightly clenched anus and her pussy. He spat on his fingers and wetted her clit. Pleasure cannoned through her as he massaged it firmly. Despite everything, she knew that if he kept on, she would have an orgasm. This was how it was with her, she might loathe the person frigging her, but her clit didn't know the difference between one finger or another, one surface or the next; just as long as the strokes were right and would bring about a climax.

Rub me, go on! she wanted to shout, but then bucked as he slapped her bottom hard with his free hand. The blow burned, spreading heat all over the area. He smacked her again and she winced and writhed and tried to get away from the steady blows. And all the time he maintained friction on her clit. The punishment was terrible and she could smell his sweat and aftershave, and the pungent odour of his cock. Her only point of reference was the deer flogger that had produced a weird dichotomy of pain and pleasure.

I'm as kinky as he is! she thought in alarm. And this is what Ray gets off on, according to Diane. I must have denied it for years, certainly when we were together before, and I don't really know if I want it now. I think I'd rather be straight. But he was giving her no choice. Alternately slapping her rump and rubbing her bud.

'Dirty slut! Consorting with Cavaliers!' he growled, and her bottom stung beneath his palm. 'Things are going to change from now on. You'll be with me, Amber.'

'I won't. I refuse to be bullied,' she shouted, battling with tears.

'You know what will happen if you give me trouble, don't you? I've said I'll put in a complaint about the parking outside your shop.'

'You can't do it,' she blazed. 'I've a friend who is a barrister and she'll advise me. You'll find yourself in a very tricky position indeed.'

'Be quiet, tart!' Duncan stormed, really getting into the

swing of it now. His arm rose and fell and her climax was close. She wanted him to stop; yearned for him to go on. Her clit was poised on the brink, the spasms gathering and about to pour over, then:

'Good God! Amber, are you all right?' Jason asked as he came in at the door. She had forgotten she had given him a key so that he could keep an eye on things if she was away.

Duncan looked up and Amber turned her head and stared at Jason. All right? 'No, I'm not,' she said and started to cry, while her clit, that disloyal little tyrant, throbbed with disappointment.

'Let her go,' Jason said quietly to Duncan. 'I don't know who you are, but it seems that this has gone on long enough.'

'Sod you!' Duncan snarled and tumbled her from his knee unceremoniously. He pushed his cock into his trousers and zipped up. 'This has nothing to do with anyone except Amber and me.'

Jason held out a hand and helped her to her feet. Mercifully her skirt obeyed the law of gravity and slithered down to cover her. 'Is what he says right, Amber? Do you want me to bugger off?'

'No,' she said. 'It's him who should leave.'

'Right then, mate,' Jason said, fronting him up, and Amber remembered that he had been a market trader for most of his working life, as tough as old boots. 'Out you go.'

Duncan picked up his jacket, glared at Amber and said, 'Don't forget my influence with the council.'

'If you do anything to harm my business, then I'll ask the barrister, Prudy Hemming, to deal with it,' she answered, out-staring him till he could no longer meet her gaze and strode from the room. Jason and Amber went with him, just to be on the safe side, and she closed the door firmly after him.

'What was all that about? Did I spoil something?' Jason wanted to know.

'I've already told you about being kidnapped. Well, that was Duncan Crompton, an ex and now a Roundhead who wants to convert me,' she said, a bit shamefaced. If Jason hadn't interrupted them, she would have been in post-orgasmic nirvana by now.

Jason grinned; he was just too all seeing. 'Fancy a bit of rough treatment, do you? I expect I can come up with the goods.'

'No, it's all right,' she said, rescuing her knickers from under the bed.

'You don't have to put them back on unless you want to,' he said charitably. 'Don't mind me. In fact, I rather like it when you're bare down there. Just as well I arrived, isn't it? He seems to be quite a nasty piece of work, threatening you like that.' He adopted a ringing, cultured tone, declaiming like an actor in a TV play, 'The fellow's a cad, an absolute bounder, and a blackguard, to boot. I'll have him barred from the club.'

She laughed for the first time in hours. 'I really am glad to see you,' she said. 'What were we going to do?'

'Plan our strategy for the forthcoming sale in the morning. We might well find that pram. It's the sort of house that must once have been swarming with kids and nannies and a proper nursery,' he answered, giving her a sharp, concerned glance. 'How about you tidying yourself up and I'll take you to that new Thai restaurant in the High Street? It has a glowing reputation.'

He absented himself and she heard R&B pounding from her hi-fi. One of his discs and she supposed she might learn to live with it. At least it wasn't Country & Western. Live with it? *Live with him*! But I don't want to live with anyone, she argued with herself as she did a repair job on her face. He's another dealer. He wants to pick my brains and take away my customers.

The restaurant proved to be excellent. Jason was a critical gourmet, knowing his food and fussy about the cleanliness of the kitchens and the service provided by the staff. He could find nothing to complain about at the Lotus Blossom. He drove there and back and Amber was able to shuck off all responsibility. They talked shop over the meal and agreed to leave at dawn, then they could view everything in the manor and be ready for the start at ten o'clock. This appealed to her hugely. The anticipation of a bargain never failed to make her tingle.

'Coming in for coffee?' she asked when they reached Collectibles. This sounded crass and she hoped he wouldn't read more into it than she intended.

'Only if I can make it,' he agreed fussily.

'You're welcome. I've been cooking and making coffees and teas for over twenty years and am heartily sick of it,' she said, dropping her bag and wrap on the settee and following him into the kitchen. 'That is the best thing that's ever happened to me,' she added, gesturing towards the shiny white dishwasher. 'I genuflect every time I go by it.'

'Lucky old robot,' he said, smiling at her as he prepared the freshly roasted beans and put them in the percolator. 'If I wasn't doing this, I suppose we'd be poking up with Instant.'

'Dead right,' she replied and perched herself on a stool near the table, tucking her feet on the struts underneath. This position made her bottom smart and brought her cleft into contact with the cane-woven seat, and she was sharply aware that she had been stopped from coming, just when she was about to ride waves of extreme pleasure.

She looked at Jason through fresh eyes, though aware that her interest lay in the fact that he was the only male around at that particular moment. Even so, this didn't usually sway her judgement. All she had to do to relieve her frustration was go off somewhere private and have a wank.

He had proved to be a friend though, despite her early doubts. He made her laugh, and was a shrewd operator. She'd learned a lot about the trade through him. He found a tray and carried the coffee to the sitting room.

'Do you mind?' he asked, and when she shook her head, got the CD from his pocket and put it on.

They sat there drinking coffee in companionable silence, apart from the music, and Amber eased herself among the cushions, and he said, 'Is your behind sore? It should be. He was certainly laying on the smacks.'

'It'll go soon,' she answered and when he held out his arm, she went into it, thinking, this is nice.

He kissed the top of her head, and she inhaled his smell. His hair had a lemon-grass scent, not dissimilar to Camilo's. In fact, out of all the men she had screwed over the past months, these two were the most alike. Rupert was a person to revere, though she had ceased giving him a soap-opera-hospital-drama doctor's halo. Ian she was fond of, but unsure of his sexual proclivities. He would be unreliable in this respect when he'd been at the bevy. Camilo was wonderful, but so far away. Duncan a non-starter. So this left Jason.

'I've brought you a present,' he said.

'Oh? Goodie. I like presents,' she replied, snuggling in.

'Heave up a minute, then,' and he shifted over and reached for his denim jacket. 'Hold out your hand,' he ordered.

She did and looked down at the strange little object he placed there. 'What is it?'

'I'm continuing my lecture and demonstration of vibrators tonight, Mrs Challonor,' he said solemnly. 'Not old ones, this time, but the latest in technology. It seems ridiculous to always produce phallus-shaped dildos. Not much good for the clitoris. This, on the other hand, is designed especially for female pleasure.'

Amber ran her fingers over it; it was about four inches long and looked like a pink, slightly curved mobile phone. 'How is it switched on?' She was eager to give it a whirl.

'It has a ten-speed, push button remote control. Isn't it nice to touch? Made of material called Cyberskin. It stays warm, a cosy little playmate for your muff. Try it.' He worked the control and it started to vibrate gently.

She couldn't wait, the familiar noise bringing back heated memories of other sex-toys she had used. None of them had ever let her down; satisfaction guaranteed. Jason helped her, hitching up her skirt, easing off her briefs and placing the throbbing object against her clit. It fitted perfectly.

'Oh, God . . .' she moaned.

He put it in her hand, saying, 'Hold on a minute. There's something I want to try.'

'Hurry,' she panted, unable to keep her pubis from rising, seeking the delicious sensation brought about by the small but superb vibrating thing.

Jason was taking off his shoes, his socks and then his jeans. 'Stand up,' he said. 'And lean over the back of the sofa.'

She dropped her skirt and he positioned her as he wanted her. He pulled his shirt over his head, then had her bend from the waist, legs splayed, pussy fully exposed from behind. He took the vibrator, switched the power up a notch, then applied it to her clit. She sighed and stuck her bottom out, and then felt the head of his cock easing into her. This fullness was just what she needed, the vibrator, his fingers pinching her nipples, the way she was impaled on him bringing her closer.

'Are you coming?' he asked, moving inside her with such force that she was almost lifted off her feet.

The vibrator thrummed and his cock pummelled her and fireworks burst in her brain as she rocketed off into an intense climax. He quickened his pace and nipped the back of her neck in the violence of his own orgasm. He killed the vibrator, slumped on her for a moment as she hung over the couch, then he moved, helped her up, cradled her in his arms and kissed her with genuine affection.

'Bed,' he said. 'We've an early start.'

She wandered into the bathroom with him, watching as he flushed the condom and then stepped under the shower, beckoning her to join him. He washed her carefully. 'Your van or mine?' she asked.

'We'd better take both. I've a feeling we're going to do rather well,' he said, lathering her crotch and making whorls in her bush. 'Let's take a break soon. We could hop on Eurostar and go to Paris. The flea markets aren't what they were ... too many amateurs using the Chunnel to cream off all they can. But I've still got contacts who keep anything especially interesting for me.'

'I'd like that,' she replied, weak at the knees and supporting herself with her hands on his wet shoulders. 'But there's one thing we've got to get straight. I'm going to Spain in October to stay with Camilo.'

'He of the tight pants and fancy footwork?'

'That's him. And I'm still wanting to attend some of the musters next year, and I shall probably accept dates with Ian and Rupert in the interim.'

'So? What's the problem?' he answered casually, giving her backside a light slap.

And she knew there wasn't one. Jason would give her plenty of rope – maybe even enough to hang herself – but she wasn't sure that she could do the same for him.

It was after midnight when the phone bleeped. Amber reached across to the nightstand and picked up the receiver. Jason slept on, curled on his side, his back to her.

She rather resented having to share her bed – it wasn't just him – anyone. I've been alone too long, she thought. It's made me selfish.

'Yes?' she answered, cursing the caller who had awakened her from a dream in which she was about to walk on to the stage and start singing the role of Tosca, but half hoping it was Andy or Chris.

'Rupert here. Sorry to call so late, but I've been at the clinic. A tricky operation and the patient hadn't responded well to the anaesthetic. I was called out to check on her. She's doing fine now, thank God.'

Amber went mushy. There was something just too appealing about this large, handsome man caring for the sick. Pictures of him flashed across her inner eye in quick succession; attired in surgical gear, big hands in rubber gloves, hair covered and only his eyes showing above the mask; or as the Prince Palatine, in vibrant blue and silver lace, chasing dastardly, dishonourable Roundheads, like Duncan.

'Hi, Rupert,' was all Amber could manage, keeping her voice low, hoping Jason wouldn't speak or fidget or betray his presence in any way.

'I've been summoned to appear at the Silver Banner Ball in London. They like me to turn up as Prince Rupert,' he said. 'It's sometime in November. Will you come as my partner? We could stay there a couple of nights and take in an opera at Covent Garden. What do you say?'

Sue will have to make me a new gown, something exquisite and totally true to period, she thought with computer speed. November. I shall have been to Spain and France by then. Rupert, Rupert – her skin crawled and her heart pounded as she schooled herself to make a controlled reply.

'I think I can manage that,' she said coolly.

'Splendid. And there will be other events, too,' he answered, then added, 'Are you alone, Amber?'

'Dear me. How ungallant, Your Highness,' she reproved primly. 'That's no question to ask a lady.'

She heard him chuckling, and then he said, 'In that case you won't mind if I come over? I could do with some company. I'm hyped up and can't sleep.'

Bugger! she swore to herself. Was there ever a woman so bedevilled on all sides by attractive men?

'Not tonight,' she prevaricated. 'I'm up at dawn to go to an important sale. How about tomorrow evening?'

'About eight?' he asked, and sounded as if he wanted to linger, and go on talking to her. Was he lonely, perhaps, in his beautiful apartment?

'Fine,' she replied and spoke quietly, for Jason had stirred, rolling over and flinging an arm across his eyes, but still deeply asleep.

'Good night, Amber,' Rupert said.

'Good night,' she murmured and replaced the phone on its cradle.

I can't let him go, not this one, not were it never so, my prince-cum-surgeon, she thought crazily. If I had to choose a man to take with me to a desert island, it would have to be him, surely? One day I'll settle down, but it doesn't have to be yet.

Visit the Black Lace website at
www.blacklace-books.co.uk

LOOK OUT FOR THE ALL-NEW BLACK LACE BOOKS – AVAILABLE NOW!

All books priced £6.99 in the UK. Please note publication dates apply to the UK only. For other territories, please contact your retailer.

WICKED WORDS 7
Various
ISBN O 352 33743 5

Hugely popular and immensely entertaining, the *Wicked Words* collections are the freshest and most cutting-edge volumes of women's erotic stories to be found anywhere in the world. The diversity of themes and styles reflects the multi-faceted nature of the female sexual imagination. Combining humour, warmth and attitude with fun, filthy, imaginative writing, these stories sizzle with horny action. Only the most arousing fiction makes it into a *Wicked Words* volume. This is the best in fun, sassy erotica from the UK and USA. **Another sizzling collection of wild fantasies from wicked women!**

OPAL DARKNESS
Cleo Cordell
ISBN O 352 33033 3

It's the latter part of the nineteenth century and beautiful twins Sidonie and Francis are yearning for adventure. Their newly awakened sexuality needs an outlet. Sent by their father on the Grand Tour of Europe, they swiftly turn cultural exploration into something illicit. When they meet Count Constantin and his decadent friends and are invited to stay at his snow-bound Romanian castle, there is no turning back on the path of depravity. **Another wonderfully decadent piece of historical fiction from a pioneer of female erotica.**

Coming in January 2003

STICKY FINGERS
Alison Tyler
ISBN 0 352 33756 7

Jodie Silver doesn't have to steal. As the main buyer for a reputable import and export business in the heart of San Francisco, she has plenty of money and prestige. But she gets a rush from pocketing things that don't belong to her. It's a potent feeling, almost as gratifying as the excitement she receives from engaging in kinky, exhibitionist sex – but not quite. Skilled at concealing her double life, Jodie thinks she's unstoppable, but with detective Nick Hudson on her tail, it's only a matter of time before the pussycat burglar meets her comeuppance. **A thrilling piece of West Coast noir erotica from Ms Tyler.**

STORMY HAVEN
Savannah Smythe
ISBN 0 352 33757 5

Daisy Lovell has had enough of her over-protective Texan millionaire father, Felix, and is determined to get away from his interfering ways. The last straw is when Felix forbids her to date a Puerto Rican boy. Determined to see some of the world, Daisy goes storm chasing across the American Midwest for some sexual adventure. She certainly finds it among truckers and bikers and a state trooper. What Daisy doesn't know is that Felix has sent personal bodyguard Max Decker to join the storm tour and watch over her. However, no one can foresee that hard man Decker will fall for Daisy in a big way. **Fantastic characterisation and lots of really hot sex scenes across the American desert.**

SILKEN CHAINS
Jodi Nicol
ISBN O 352 33143 7

Fleeing from her scheming guardians at the prospect of an arranged marriage, the beautiful young Abbie is thrown from her horse. On regaining consciousness she finds herself in a lavish house modelled on the palaces of Indian princes – and the virtual prisoner of the extremely wealthy and attractive Leon Villiers, the Master. Eastern philosophy and eroticism form the basis of the Master's opulent lifestyle and he introduces Abbie to sensual pleasures beyond the bounds of her imagination. **By popular demand, another of the list's bestselling historical novels is reprinted.**

Coming in February

LIBERTY HALL
Kate Steward
ISBN O 352 33776 1

Vicar's daughter and wannabe journalist Tess Morgan is willing to do anything to pay off her student overdraft. Luckily for Tess, her flatmate Imogen is the daughter of infamous madam, Liberty Hall, who owns a pleasure palace of the same name that operates under a guise of respectability as a hotel. When Tess lands herself a summer job catering for 'special clients' at Liberty Hall, she sees an opportunity to clear that overdraft with a bit of undercover journalism. But when she tries to tell all to a Sunday newspaper, Tess is in for a shocking surprise. **Fruity antics aplenty in this tale of naughty behaviour and double crossing.**

THE WICKED STEPDAUGHTER
Wendy Harris
ISBN 0 352 33777 X

Selina is in lust with Matt, who unfortunately is the boyfriend of the
really irritating Miranda, who was Selina's stepmother for several years
until her poor old dad keeled over years before his time. When Miranda
has to go to the US for three weeks, Selina hatches a plan to seduce the
floppy-haired Matt – and get her revenge on the money-grabbing
Miranda, who Selina blames for her dad's early demise. With several
suitors in tow, the highly sexed Selina causes mayhem, both at work – at
the strippergram service she co-runs – and in her personal life. **Another
hilarious black comedy of sexual manners from Ms Harris.**

DRAWN TOGETHER
Robyn Russell
ISBN 0 352 33269 7

When Tanya, a graphic artist, creates Katrina Cortez – a sexy, comic-strip
detective – she begins to wish her own life were more like that of
Katrina's. Stephen Sinclair, who works with Tanya, is her kind of man.
Unfortunately Tanya's just moved in with her bank manager boyfriend,
who expects her to play the part of the executive girlfriend. In Tanya's
quest to gain the affection of Mr Sinclair, she must become more like
Katrina Cortez – a voluptuous wild woman! **Unusual and engaging story
of seduction and delight.**

Black Lace Booklist

Information is correct at time of printing. To avoid disappointment check availability before ordering. Go to www.blacklace-books.co.uk. All books are priced £6.99 unless another price is given.

BLACK LACE BOOKS WITH A CONTEMPORARY SETTING

☐ THE TOP OF HER GAME Emma Holly	ISBN 0 352 33337 5	£5.99
☐ IN THE FLESH Emma Holly	ISBN 0 352 34498 3	£5.99
☐ A PRIVATE VIEW Crystalle Valentino	ISBN 0 352 33308 1	£5.99
☐ SHAMELESS Stella Black	ISBN 0 352 34485 1	£5.99
☐ INTENSE BLUE Lyn Wood	ISBN 0 352 34496 7	£5.99
☐ THE NAKED TRUTH Natasha Rostova	ISBN 0 352 34497 5	£5.99
☐ ANIMAL PASSIONS Martine Marquand	ISBN 0 352 34499 1	£5.99
☐ A SPORTING CHANCE Susie Raymond	ISBN 0 352 33501 7	£5.99
☐ TAKING LIBERTIES Susie Raymond	ISBN 0 352 33357 X	£5.99
☐ A SCANDALOUS AFFAIR Holly Graham	ISBN 0 352 33523 8	£5.99
☐ THE NAKED FLAME Crystalle Valentino	ISBN 0 352 33528 9	£5.99
☐ ON THE EDGE Laura Hamilton	ISBN 0 352 33534 3	£5.99
☐ LURED BY LUST Tania Picarda	ISBN 0 352 33533 5	£5.99
☐ THE HOTTEST PLACE Tabitha Flyte	ISBN 0 352 33536 X	£5.99
☐ THE NINETY DAYS OF GENEVIEVE Lucinda Carrington	ISBN 0 352 33070 8	£5.99
☐ EARTHY DELIGHTS Tesni Morgan	ISBN 0 352 33548 3	£5.99
☐ MAN HUNT Cathleen Ross	ISBN 0 352 33583 1	
☐ MÉNAGE Emma Holly	ISBN 0 352 33231 X	
☐ DREAMING SPIRES Juliet Hastings	ISBN 0 352 33584 X	
☐ THE TRANSFORMATION Natasha Rostova	ISBN 0 352 33311 1	
☐ STELLA DOES HOLLYWOOD Stella Black	ISBN 0 352 33588 2	
☐ SIN.NET Helena Ravenscroft	ISBN 0 352 33598 X	
☐ HOTBED Portia Da Costa	ISBN 0 352 33614 5	
☐ TWO WEEKS IN TANGIER Annabel Lee	ISBN 0 352 33599 8	
☐ HIGHLAND FLING Jane Justine	ISBN 0 352 33616 1	
☐ PLAYING HARD Tina Troy	ISBN 0 352 33617 X	
☐ SYMPHONY X Jasmine Stone	ISBN 0 352 33629 3	

BLACK LACE NON-FICTION

☐ THE BLACK LACE BOOK OF WOMEN'S SEXUAL   ISBN 0 352 33346 4   £5.99
   FANTASIES   Ed. Kerri Sharp

To find out the latest information about Black Lace titles, check out the website: www.blacklace-books.co.uk or send for a booklist with complete synopses by writing to:

> Black Lace Booklist, Virgin Books Ltd
> Thames Wharf Studios
> Rainville Road
> London W6 9HA

Please include an SAE of decent size. Please note only British stamps are valid.

Our privacy policy
We will not disclose information you supply us to any other parties. We will not disclose any information which identifies you personally to any person without your express consent.

From time to time we may send out information about Black Lace books and special offers. Please tick here if you do <u>not</u> wish to receive Black Lace information.   ☐

Please send me the books I have ticked above.

Name ....

Address ....

....

....

....

Post Code ....

Send to: Cash Sales, Black Lace Books, Thames Wharf Studios, Rainville Road, London W6 9HA.

US customers: for prices and details of how to order books for delivery by mail, call 1-800-343-4499.

Please enclose a cheque or postal order, made payable to Virgin Books Ltd, to the value of the books you have ordered plus postage and packing costs as follows:

UK and BFPO – £1.00 for the first book, 50p for each subsequent book.

Overseas (including Republic of Ireland) – £2.00 for the first book, £1.00 for each subsequent book.

If you would prefer to pay by VISA, ACCESS/MASTERCARD, DINERS CLUB, AMEX or SWITCH, please write your card number and expiry date here:

....

Signature ....

Please allow up to 28 days for delivery.